ABOVE WORLD

WITHDRAWN

ABOVE WORLD

JENN REESE

CANDLEWICK PRESS

This is a work of fiction. Names, characters, places, and incidents are either products of the author's imagination or, if real, are used fictitiously.

Copyright © 2012 by Jenn Reese

All rights reserved. No part of this book may be reproduced, transmitted, or stored in an information retrieval system in any form or by any means, graphic, electronic, or mechanical, including photocopying, taping, and recording, without prior written permission from the publisher.

First edition 2012

Library of Congress Cataloging-in-Publication Data

Reese, Jenn.
Above World / Jenn Reese. — 1st ed.
p. cm.
Summary: In a future of high technology and genetic modification, the Coral Kampii, like legendary mermaids, live isolated from the Above World, but when the devices that allow them to breathe underwater start to fail, thirteen-year-old Aluna and her friend Hoku go to that forbidden place to find help.
ISBN 978-0-7636-5417-7
[1. Science fiction.] I. Title.
PZ7.R25515Abo 2012
[Fic] — dc23   2011013668

12 13 14 15 16 BVG 10 9 8 7 6 5 4 3

Printed in Berryville, VA, U.S.A.

This book was typeset in Plantin.

Candlewick Press
99 Dover Street
Somerville, Massachusetts 02144

visit us at www.candlewick.com

For every kid
who wants to save the world

———

And for Stephanie,
who frequently saves me

WITHDRAWN

"THE WORLD CANNOT CHANGE FOR US;
THEREFORE WE MUST CHANGE OURSELVES FOR THE WORLD."

—*Ali'ikai of the Coral Kampii,*
born Sarah Jennings

CHAPTER 1

ALUNA SWAM TOWARD the abandoned outpost, her heart pounding, her breathing necklace pulsing at her throat. She kicked her legs harder, wishing it were tomorrow. Wishing she already had her tail. With a tail, she could speed through the water, fast as a dolphin.

Goldenfins and shiny-blues darted out of her way. Most of the sun's light was gobbled up by the ocean above her, but she could still see every frond of kelp, every sprout of rainbow coral, every pair of eyes hidden deep in a hidey-hole. The ancients had blessed the Kampii with everything they needed to survive underwater: powerful tails, thick bones and tough skin, adaptable vision, breathing necklaces . . . everything except the ability to fix their own tech when it started to fail.

"Hurry up," she called to Hoku. The thick ocean swallowed the sound, but the tiny artifact in her throat sent her words directly to the artifacts in Hoku's ears . . . despite the fact that he was trailing ten meters behind her.

"I'm swimming as fast as I can," Hoku said. "You know, there might be a reason the outpost is forbidden. Maybe it's overrun with Deepfell."

"Deepfell don't hunt this far into the shallows," Aluna said, hoping she was right. She and Hoku would both be fish food if she wasn't.

"I think we should turn back. My grandma will worry if I'm not in the nest for dinner."

Aluna swung her body upright and treaded in the current. She could see Hoku in the distance, swimming slowly with his pale, scrawny legs and terrible technique. "Four Kampii have died in the last three moons, and the Elders want us to believe their deaths were all accidents? They're hiding something, something important. The ancients lived at this outpost for years before the City of Shifting Tides was even built. I know it holds the answers."

Silence.

"And who knows?" she said. "Maybe we'll find a few artifacts for your workshop. . . ."

"Oh, tides' teeth," Hoku said. "I'll be there in a flash."

He caught up, his freckled face red from the effort. And from thinking about artifacts, no doubt. Hoku could stay hunched over his workbench for days when he got a new piece of tech.

"We'd better find something good," he said with a grin.

She laughed and kicked off. "Let's swim. We only have a few hours before full dark."

But instead of fading into blackness, the ocean grew brighter as they swam. Aluna drifted to a stop before a shimmering dome of white light. It looked as if the moon had fallen into the sea and lay buried halfway in the sand.

"A glowfield!" Hoku said. "It takes forever to breed the right jellyfish and to get them to knit together in the correct pattern. You were right—whatever the Elders are hiding, it must be important."

"How do we get through the barrier?" Aluna unfastened the knife strapped to her thigh and swam closer. Thousands of jellyfish floated in a vast web, their tentacles intertwined so closely that not even a hermit crab could slip through their embrace. She looked for a spot with fewer tendrils and readied her blade. "Maybe we can cut a hole."

"Oh, it's not difficult to cut through the jellyfish,"

Hoku said absently. "The hard part is resisting the paralysis they cause."

"Paralysis?" Aluna yanked her weapon away from the jellyfish and bolted backward. "Next time, make that the *first* thing you mention, okay?"

She looked closer and spotted fish stuck to the glowfield like shells woven into her sister's hair. Some of the fish struggled weakly, but most were dead and partially eaten. She had no intention of sharing their fate.

"I can see buildings!" Hoku said, peering between jellyfish. "The ancients conducted experiments here, back when they were figuring out how to work with the ocean spirits, before the first Kampii colony was founded. I wonder if any of their equipment still works."

Aluna squinted through the tendrils, careful to keep her distance. A cluster of barnacle-covered domes sat in the middle of the glowfield, silent and serene. In the white jellyfish light, they looked like pearls.

"Sarah Jennings must have come here," Aluna said wistfully. "This was her home before she founded the City of Shifting Tides and saved us all from the Above World."

"Aluna," Hoku whispered.

"We've got to get inside," she said. "The Elders want to keep us out, and I want to know why."

"Aluna," he whispered again, his eyes wide and focused on something behind and above her. "I don't think it's *us* the Elders are trying to keep out."

Aluna clamped her mouth shut and looked up.

She felt the water grow cold as the deadliest predator in the ocean glided a few meters above their heads. Pointed snout, black pebble eyes pressed into pale flesh, rows of sharp teeth still trailing scraps of meat from its last meal.

Great White.

The shark lazed its way through the water, looking. Listening. Smelling.

Aluna was sure it would hear their hearts pounding or see the necklaces pulsing at their throats. *Be still as a starfish,* she told herself. *Be calm as Big Blue.*

The shark glided over them and zigzagged around the curve of the glowfield, as if it were searching for an entrance.

When the creature was almost out of view, Hoku kicked his feet against the current to maintain his position. It was a small, unconscious move. He probably didn't realize he'd even done it. But Aluna noticed, and Great White did, too.

The shark twisted sharply, attracted to the sudden motion. In one moment it was swimming away, and in the next it was streaking through the water right at Hoku.

"Swim!" Aluna yelled, but he didn't move. His arms drifted at his sides, his legs hung useless below him. He just stared at the shark.

Aluna vaulted up from the ocean floor, waving both legs and both arms, and screamed, "Over here, you big guppy! Fight me instead!"

Great White ignored her.

Only one thing left to try. She flicked the point of her knife across her palm, fast and deep. A tiny red cloud puffed up from the wound. Her skin would knit itself back together quickly, thanks to the ancients who designed it, but even one drop was enough. Sharks could smell blood from kilometers away. There was nothing they loved more.

Great White twitched. Aluna gasped, her vision suddenly eclipsed by the shark's pale, monstrous body speeding toward her, fast as a harpoon. Deep battle scars marred its muzzle. Its great maw hung open, big enough to swallow her whole.

She switched the grip on her knife so that the back of the blade rested against her forearm. *The knife is not a tool that you "use,"* her brother Anadar always said. *The knife is an extension of your arm. As soon as you pick it up, it becomes a part of you.*

She knew she couldn't hurt the shark, not without a thick spear and the skill to drive it deep into the monster's gills, but it wasn't expecting her to fight back at all. Sharks never expected that. If she could slash it on the nose a few times before it bit her, it might decide she wasn't worth the effort.

The shark closed in. Aluna yelled and punched her knife at its nose. Great White dodged at the last moment and *flash!* A bright-green beam of light erupted from a spot above one of its pitiless black eyes.

Glowing lines crisscrossed Aluna's body. The shark had cast a net over her—a net of light! She watched the net move across the dark skin of her arms and legs and over the tight seal leather that covered the rest of her. The green light shimmered in the current, dancing and flickering like moonlight on the waves. It didn't hurt. In fact, she couldn't feel it at all.

"Move!" Hoku yelled. His voice reverberated in her ear and woke her from her stupor.

She straightened her legs, lifted her arms, and dropped like a stone through the water. She hit the ocean floor and flattened herself against it. Lots of sea creatures hid themselves in the sand. She tried to be one more. The shark's flickering green gaze refracted through the water where she had been, as if it were looking for her.

Aluna saw Hoku not far off, dug into the sand, just like her. "What's going on?" she whispered.

"I don't know," Hoku said. "I've never seen tech like that. And I've definitely never seen it coming from a shark!"

The creature darted left and right, searching.

Great White had legendary patience, while Aluna was renowned among the Coral Kampii for exactly the opposite. She couldn't stay here forever. She had to take a chance.

"Wait till it chases me, then circle back to the city," she whispered. "Don't follow me, no matter what."

She secured her knife in its sheath and waited. When Great White's mysterious green light was farthest away, she pulled herself into a crouch, pressed her palms together over her head, and kicked off.

"Aluna, what are you doing?" Hoku yelled.

"Saving us," she said simply, and swam for her life. For both of their lives.

CHAPTER 2

SWIFT AS A SEAL.

Aluna could feel Great White behind her, mouth agape, hunting. Its glowing net formed around her once, and she darted out of it as fast as she could. She tucked her chin to her chest to minimize her drag in the water and kicked harder. *Nothing could hold her. Nothing would stop her.*

She swam through a school of sunstripes, trying to confuse her scent. Great White dragged its green light through the water, searching for her. She ducked under coral and around rocks. Never in all her life had she wanted to see one of her brothers so badly. She'd even be grateful to see her father. Not even Great White could scare him.

If the shark hadn't been throwing out its net, it would have caught her in one flash of a tail. Whatever game it was playing, that game was saving her life. So far. The rest of the saving was up to her. If she could just make it to the kelp forest near the city! Great White would never be able to navigate between those thick, sticky strands.

The first tufts of seaweed were young and sparse, easy to weave between. Easy for Great White, too. It powered through the fronds as if they didn't exist. Aluna tried to stay calm and focus on her technique. She'd never swum this hard and this long before, even when she'd secretly followed her brothers on their hunting trips. The breathing shell at her throat pulsed faster, sucking air from the water and feeding it to her lungs.

The kelp thickened. Long strands of green brushed her face and slid across her legs. She tried to keep her bearings. It was easy to get lost in a big kelp forest like this one — and dangerous. You could swim for days without finding your way out. She'd heard some Elders talking about a kelp jungle somewhere that was too treacherous to enter at all. Strange things lived there, they said. Creatures with unnatural bodies cried like babies to lure you in, then devoured you with a hundred tiny mouths.

That kelp jungle was high on her list of places to find.

Soon, she had trouble navigating between the tall, sticky stalks. She slowed and used her hands to make a path through the towers of green. Behind her, Great White slowed to a stop. Its green light bounced off the dark kelp, creating a field of dancing shadows. Aluna drifted silently, afraid to move. A few heartbeats later, the shark's glowing net veered off, grew dimmer, and disappeared.

Great White had gone in search of easier prey.

Aluna took her first big, slow deep breath. *Almost home.* She'd be safely in the City of Shifting Tides before full dark, and hopefully, so would Hoku.

A tendril of kelp wrapped itself around her ankle and she kicked it off. Another wrapped around her wrist. She tried to shake it off, but it clung tight. She unsheathed her knife to cut the kelp from her arm, but it wasn't kelp that had grabbed her. It was a hand. A girl's hand. Aluna looked up into a pretty face and a pair of blank white eyes.

Makina.

They'd been friends until last year, when Makina had undergone the ceremony of transformation and grown her tail. Since then, they'd barely spoken.

Makina hung in the tendrils of kelp, swaying softly

in the current. Her eyes glowed white and full, as if tiny moons had eclipsed her pupils. Dozens of thin braids drifted around her face. Her hand, stiff and clawed, had somehow grabbed Aluna's wrist.

"Makina," Aluna whispered, blinking away sudden tears. Her gaze fell to her friend's throat, to the little shell pressed hard into Makina's flesh. No pulsing glow. She wasn't breathing.

Makina was dead.

Aluna stared at her, remembering her face in life, remembering how proud Makina had been of that silly long hair and all those braids. How she always wanted to come over when Aluna's three brothers were home. Aluna wore tight sealskins in order to swim faster, but Makina cared more about her looks. Her delicate fish-scale blouse perfectly complemented the silvery shimmer of her new tail and the pale, gauzy skirt she wore over it.

Gently, Aluna pulled her free of the kelp. The sticky fronds had wrapped around the girl's legs and torso, but not tightly. Makina could have freed herself easily. The seaweed must have attached itself after she had died, not before.

But there was no blood. Makina hadn't been bitten or punctured. Aluna stared at the breathing shell attached to Makina's neck, suddenly suspicious. She reached out a finger to trace the seahorse design. As soon as she touched it, the shell dislodged and drifted toward the ocean floor. Aluna caught it in her hand.

Aluna saw two small, dark holes in Makina's throat where the shell had been attached. Empty holes. The breathing shell's two slender tubes should have been burrowed there. Those tails held the shell in place as it filtered air from the water and delivered it to the lungs.

Without air, Makina had drowned.

Aluna opened her hand and stared at the broken shell nestled in her palm. A name was carved on its back in tiny, perfect letters. The Elders had spoken the name a dozen times before, always in hushed voices, always when they thought no one could hear them. She couldn't read, but Hoku could, and he'd written the letters for her to see.

HydroTek.

Makina wasn't the first to die like this, and Aluna knew that she wouldn't be the last. The City of Shifting Tides was fading, one Kampii at a time, and the Elders weren't doing a thing to stop it.

Aluna squeezed the necklace in her fist. *Makina was dead.* Suddenly, it didn't matter that Great White had almost caught her. It didn't matter that her legs ached and her eyes burned and her head was starting to pound.

She wanted answers.

CHAPTER 3

I WISH they hadn't taken the necklace," Hoku said. "If I could examine one, maybe I could figure out why they're breaking. They must need power to operate, but where is it coming from? Elder Peleke won't tell me. I wonder if he even knows." He looked at his hands, wishing he had his tools. Wishing he had something to focus on besides Makina's death and Aluna's anger.

"Of course they took the necklace," Aluna stormed. "They're going to act as if none of this ever happened, same as always. One death might be an accident, but Makina was the fifth. How can they ignore five?"

She was swimming circles around her nest, her eyes red rimmed and wild. They'd spent the last hour remembering everything they could about Makina. Now he just wanted to eat some fish and go to sleep. Predictably, Aluna's mood had gone in the other direction.

"They had no right to hide her away like that!" she said.

"Not everyone wants to see . . ." *The body,* he thought. When had Makina stopped being a person and become just another object? "She had a lot of friends, and her parents weren't even in the crossway when you brought her in. Maybe—"

"And they wouldn't even answer my questions about the necklace! Now the Elders are off 'conferring.'" She snorted. "That's all they ever do. Talk, talk, talk. They never actually *do* anything."

"But your father . . ."

Aluna waved her hand. "He's the worst."

Aluna and her father were like a pair of fighting eels—always going for each other's throats. Elder Kapono intimidated the entire city, and scared the ink out of Hoku, but Aluna was never cowed. She seemed to think it was her duty to defy him.

"The Elders are probably talking at the council dome," she continued. "Eating clams and sucking coralfruit juice and gossiping like younglings. If only we could hear through the sound shield!"

"Well, maybe . . ."

Aluna stopped her swishing and swam over to him, her eyes intense.

"Well, what?"

Oh, crabs and krill. Why did he always have to open his mouth? He shrugged, suddenly embarrassed. "I've been working on this device, this new artifact. You put it over your ear and it increases the distance you can hear. I thought if I made it strong enough, we could talk at night when we're both in our nests." He'd intended to give her the artifact as a gift when she got her tail, as a way for them to stay in touch even when she was off with all her new friends. So much for the surprise.

"And you think it will work through the sound shield?"

"It might. I couldn't find a way to make us talk louder, so I found a way to make the artifacts in our ears pick up sound better."

"Brilliant!" Aluna said.

"Well, I, uh—it's not—"

"We can try it out right now. Let's go!"

Aluna bolted for the room's hatch and darted into the passageway. Hoku smiled and followed her back to his family's nest.

Tomorrow was the ceremony of transformation, when he'd watch Aluna trade her legs for a tail. Tonight was all he had left before everything changed, before she became a full Kampii and left him behind. One last night of trouble and danger to get him through the months of loneliness that would surely follow.

Hoku's family lived in the sand-side part of the city, where the nests were small and carved right next to each other at the bottom of the coral reef. Few rays of sun penetrated the water sand-side, and the current was nowhere near as strong and refreshing as it was in the city's main channels. Overall, the sand-side was dark, dingy, and depressing.

His mother always talked about moving to a moon-side nest, but he and his dad knew that would never happen. The old moon-side Kampii families passed their homes to their children, and the Elders had long since forbidden the carving of any new ones in the "good" areas. Something about the structural integrity of the coral, Elder Peleke had said. Hoku had a feeling there was more to it than that, but he never questioned the social injustice of it all out loud. Who would listen to a lowly sand-sider, anyway?

Aluna would, if he ever found the courage to talk to her. She never said anything about his family's nest or status, or her own. Fresh, clean currents flowed through her family nest. Glow-in-the-dark spirals and starfish and seashells decorated every surface. Even their resting sticks bore the hand-carved Shifting Tides seahorse emblem. But despite everything Aluna had and everything he didn't have, not even the tiniest hint of disgust or pity ever showed on her face. She was just Aluna, same as ever.

When they got to his nest, both his parents were out on work assignments and his grandma Nani was napping. *Good.* He didn't want to answer any questions about what they were doing.

They swam through the cramped tunnel to his room. There was nothing he loved more than his workshop, except getting the chance to show it off. He immediately darted to his desk, hooked his knees around his worn resting stick, and tapped on the lantern to wake up the lightning fish inside. The fish darted back and forth, faster and faster, their bodies glowing brighter and brighter.

"You've been busy!" Aluna said, nodding to the new jars of artifacts hooked to the ceiling and secured to his desk.

He shrugged. "Elder Peleke still won't take me on as an apprentice, so I have to learn everything myself. Which means lots of failed experiments," he said. "I haven't gotten anything to work in weeks, except for the Extra Ears."

"Extra Ears? Is that what you're calling the hearing artifact you made?"

"You like it?" he asked. "I like coming up with

names for the artifacts almost as much as I like making them." "Extra Ears" was a vast improvement over his first two naming attempts, "Hearing Helpers" and "Ears x 10."

He reached for his "in progress" jar, carefully removed the Extra Ears artifacts, and placed them on the sticky plate attached to his desk. He loved his sticky plate; it had been in his family for generations. The flat square of metal grabbed other metal things and clung to them. Magic, his mother called it, but his grandma pronounced it "magnet."

"How do they work?" Aluna reached for one of the Ears, but Hoku batted her hand away.

"No touching! They're very delicate. I think we both remember what happened the last time you tried to help." He looked up at the jar labeled SHARK DETECTOR and the mangled metal bits inside. Such a waste.

"I forgot what a snoot you are with your bits of metal," she said, but she didn't reach for the artifacts again.

"I have to be careful," he said. "If I do something wrong, I might break the artifacts already in our ears. And then we won't be hearing anything besides whales and waves."

The Extra Ears on his sticky plate looked like tiny plugs attached to bent pieces of coated wire. He plucked one gently from the plate and tightened two tiny screws. It didn't matter what they looked like; it only mattered that they worked. And they did. He'd tested one the night before and overheard the neighbors fighting three nests away. Once he perfected the design and showed it to the Elders, Elder Peleke would have to take him on as an apprentice, even though he was a lowly sand-side kid and not the son of someone important.

"Ready!" Hoku said.

Aluna drifted over and held her short hair out of the way. Hoku pressed the artifact against the inside of her ear, then wrapped the wire around the outside to secure it in place.

"By the tides!" Aluna said.

"What? What do you hear?"

"A mumble-jumble mostly, but I can hear that little squid Jessia gossiping to someone about the boy she likes — oh!" Aluna looked at him and giggled.

"What? Who is she talking about? Tell me!" he begged. Jessia had smiled at him that very morning. She had nice teeth. He grabbed the other hearing artifact and scrambled to affix it to his ear with none of the delicacy he'd used with the first one.

"Oh, she's moved off. I can't hear her anymore. Too bad!" Aluna said. "Are freckles really that cute? I hadn't noticed. But now that old fish Moke is going on and on about what he wants for dinner."

"Shhh!" Hoku said, but she was right. All he could hear was Moke talking about fish. He couldn't hear Jessia at all. Had Aluna made the whole thing up? This wouldn't be the first time she'd teased him about one of his crushes. He put a hand to his cheek. He had a lot of freckles.

"Hoku, these Extra Ears are amazing. You're a genius," Aluna said, and he instantly forgave her.

"Let's get to the council dome," he said. *And see how much trouble we can find.*

CHAPTER 4

THE ELDERS' VOICES were faint, but when Hoku clung to the council dome and pressed his Extra Ear against the slick, opaque surface, he could make out the words. Aluna followed his example.

". . . simply ridiculous," Elder Maylea said. "It's already dangerous enough sending our trade team to the Human settlement. Who knows what horrors have overtaken the rest of the Above World. The ancients came to the City of Shifting Tides for a reason, and that reason has not changed."

"The surviving Humans have reverted to barbarism and worse," said Elder Peleke. "Our scouts have seen Humans with fingers made of knives, with artificial eyes that burn like fires! And the Humans that do not reshape themselves with tech simply cower in their villages or wage senseless, bloody wars with their neighbors." He grunted. "Theirs has always been a savage heritage."

"Their heritage is the same as ours, Peleke," Aluna's father said. His voice, even through the sound shield, resonated stronger than the rest. "A few hundred years of separation does not erase the thousands of years that came before. We were all Humans once."

"But our security is based on the fact that none of the Above Worlders know where we are," Elder Maylea said. "Sarah Jennings went to great lengths to keep our location a secret. Not even the other Kampii tribes know where to find us, and we are still three dozen years away from the next Exchange. The more contact we have with others, the greater the risk."

"Yes, there is safety in isolation," Kapono said. "But are we afraid of contact for the right reasons? Are we jumping at sharks, or just at their shadows? We could use the outpost at Seahorse Alpha to communicate with other colonies, to learn about our past, to plan for our future! And yet, Seahorse Alpha has never even been opened in my lifetime. We have imprisoned it in a glowfield, as if knowledge itself were dangerous." Kapono lowered his voice and spoke slowly. "As long as our gaze remains inward, we will never truly know what is happening in the Above World."

The Elders fell silent. Aluna and her father were so alike, Hoku thought. More alike than either of them realized.

Elder Inoa's voice broke the quiet. "Are you suggesting that we reject the ways of our ancestors, reject the very will of Sarah Jennings herself? That we rejoin the Above World while we are at our most vulnerable?"

Rejoin the Above World!

Hoku couldn't believe what he was hearing. The Above World had always seemed like a dream to him, a world filled with endless artifacts and machines and people who knew how to use them. Sometimes he wished he'd been born in ancient times, before the Kampii gave up that wondrous, mechanical life.

But he'd heard other stories, too. Tales of Humans with poisonous weapons for arms and with hearts of cold metal, who roamed the Above World killing whomever they wanted. With the Deepfell hunting the oceans and those Humans on dry land, the only safe place in all the wide world was right where they were: hidden in the City of Shifting Tides.

There was a silence in the council dome. Hoku pressed his ear harder against the dome's surface, afraid that he'd miss Kapono's answer. His heart pounded and the breathing shell at his neck pulsed rapidly to keep up. Half a meter away, Aluna's shell pulsed just as fast, her eyes wide.

The silence seemed to last forever. Then Aluna's father said, "No, no. Of course not. You all know how I feel about the Above World. It's too dangerous, too unpredictable. My allegiance has always been, and will always be, to the Coral Kampii and our founding principles. I believe I have already proven my loyalty."

"My mother," Aluna whispered to Hoku. "He's talking about my mother. He could have gone to the Above World when she got sick. I bet the Humans had medicines that could have saved her. But he didn't. He let her die instead. To him, that's loyalty."

Hoku looked at her, saw her lips pressed together and her brown eyes fierce. He didn't know what to say. He never did. Aluna's loss made him feel guilty that he still had his own mother. Guilty, and grateful.

Elder Inoa said, "Yes, of course you have proven your loyalty. No one thinks otherwise. But we must stay hidden as long as possible, if not forever. It is who we are. We must trust the Elders before us and keep the Seahorse Alpha outpost secure. Exposing our people to the information inside will only cause more strife. Kampii must not fight Kampii. Not ever again."

Aluna whispered, "The outpost! We have to—"

"Even so," Elder Kapono said, and Aluna clamped her mouth shut so they could hear. "Heed my words: this is not the last death our people will suffer."

"It is not," Elder Peleke agreed. "But as you know

better than anyone, in dark times, some Kampii must die to preserve the way of life for the rest."

The Elders all spoke their agreement at once.

"We will encourage more pregnancies," Elder Inoa said. She herself had borne eight children, and she never let anyone forget it. Fertility was a great badge of honor for the women in the City of Shifting Tides.

"Yes, more pregnancies," Elder Peleke said. "We can offer incentives. Our reasons need not be apparent."

"Then the matter is settled," said Elder Maylea. "We will weather this storm as we always have. As Sarah Jennings would have wanted us to. By the moon!"

The other Elders repeated, "By the moon!"

"The next order of business is the taxation of whitefish harvests from the sand-side farmers—"

"Enough," Aluna said. She let go of the dome and drifted from its surface. She ripped off her Extra Ear and held it out. "Here, take it. I don't want it anymore."

Hoku stared at the artifact pinched between her fingers.

This is not the last death. Some must die . . .

"Take it," she repeated.

He did. In the dome below, he could hear the Elders arguing about harvest rights. He quickly removed his own Extra Ear and shoved them both into one of his pockets.

"What should we do?" he asked her. Aluna always knew what to do. She always had a plan. No matter what, he could count on her to tell him where to go.

This time, she laughed. It wasn't a happy sound.

"What should we do? Pass the tides, like good little fish," she said. "And hope that the next Kampii to die isn't someone we love."

CHAPTER 5

ALUNA SAID GOOD NIGHT to Hoku and swam for her nest, her thoughts dark. She kept seeing the same images, over and over: Makina's dead white eyes, the broken necklace in her palm, Hoku's worried face pressed against the council dome. How could she live a normal life knowing it was only a matter of time before someone else died?

Then again, maybe she *wouldn't* be living a normal life. Maybe her own necklace would be the next to fail.

She changed direction and headed for the training dome. A few weapon drills would calm her tumultuous mind. Most days, they were the only thing that could. If only she were allowed to be a hunter like her brothers!

She loved fighting—the emotional rush, the way her mind and body worked together, the rare feeling of power and control, even if it was just over herself. And she was good at it, too. But girls were forbidden to do anything the Elders deemed dangerous while the Coral Kampii population was below its "minimum safe level." And now, with the Elders wanting more babies, she'd be lucky to do anything as deadly as shucking a mussel or skinning a fish.

Her brother Anadar was in the dome when she got there, going through a complicated spear set. Aluna treaded by the entrance, not wanting to distract him. Besides, she loved watching the swish of his long spear as it pierced the water. He wasn't as strong or naturally talented as their older brothers, Pilipo and Ehu, but he worked harder and had more patience. And so far, he'd kept her training a secret.

When Anadar finished his series of moves, he saluted the old stone warriors' shrine at the north curve of the dome and turned to her.

"I thought I might see you tonight, after every-thing," he said, and that was all the mention he made of Makina. But there was a look in his eyes, a sadness, and Aluna wondered if he didn't need this session as much as she did. Not that they could actually talk about it. Unless Daphine was part of the conversation, Aluna and her brothers stuck to the same three topics:

eating, hunting, and which one of them would win in a fight.

"Well, what are you waiting for?" he said. "Grab your spear."

Aluna grinned and darted for the weapons stuck to the nearby wall with jellyfish goo. A few of the spears had only one point, but most had sharpened metal tips on both ends. She chose the shortest, sturdiest spear, to match her smaller stature. One day, she'd wield the longer sinuous weapons and make them dance in the water, just as her brothers did.

"This is your last lesson before you get your tail, so let's make it a good one," Anadar said in his best grown-up teacher voice. "I want to see every spear set you've learned so far."

She groaned. "All of them? But I want to learn something new!"

"Then you better find enlightenment in a set you already know."

Aluna sighed and swam to the center of the dome, about three meters above the sandy floor. Before she started training, she'd thought the weapon sets were beautiful, but stupid. The hunter performed a series of moves with the weapon, but without an opponent. Some of the spear twirls and positions looked far too elaborate to ever be useful in a real fight. But after she learned her first set—Spear in Six Directions—she began to understand. The sets conditioned the body to understand the weapon, to feel its ebb and flow. And they were much harder than they looked. She never concentrated more than when she was learning a new series of moves.

She faced north, saluted the shrine and her brother, then began.

Her body did most of the work. It knew the moves, directed the spear to poke or slash, twist or spin. Her mind focused on *intent*. It was not enough to go through the motions. She had to understand what each of them meant. She had to give them heart, imbue them with her spirit. She wasn't just poking the point toward the sand; she was driving it into the gills of an imaginary Great White.

After Six Directions, she performed two dolphin-style sets called Chase the Seal and Playing in the Surf that involved tumbles and quick changes of direction. By the end of the second one, her breathing necklace was pulsing so fast that she thought she might pass out.

"Go on," Anadar said. "There is no time to catch your breath in the middle of a fight. Push."

Push through the exhaustion. He'd been telling her that since the first day she picked up a knife. *The only limits you have are the ones you set yourself.*

Aluna saluted and began Devil in the Depths, a

shark-style set with fast, sharp movements. Her arms wobbled, and the first few strikes were sloppy. She *pushed,* and found a second wave of strength.

When she had finished the rest of her sets, she stopped treading and drifted to the ocean floor. Her breath came in great gasps, and she held her side to ease the cramp in her ribs. Her spear hung lifeless from her hand. If Great White attacked right now, she'd almost welcome its jaws.

"Not bad," Anadar said. "A little messy at times, but you maintained good speed and power. Let's go over the spinning combination in the White Coral set. I think you have the wrong grip in one part."

Aluna looked at him. Was he serious? His brown eyes sparkled their response. *Tides' teeth*—he was.

She pulled herself upright with a groan, adjusted her hands on the spear, and adopted the White Coral stance.

Push.

Her father was waiting for her when she got back to the nest. His tail curled around his resting stick in the common room, the resting stick no one else dared use. He didn't look at her when she entered but stared at his dinner pouch, seemingly transfixed by whatever food Daphine had prepared for the family that night.

Aluna hurried through the room, eager to collapse and savor her well-earned exhaustion. She had almost made it to the other side when her father spoke.

"That girl should never have been in the kelp forest alone," he said. "Her death was an unfortunate accident."

Aluna stopped and twirled to face him. "An accident?" The anger and frustration she'd just purged from her system returned in one flash of a tail. "How can you say that? It was her necklace!"

His eyes flickered wide, but he recovered quickly from the surprise. "You're talking nonsense. The girl made a foolish mistake and she died for it."

"But you know it's the necklaces," she sputtered. "And you know more people are going to die just like Makina!"

You let my mother die, too. You chose the City of Shifting Tides over your own wife. She couldn't say the words out loud. Not to him. But they both felt the accusation floating there, an invisible barrier always between them.

"Lower your voice," he hissed. "I know the girl was your friend, but if I tell you her death was an accident, then you'll believe it was an accident. Do you understand me?"

Tears pooled in her eyes and she blinked them into

the ocean. "The Elders listen to you. I know they're afraid, but they listen to you. They would follow you anywhere." *Even to the Above World.*

He gave a harsh laugh. "No one will follow a man who can't even control his own daughter."

"So this is my fault somehow?" she said. "What if Anadar is the next Kampii to die? Or Daphine?"

Her father's brow darkened. "You are too young to understand what's happening. You know nothing of the Above World and its horrors. Grow up, Aluna. You're about to get your tail, and you're still acting like a child."

She glowered, her blistered hands curling into fists. She couldn't speak, not without screaming. Where was the proud, honorable man the rest of the Kampii saw when they looked at her father? All she saw was a coward. A coward who was perpetually disappointed in her.

"Get out of my sight," her father said, and she did.

CHAPTER 6

TRADITIONALLY, her mother would have fixed her hair before the ceremony. Aluna had to make do with her sister.

"Stop moving," Daphine chided. "This would be easier if you'd grown your hair out. I can't get this shell woven on."

"Tides' teeth, how many shells do I need?" They'd been at this for more than an hour. Her head felt like a basket of clams.

"Shhhh," Daphine said.

"Who did this to you, before your ceremony?" Aluna asked, surprised that she didn't already know the answer. Their mother had died a week after Aluna was born, a few tides before Daphine got her tail.

"I did it myself," Daphine said.

Aluna could hear a mix of pride and hurt in her sister's voice, and that hollow, aching echo of silence that remained the only acknowledgment of their loss. She heard the echo in her brothers' voices sometimes—and in her father's voice on those rare occasions when he wasn't yelling at her. But Daphine, who had suffered the most, rarely let it show. When she did, it made her look vulnerable. It made her seem young.

Aluna squirmed. "I bet it didn't take this long when you did it yourself," she said crossly. She'd rather her sister be angry than frail.

Daphine snorted. "It took longer, and half the shells fell out right before I swallowed the Ocean Seed."

"Ha!" Aluna poked at a group of pearls clustered at her temple. "That must have irked the Elders. They like everything to go steady as tides. Remember when Ehu sneezed during his ceremony and Elder Peleke got so flustered he forgot a line of the ritual?"

Daphine laughed. The sound lifted Aluna's heart. If her sister's quiet despair could make others weep without even realizing why, then her laugh could bring sunlight to the abyss. Her three brothers had almost as much power. Pilipo and Ehu were the city's best hunters, and Anadar would be, too, one day. Other Kampii looked up to them. Someday, they'd all be as respected as her father.

All of them except her.

She'd been telling herself for years that getting her tail would change everything. Once she looked like a real Kampii, she would suddenly become an invaluable member of the community and earn her siblings' respect. Maybe even her father's respect, too. But now, on the day of the ceremony, she faltered. Maybe a tail wouldn't change enough. Maybe it wouldn't change anything at all.

"There," Daphine said, and swam back a bit to admire her handiwork. "Pretty as a porpoise."

"Hey!"

Daphine laughed again, and Aluna forgave her the insult.

Aluna treaded water with six other girls and eight boys in a tiny cove near the ritual dome. The ceremonial robes fit loosely around her arms and legs, irritating her. She preferred her tight, sleeveless hunting leathers, designed for protection and speed. Dresses made her feel stupid, like she was trying to look as pretty as Daphine, when everyone knew she never would be.

Despite the company, Aluna had never felt more alone. The other girls whispered to one another and kept looking at their legs. Soon they'd swallow the Ocean Seed and the ancestors would bestow their blessings. Their legs would change into tails. At thirteen, they'd finally be true Kampii.

The transformation took several tides and was extremely painful. A rite of passage, the Elders called it, as if that somehow explained why it had to hurt. But everyone—every adult Kampii in the City of Shifting Tides—agreed that the pain was worth it.

Elder Inoa came to fetch them. A fit Kampii in her late fifties, Inoa wore a bright-white robe cinched at the waist with a green cord and decorated with pearls and sparkle shells. Eight thin bracelets slid up and down her right arm, one for each of her children. Her flowing skirt was embroidered with the ancient Kampii seahorse and billowed around her tail in the morning current.

Aluna's chest swelled. She looked at her companions and saw the same mix of pride, excitement, and terror reflected on their faces. They followed the Elder in an ordered line, as they had seen Kampii do in years before this.

It looked as if the entire population of the City of Shifting Tides had come to watch the festivities. Kampii clustered around the entrance hatch to the ritual dome, cheering and shouting blessings of luck as Aluna and the others swam by. Spectators weren't allowed inside the dome during the ceremony, but that didn't stop Kampii from pressing their faces to the dome's glassy surface and watching from the outside.

Once Aluna entered the ritual dome, the mood

changed completely. The dome's sound shield dulled the cheers to a distant murmur, and its curved glass walls had been darkened to black. The spectators could see in, but Aluna and the other ceremony participants couldn't see out. The Elders had granted them the illusion of privacy.

Daphine and Hoku were out there somewhere, but her brothers were not. On ceremony days, the hunters had to catch three times as many fish for the feast. Pilipo, Ehu, and Anadar were scouring the ocean, swimming far and fast, looking for prey to honor the ocean spirits and their ancestors.

Elder Inoa shut the entrance hatch, and the world fell silent. Aluna followed the others to a small cluster of resting sticks dotting the center of the dome, wishing her heart would slow to its normal pace. Or at least stop beating so loudly in her head. She wrapped her legs around her resting stick, careful not to bend her knees too tightly. If past ceremonies were any indication, the Elders would drone on and on. She didn't want her legs falling asleep or going numb.

"First to speak will be Elder Kapono," Elder Inoa said, and took her place with the other Elders. Aluna's father swam forward.

In his ritual clothes, he looked even more intimidating than usual. His flowing white tunic emphasized his dark skin. Shells and bits of kelp had been woven into his long, graying braids. Had Daphine done his hair before or after hers? If he cared that his youngest daughter was among the initiates this year, he didn't show it. His gaze passed over her as if she were a hermit crab, beneath his notice.

Her father spoke about the city's history. She'd heard the story a million times, but she had to admit, her father told it well.

Long ago, they had all lived in the Above World with the other Humans until the first Elder, Ali'ikai who-was-born Sarah Jennings, led them away from the disease and the famine and the war and made them a home under the waves. Only Sarah Jennings maintained contact with the Humans, the other Kampii colonies, and other splinter people. She became the Coral Kampii's first Voice. But conditions in the Above World worsened. Sarah Jennings fell ill during one of her missions, and after she died, the Kampii vowed to limit their contact with the Above World forever.

As the Elders lectured about honor and duty, Aluna's thoughts drifted back to the kelp forest, back to Makina. She could almost feel the girl's dead hand clutching her wrist, could almost see Makina's fog-filled eyes, as if she were swimming right in front of her. How long would that memory haunt her?

When Elder Inoa began handing out the ceremonial bowls, Aluna almost dropped hers. Elder Peleke was talking about responsibility at that very moment. Her father scowled. Aluna tightened her grip on the bowl and tried to focus.

Elder Peleke called their names. Aluna rose first and slowly swam forward. Elder Inoa used a pair of tongs to pluck an Ocean Seed from the ritual container that only the Elders could open. The seed glowed red-hot as she dropped it into Aluna's bowl, but it sizzled and cooled quickly in open water. The seed was small, no bigger than a pearl, and a dingy brownish gray.

"The color of the stormy sea," the Elder said. "A symbol of change."

CHAPTER 7

*C*HANGE, thought Aluna. Not a word that got a lot of use in the City of Shifting Tides. The Elders would rather die than do anything that would alter the Kampii way of life. Or, at least they were willing to let *other* people die.

Elder Inoa began to speak about tradition, and Aluna felt movement in her chest, a quiet tension building slowly, like a wave.

"Events in the Above World come and go," the Elder intoned. "The Humans and the other splinters fight their wars and destroy their resources. We of the sea, of the coral, of water . . . we remain strong and unwavering. We persevere. We thrive."

Aluna snorted. She hadn't meant to, but it just came out. The eleven Elders and the other supplicants all turned to stare.

She bit her lip and lowered her gaze, trying to fight the anger growing inside her. How could they be "thriving" if innocent girls like Makina had to die? And if more and more Kampii would die just as she had? Hiding from the rest of the world while your failing tech slowly killed you was in no way the same as "thriving."

Elder Inoa began again. "We Kampii have always kept ourselves apart. We have not succumbed to the weakness that ravages the Above World. We have maintained our culture and grown our civilization even as the rest of the world suffers darkness and misery."

Aluna rolled her eyes and muttered to herself. The girl next to her shifted uncomfortably.

"Silence!" Elder Peleke bellowed. Then, with more dignity, he turned to Elder Inoa and said, "Please continue, Elder."

Elder Inoa tucked a tendril of pale hair into her coral headpiece and continued, but not without a long, dark look in Aluna's direction.

"While the Above World destroys itself, our colony grows. . . ."

In the distance, a whale sang. It was a sad, melancholy sound that cut through the water like a harpoon. *All whales are pessimists,* Hoku had told her once.

He was probably out there now, wondering what she'd done to anger the Elders. She'd tell him later, along with some embellishment. Hoku loved a good story.

But what if . . . what if Hoku were next? What if it had been *his* body she had found in the kelp forest? What if he died, afraid and alone, and the Elders had hidden him away like Makina, as if he had never even existed?

Aluna stared down at the ugly seed in her bowl and clenched her teeth. *Calm as Big Blue*, she told herself. But she didn't feel calm. She didn't even truly want to *be* calm. The wave inside her chest grew like a tsunami, pulling thoughts and energy from every part of her and growing bigger and bigger.

She unwrapped her legs from the resting stick and floated up.

"On your stick, Aluna," her father said, the first words he'd spoken directly to her since their fight the night before. His tail swished.

"No," Aluna said. The wave inside her crashed and rolled, thunderous loud. Elder Inoa was staring at her, mouth agape, breathing shell pulsing at her throat. "I can't listen to this anymore," Aluna said. "Our city isn't *growing*. The Coral Kampii aren't *thriving*."

"Daughter, enough!" her father yelled. Aluna

cringed, but couldn't stop the anger now that it had begun to flow. She turned on him.

"Makina is just the latest victim of our ignorance, but there have been others. Too many others. My mother died, too," she said, knowing it would hurt him. Wanting it to hurt. She couldn't say it to him last night, in private, but she found her voice now in front of everybody. "You could have gone to the Above World for help when she got sick, but you let her die. Now our necklaces are breaking, and we're still hiding in our shells."

Her father swam forward, his eyes dark, his mouth twisted. She'd never seen him so angry.

"Aluna, daughter of Leilani," he said, her mother's name sounding like an insult, his shame at being her father evident in every syllable, "if you do not apologize to the Elders and return to your stick, you will be asked to leave this sacred place immediately."

But she wasn't done. Not yet. She stared right into her father's eyes. "If you won't find HydroTek and ask for help, then I'll go to the Above World and do it myself."

He stared back at her, his eyes dark with the promise of further punishment. It took all her strength not to cower before him. Silence filled the dome.

Finally, he said, "This girl is deemed unworthy of

citizenship in the City of Shifting Tides and will not pass into adulthood this day. What say the council?"

"By the moon," the Elders agreed in unison, clearly relieved.

"Leave now, *child*," her father said through gritted teeth, "and return to your foolish games."

The wave of anger inside Aluna roiled and churned. She lowered her gaze and fought it back. If she opened her mouth again, she had no idea what would come out. Her father would never forgive her for this. Never. Her entire family would suffer in their standing because of her.

She swam toward the exit hatch slowly. Her body shook, her legs threatened to turn to jelly, but she kept them moving.

When she got close to the exit, Elder Peleke called to her. "Leave the bowl, girl. You will return in no less than one year's time to have your loyalty to the Kampii reassessed."

Aluna lowered herself to the ground. She stared at the Ocean Seed. How could something so small and ugly be so powerful? Her back was to the Elders. Before she placed the bowl on the sand, she snatched up the seed and hid it in her fist. The tiny nugget burned painfully hot against her palm. She said nothing and swam solemnly to the exit.

As the hatch snicked shut behind her, Aluna heard

Elder Peleke say, "Even our glorious city can produce, on occasion, a bad fish. . . ."

She swam to her cave before Daphine or Hoku could catch up to her. Why had she taken the Ocean Seed? She had no plans to use it, at least not now. Where she was going, she needed legs.

Aluna opened the small pouch she wore around her neck and pulled out the shiny silver ring that had once been her mother's. She kissed the ring's single purple stone as she did almost every night, then placed the stolen Ocean Seed within the ring's circle and tucked both back into the pouch.

She ripped off her ceremony clothes and dressed in a pair of worn leggings and the top Ehu had given to her the first time she'd killed a shark. Daphine had sewn the shark's teeth around the neckline in a clever pattern. Whenever Aluna wore it, she felt fierce.

She strapped on her knife and tossed a few pieces of cured fish into a small net secured to her waist sash. At the opening to her room, Aluna paused. She looked back at her swirly, glowing cave, at her comfy sticky-sponge bed, at her secret stockpile of spearheads and pretty shells, and wondered if she'd ever see any of it again.

Or if she'd ever see Hoku. The Above World was no place for a youngling like him. If she told him where she was going, he'd insist on coming with her. Keeping herself safe was going to be enough of a challenge. Keeping them both safe would be close to impossible.

The Elders were wrong. She wasn't a bad fish. To her, duty meant something other than doing what you were told. To her, duty meant doing whatever you had to do for the good of the Kampii . . . regardless of the consequences. If the Elders had their way, they'd all ignore their problems until the whole colony dwindled away into nothing.

Aluna left the nest and snuck out of the city, avoiding the major currents and crossways and sticking to the shadows like an eel. Once she was free of the coral reef, she swam upward, toward the sun, and toward the shore.

CHAPTER 8

$\mathcal{H}$OKU WATCHED from outside the ritual dome, crammed between a Kampii woman who kept shoving him with her tail and a huge mussel farmer whose son was inside the dome with Aluna. The big Kampii kept asking what the Elders were saying, but no one answered him. No one knew.

Except Hoku. With his Extra Ears, he'd heard everything that had happened. Only he wished he hadn't. He wished he'd never brought his stupid tech to the ceremony in the first place. He hated seeing his best friend humiliated, especially when he was powerless to help.

Well, he could do something now. He could find Aluna and distract her. They could hunt tasty starbellies or find a wreck to scavenge. They could head back to the glowfield with a plan for disrupting the jellyfish and fending off Great White. He could get himself into trouble, if necessary, so that she could come and save him. That always cheered her up. Usually, it cheered him up, too.

He pushed his way through the throngs of Kampii now gossiping about Aluna's exit from the ceremony. He wanted to scream at them all, to tell them to be quiet, to leave her alone. He heard Kapono's name mentioned, and Daphine's, too. They'd be talking about Aluna and her whole family for moons.

He swam to the broken dome first, and then to their secret meeting stone. No Aluna. He checked the abandoned hull outside the city, the perimeter of the kelp forest, and her secret stash of weapons near the training dome. Nothing.

Finally, he went to the monument, the final resting place of Ali'ikai-born-Sarah Jennings. The monument was made from a smooth white stone unlike anything else in the city. Sarah Jennings's face was carved into an oval on one side. Her hair was short and wild like Aluna's, her eyes dark and severe. Aluna called them strong.

Aluna snuck away to the monument often, usually after a fight with her father. She didn't want anyone to know, so Hoku pretended he didn't. Sometimes she left offerings propped up against the structure's base—artifacts from their scavenging runs, glittering shells, shark teeth. The sort of things he brought home to show his mother.

Aluna wasn't at the monument, and there were no new offerings. The tight knot growing in his stomach was trying to tell him something. Something he was trying even harder to deny.

When he'd heard her get kicked out of the ceremony, a small selfish part of him had rejoiced. One more year! One more year of being best friends and doing everything together. One more year, and then they'd both be facing the ceremony together. He wouldn't get left behind.

But he got left behind anyway.

By the end of the day—or maybe by tomorrow morning, since Aluna had a reputation for disappearing—the city would organize a search. Everyone would forget they were angry at her and band together to save one of their own. But they wouldn't find her, because she wasn't missing. She was *gone*. On purpose. To the Above World.

To save the Coral Kampii all by herself.

He flipped a starfish onto its back with his foot. She hadn't asked him to go. He would have been useful to her in the Above World. He knew a lot more about tech than she did, and about other things, too. He'd read every book in the city at least three times, which wasn't that impressive when you considered the city only had a few dozen books. But most Kampii knowledge passed from one generation to the next through stories and lectures—Aluna and most of the other Kampii couldn't read at all.

She should have asked him to go. He flipped the starfish again, then headed back to his nest to settle in for a long day of worrying.

His parents were out helping with preparations for the feast—the feast that would no longer be in Aluna's honor. He'd been looking forward to the celebration, had even planned on asking Jessia to dance. He couldn't go at all now, not without Aluna. He grabbed some clams from the kitchen and swam down the cramped tunnel toward his room.

"Boy!" his grandma called from her cave. "Boy, get in here."

He swam to her nest and hovered in the archway, gripping the smooth coral with his hands to keep from drifting. Grandma Nani had a window in her nest. Most days, she stared out it for hours, her old, saggy tail draped around a worn resting stick that his father should have replaced years ago. She kept her hair short. "So no imbecile tries to stick shells in it," she always said.

Grandma Nani had been old when Hoku was a youngling, and nowadays she seemed like an ancient. Like someone out of the old legends. Her father had come from a distant Kampii colony during the last Exchange. He had swum a whole year to get here and had filled Grandma Nani's head with wild stories about his travels. Hoku didn't know what his grandma saw out that window of hers, but he was sure it was more than just a handful of fish or the occasional eel.

"Did you want something, Grandma?" he asked. Maybe she wanted lunch, or another covering for her sticky bed.

"I want you to tell me what happened," Grandma Nani said, her back still to him. "Why aren't you at the ceremony? Your friend is getting her tail today. You should be there to support her."

Her words struck him like a harpoon to the heart. He couldn't speak at first, not with so many thoughts and feelings swirling inside of him. And then, when he found his voice, it all came tumbling out. He told her everything. Not just what happened during the ceremony, but about Makina and necklaces. About where he'd looked for Aluna. About where he feared she had gone.

Grandma Nani bobbed quietly on her resting stick

and said nothing until he was done. Then she reached over and took his hand between both of hers.

"You're right, child," Grandma Nani said. "That's exactly where the girl has gone."

"But how—?"

"Because your friend knows what must be done, and she knows no one else will do it," she snapped. "And because that's what I would have done, back when my body and my mind did what I asked."

"But the Elders—"

"Are scared and shortsighted." She waved her hand, as if dismissing the entire council. "They think the answer is turning inward. They think they're honoring Sarah Jennings and our ancestors." She snorted and turned to face him again. "They've forgotten that our ancestors were pioneers. Adventurers. Heroes!" She unwound her tail and swam over to one of the dozens of cubbyholes carved into her wall. "They've forgotten what it means to be brave."

She pulled out a small box no bigger than one of his artifact jars. It shimmered in the water, part silver, part pearl.

"Come here, boy," she said. "This is for you."

He swam over, his eyes focused on the box. An artifact! Why had she kept it hidden all these years? He ran his fingers over the ornate design of a woman on the lid.

"She doesn't look much like a Kampii," he said.

"Because she's not a Kampii. She's a mermaid," his grandma said. "Humans have always longed for the sea. She's the dream that eventually gave us life."

"What's inside?"

Grandma Nani snorted again. "Secrets. Mysteries. I have no idea. My father came from far away, but my mother's family has been here since the beginning. My great-grandfather said this box belonged to Sarah Jennings herself, and I believe him. Maybe it holds her memories of the Above World. Maybe it holds far more."

"Sarah Jennings!" he said. "But how come we have it? Wouldn't she have given it to one of the moon-side families?"

"She was a smart woman, child. Smart in more ways than just books and people," his grandma said. "This box found its way into our family for a reason, and you're going to discover what that reason is."

He wrenched his gaze from the box and looked at her. "You've never opened it?" The idea of possessing a box and never opening it seemed impossible to him. Maybe it was booby-trapped. . . .

She chuckled and handed the box to him. "No, boy, I haven't. It's a water safe. I didn't want to compromise the seal."

Hoku took the box, reveling in the complexity

of the design. A thin coating of transparent material kept the silver from eroding in the salty ocean water. He found a small flap on the front, hiding six glowing numbers and a button. A combination lock!

"No, I don't know the combination. That's another mystery for you to solve," Grandma Nani said. "It needs to be opened in air. I have no need of Above World artifacts, but you, however . . ."

Hoku's mouth slid open.

"You heard me," Grandma Nani said quietly. "Don't be as blind as the Elders, boy. Your friend is showing you the way."

"But Mom and Dad—"

"Will survive," she said briskly. "Only the young can save us, boy. Only those without tails can walk between worlds." She rested her old hand on the top of his head. The weight steadied him in the current.

Hoku looked at the silvery water safe. A great whirlpool was forming inside his belly. Not just of fear, although there was certainly some of that, but of excitement. It swirled inside him, faster and faster, until it was all he could feel.

Grandma Nani nodded and smiled. "Hoku, my boy, it's time you had an adventure."

CHAPTER 9

Hoku packed quickly, his mind filled with thoughts of artifacts. He wanted to bring everything: his bubble jars, his sticky plate, his collection of tools, a few spools of wire, and maybe some food. But he wasn't exactly a strong swimmer, and he had a long way to travel. In the end, only the mermaid box and some of his essential tools made it into his satchel. He slipped a few smaller items into the pockets of his clothes. Just in case.

To the Above World!

Aluna would make fun of him for choosing gadgets over food, but what did they really know about the Above World? Maybe food was plentiful. Maybe there were magic seeds in the water safe that would keep them fed for the rest of their lives. Maybe Aluna could easily hunt for their dinner every night. Or maybe they'd both be dead before their stomachs even started to grumble.

Even that last thought didn't deflate his enthusiasm.

Hoku kissed his grandma good-bye, but she hardly seemed to notice. She was back at her window, staring. He gave her a message for his parents, a simple "I have to do this, don't worry, I love you," and repeated it until she nodded and promised to deliver it.

Leaving the city was easy. His parents were still at work, and no one ever paid much attention to him. A nobody kid, off to do something unimportant.

This time, they were wrong.

Hoku swam toward the surface slowly, pausing every few meters to recite the ritual of ascent. One did not leave the depths of the ocean lightly. If you rose too quickly through the water, the ocean spirits exacted a price. They might decide to give you a rash, or take your sight, or even kill you. Aluna usually spoke the ritual quickly, impatient to keep swimming. He hoped, wherever she was, that she'd been more careful this time.

And that he'd be able to find her. The Above World was big. Not ocean big, but far larger than the coral reef that hid the City of Shifting Tides. They might never be reunited.

While it was true that the ancients had been obsessed with learning, building, and experimenting, just like him, they'd also destroyed themselves with wars and sickness. What part of their legacy remained? Would he and Aluna stumble on an ancient disease or kill themselves with a weapon disguised as something else?

Why were wonder and danger always so tightly interwoven?

He swam a meter under the ocean's surface and used the shimmery streaks of sunlight and the currents to maintain his trajectory. He was getting closer and closer to the shore. He'd passed the first two of three resting rocks the Kampii used when they journeyed to trade with the Human village. The Trade Rock itself was next. He surfaced and saw it in the distance—the big, flat rock where the Kampii's Voice bargained with the Humans.

And there she was now! Daphine's silhouette was unmistakable. Aluna's sister sat on the rock in a classic Kampii pose, her tail displayed to its full glittering splendor. She had undone her braids, and her hair fell in a great mass around her head. She'd made herself look like the mermaid on his water safe.

Her guards—two of Aluna's brothers, Pilipo and Ehu—treaded near the rock with their weapons raised. But why were they here? The Elders would never schedule a trade mission on the same day as a transformation ceremony. Unless . . . this was about Aluna.

A boat wobbled near the Kampii, a small wooden slab carrying four people. Hoku swallowed. Four *Humans.* Aluna's brothers had told him stories about the Humans from the small village on shore, but he'd never actually seen one of them.

He swam closer, but stayed low and quiet. If Daphine or the others saw him, they'd take him back to the city. He didn't want his adventure to end before he even made it to solid ground.

He couldn't make out much detail on the Humans' faces, but he could tell from the way they held their weapons that they were scared and angry, and ready to fight. They kept looking behind them, toward land and their home.

Aluna's brothers carried three-meter ceremonial axes, more for show than killing. Hunters used knives and sleek spears and harpoons when they were actually fighting. Such monstrous blades would take forever to swing in the swift ocean currents.

Daphine's voice carried over the water, but he couldn't make out her words. He pulled out an Extra Ear so he could hear.

"I repeat: we mean you no harm. We are only looking for a girl." She held her hand out to indicate Aluna's height. "Have you seen her?" She pointed to her eyes and then to the shore.

The largest Human replied, a quick burst of frantic

words. His voice didn't sound inside Hoku's ears like Daphine's had, so Hoku swam a little closer. The Human's language was guttural and fast, but some of the words were similar to theirs. He heard "dead," "attack," "fathom," and then, repeated over and over again, "help."

Not Aluna, he told himself. *They're not talking about Aluna.*

A loud buzzing filled the air. A Human male shouted and pointed toward shore.

Two massive artifacts flew toward them, each as big as Great White. A blur of flapping insect wings kept them aloft. Mechanical dragonflies! Then he noticed the Humans riding on top of the metal beasts. Sunlight glinted off a silvery eye, and a black spike like a narwhal's horn jutted out of the other rider's forehead. Their bodies were bizarre patchworks of flesh and artifacts, almost impossible to understand.

One of the riders had no legs at all. Her torso seemed like part of the mechanical insect itself. Did these misshapen creatures really share the same ancestors as the unadorned Humans in the boat? The same ancestors as the Kampii?

"Dragonfliers!" Ehu yelled. "Swim!"

One of the Humans on the boat—a woman—shot a harpoon at the closest flier. It bounced off the vehicle's metal dragonfly head and plunked into the water. The rider let loose a volley of missiles in return.

Pilipo jumped onto the rock between his sister and the deadly bolts. He deflected most of the missiles with his ax, but one bolt lodged itself in his shoulder and knocked him back. The Human woman was not so quick. Several darts struck her in the chest. She groaned and tumbled into the ocean.

Hoku watched Daphine dive backward into the water. Pilipo flicked his hand, and one of the Human dragonfly riders clutched at his throat. A hunting dart! The dragonflier lurched in the air as the rider struggled to regain control. He didn't make it. A moment later, the great machine plunged into the ocean, its wings splashing water in great gouts until the sea sucked it under.

The other two Humans swung at the remaining dragonflier with their clubs. Hoku heard four dull clangs of wood on metal, and a light peal of laughter. The second rider, the one merged with her machine, seemed agile in the air and impervious to their assault.

"Dive," Ehu called to the Humans. "We can protect you underwater!"

Either the Humans didn't understand or they were too angry to listen to reason. They beat uselessly on the dragonflier and spewed words Hoku couldn't hear.

The dragonflier pulled away, out of reach of the

Humans. The Humans cheered, but Hoku knew better. She was simply taking aim.

Green fluid erupted from a nozzle at the front of the dragonflier.

He saw Pilipo and Ehu dive, and he knew he wouldn't see them again. Pilipo was bleeding from his shoulder wound. They needed to get away from the carnage and find someplace to hide until they could stop the flow of blood.

The Humans were too close to the dragonflier, and too slow. The green liquid splashed them. They dropped their weapons into the ocean and screamed.

Hoku tore his gaze from the Trade Rock and took three quick breaths. He heard the Humans fall into the water, the sounds of their pain muffled by the ocean's embrace. He tried to move, but his body wouldn't listen. Terror smothered him, trapping his arms and legs and squeezing at his lungs. He bobbed up and down on the waves like a lifeless buoy.

Swim! he screamed at himself. *Swim!*

And then the remaining dragonflier saw him. He could tell, even from a distance, by the way he adjusted the insect's angle, by the whirring of its wings as it prepared to attack.

Finally, he remembered his legs and dove.

CHAPTER 10

ALUNA RODE a series of waves toward the shore, breathing heavily. Trees lined the white sand beach in the distance. How straight they stood, their trunks tall and inflexible, only their leaves swishing in the wind. She'd made good time. Even if someone in the city noticed she was missing, she'd have a few hours' lead.

The ocean tumbled her to the beach and she struggled to her hands and knees. Her muscles felt weak, and not just from the marathon swim. Underwater, the ocean spirits did not pull her down toward the sand, but kept her buoyant. In the Above World, her body felt heavy and slow, as if it were stuck to the earth and being crushed by the sky.

She wobbled to her feet and gave herself another minute to adjust. Her body shivered—not from the cold but from the prickly sensation of air blowing against her wet skin.

In the ocean, the current was an old friend. You knew where it flowed and how fast. You learned how to ride it, how to hear it in your head like a melody everywhere you went. Wind was the Above World's current, but it felt wild and unpredictable. In one moment the wind pushed gently against Aluna's back, and a moment later, it knocked her to her knees.

She stood again and took a few steps. Her legs steadied. Shells and sharp sticks jutted out of the sand, but she barely felt them under her feet. The ancients had given the Kampii thick skin for warmth, and so they wouldn't bleed every time they brushed up against a piece of sharp coral or got snipped by a crab claw. She was especially grateful for that gift now.

Her breathing necklace pulsed slowly at her throat. It didn't have to work as hard up here, where it was easier to pull oxygen from her surroundings. Was she getting oxygen through her mouth and nose now, too, like an Above World Human? She huffed and snorted a few times but couldn't tell.

Hoku would know.

Her stomach twisted at the thought of him, so she walked faster. Inky night would seep into the world within a few hours. She needed someplace to rest and eat in safety. A hidey-hole or a cave, maybe.

Her right knee buckled. She dropped to the sand. Maybe the swim had been a little more exhausting than she'd thought. She squinted farther up the shore and saw a pile of driftwood sticking out of the sand. One of the pieces stuck out at an angle, creating a tiny triangle of shade. She crawled over, wedged herself under the wood, and fell asleep.

The waves nudged her awake. The tide crept up the shore and tickled her face more and more with each surge. She lifted her head and wiped the wet sand from her cheek. She could feel dozens of tiny sand crabs burrowing beneath her, could hear nameless nighttime creatures scurrying around the driftwood in the darkness. She crawled out from under her shelter and sat in the surf, arms wrapped around her knees.

The moon hovered in the darkness, as if it were pinned in place. The ocean glittered beneath it, surging and withdrawing in its happy rhythm.

She opened her food net, pulled out a hunk of fish, and whispered her thanks to the ocean spirits—and her brothers—for providing it. She chewed it slowly, denying her desire to gobble her whole supply in two or three crazy bites. Were tree leaves edible? Or tree trunks? She should have brought a bigger supply of kelp. If land animals were anything like sea creatures, she'd have to be very careful about which ones she hunted and ate. The most harmless-looking creatures had an irritating tendency to be poisonous.

Her eyes adjusted to the darkness quickly. She stashed her food pouch inside another pouch so that she wouldn't be tempted to nibble as she walked, and headed up the beach. Getting to the Above World had been her first goal. Now that she was here, it was time to meet the Humans.

She stumbled less and less as she walked. At first, her legs were being stupid. Her foot would stop short of the sand and she'd lurch forward until it hit the ground, or she'd pound her foot down, thinking it would hit the sand several centimeters after it did. The process became easier the less she thought about it. She needed to trust her body more, to stop thinking so much. The idea made her laugh. Overthinking was not usually one of her faults.

She must have come to shore farther south than she'd intended. Not surprising, since navigation was one of Hoku's hobbies, not hers. It was almost dawn when she saw the flickering glow of the Human village in the distance. She urged her legs to walk faster. Daphine said they could understand some of the Kampii language, but how much? Aluna didn't want to insult them by accident.

The smell hit her a dozen meters before she reached the first hut. Charred flesh. Smoke, acrid and foul, filled her nose. Where were the Above World's currents to whisk the odors away and cleanse the sky? She pinched her nose closed and kept her mouth shut, relying on her breathing shell to bring oxygen to her lungs. It didn't keep the stench out completely, but it helped.

As she got closer, sickly light illuminated a small cluster of huts and enclosures. The walls of the huts were a patchwork of rocks and bricks, wood planks and dried mud. Some still smoldered. Flames licked out of pits scattered around the tiny compound and ate the remains of fences and roofs. She'd heard about fire, but never seen it. In the stories Daphine told, the flames were always red and yellow. But here, in the remains of the village, the fire burned green.

She approached cautiously, her free hand clutching the hilt of her knife. As far as she could tell, the village was deserted. She peered into a hut. The inside was scorched, its contents burned to ashes.

A strange scrape on the ground caught her eye. Aluna knelt and studied the marks in the hard-packed earth. Tracks. She could follow the trail of most ground-dwelling ocean animals to discover their hidey-holes, but she had no idea what sort of creatures made these marks. Some were probably Human — they resembled the tracks she'd been leaving in the sand all day. But others were unfathomable: huge depressions the size of her entire body, lines and scuffs as if something big had been dragged.

A barely audible noise tickled the inside of her ears. A sniffle?

She walked slowly and quietly through the Human town, careful to avoid the pits where green fires still burned and coughed up smoke. Tools crafted of metal and wood burned on racks by some of the huts. She didn't know what they were for, but she bet Hoku could have figured it out.

Some of the huts had little fenced-in areas attached. White-furred animals lay dead inside, their bodies slashed with spears or knives or some other bladed Above World weapons. She moved past them quickly.

The sniffling got louder. She could hear it inside her ears, the way she heard other Kampii under the ocean. She ran toward the sound, ignoring the flames and scanning huts as fast as she could. Who was it? Had Daphine followed her? Was she hurt?

And then she found him. He sat huddled in a small hut on the edge of the village, his knees folded tight against his chest, his breathing ragged. Sniffling.

Hoku.

CHAPTER 11

SHE THOUGHT Hoku would smile and rush to her, throw his arms around her and hug her tight. Instead, he said blankly, "The whole village. Dead. Even the younglings. Even the animals."

Aluna knelt by his side. "Are you hurt? Do you know who did this?"

Hoku buried his face against his knees. She wrapped her arms around him and held him close. She'd seen him like this only once before, on the morning of the last Deepfell attack. He'd lost an uncle and a grandfather to those killers that day.

Eventually, he lifted his head and started to talk. The words spilled out in one long stream, crashing over one another like waves.

He told her about the Trade Rock. About seeing Daphine and her brothers. About the Humans. About the horrible flying people-creatures and what they did.

"Daphine and your brothers got away—I'm sure of it," Hoku said. "There's no way the dragonflier could have followed them underwater."

"But Pilipo's wound—"

"Not serious," Hoku said quickly. "He's gotten injured much worse on hunting trips. He's smart, Aluna. They all are. They'll be okay."

She let out the breath caught in her lungs and leaned her head against the wall of the hut. Her gaze fell on a small blackened object by the door. A child's doll.

"We should search for survivors," she said. "Four Humans made it to the Trade Rock. Maybe others are hiding in the village somewhere. I haven't seen any bodies."

Hoku stared down at his hands and looked as if he might throw up.

"I found . . ." He gulped. "I found a pit. It was filled with . . . The smell . . . There were arms. . . ."

"So all the stories about the kind of people who live up here . . . are true?"

Hoku nodded.

He looked so pale and thin. He probably followed her, convinced he'd find the Above World filled with artifacts and new tech. Instead, he'd been subjected to one horror after another. She'd left him behind because she wanted to keep him safe—but now that he was here, she couldn't bear the thought of sending him back. No, they were on this journey together now.

She reached into her food net and pulled out a hunk of fish. Hoku's eyes widened when she offered it to him.

"You sure?" he said. "You must be hungry, too."

"Not really," she said. "I practically ate a whole shark not too long ago. I'm fat as a whale." One lie was all it took. Hoku grabbed the fish, mumbled a quick thanks, and shoved most of it in his mouth in one bite.

"Here, look at this," he said with his mouth full. He reached into his waterlogged bag and pulled out a small glittering box.

"What is it?" she asked. Hoku was already looking better. Amazing how quickly his mood could turn when food and tech were involved.

Hoku jammed the last bit of fish into his mouth. "A water safe. Can you believe Grandma Nani had it? She said it was a gift to my family from Sarah Jennings herself."

"From Sarah Jennings?" While the thought of touching something Sarah Jennings once possessed made Aluna's heart skip, she had her doubts about Nani's claim. The old woman had once told her that a

Kampii could live for a whole year inside the belly of a whale.

Still, the box did look ancient. The silvery mermaid embossed on the lid reminded her of Daphine. She seemed so regal, so perfect. Except for being too skinny and not wearing enough clothes. "What's inside?"

His smile faded slightly. "I don't know, exactly."

"You haven't opened it yet?" He'd been shocked by the death of the Humans, and from finding their burial pit, and from the long swim, but still. This was Hoku.

"Well, of course I've *tried* to open it," he said, irritated. "The safe is locked. Look."

He lifted the flap hiding the numbers.

"If you press a number, it cycles up one until it hits nine. Then it starts over at zero again. If you press this button on the side, it tries to open." He demonstrated. Nothing happened.

"It reminds me of the secrets dome," Aluna said. "You have to blow on the conch shells in the right order so the hatch will open . . . and only the Elders know the order."

"Exactly!" Hoku said. "Elder Peleke calls it a combination lock."

"There must be dozens of possible combinations!"

Hoku frowned at her.

"Or . . . a lot more?" she said weakly.

"A whole lot more," he said. "I've already tried a

few hundred. I'm going to be systematic about it and hope they didn't pick 999999."

She looked at him. He looked at her. Hoku tapped in 999999 and pushed the button. Nothing happened.

They both grinned.

"Now that we've gotten that out of the way, let's get moving," Aluna said. "We need to find a splinter colony or another Human village. We may be swim— I mean, *walking*—for a while."

"Back when our ancestors lived, people were everywhere. I'll bet there were more Humans in the Above World than there are sharks in the sea," Hoku said.

She snorted. "There's no way there could be that many."

"It's true. How many Coral Kampii are there— a little over two thousand? We'd be a tiny village in ancient times, just a grain of sand compared to the huge cities that used to cover the land."

"Well, I don't see any of those huge cities now, and I don't want to be here if the dragonfly-people decide to come back. Can you try to focus, please?"

Hoku paled. "Focus. I can do that."

"The sand ocean is to the east," she said, remembering a story Daphine had told her about the horse people of the desert. "I doubt we'll find HydroTek so far from the water. I walked half a day from the south and didn't see anything, so I say north. I can see mountains and trees that way. Maybe mountains are like our coral reefs, and people will be living in nests carved out near the bottom."

Hoku nodded and said, "North is good. Anywhere but here is good. I want to leave this place and never come back."

Aluna glanced at the charred doll by the door. "Agreed."

They headed north, following the coast. The sand grew rockier. The sun rose in the sky, and Aluna kept a hand over her eyes to shield them from the light. Hoku did the same. A few times they stowed their packs in the sand and dove through the waves, collecting mussels and hunting crabs.

The day burned on. Aluna was surprised the Kampii hadn't sent more hunters after them, but maybe the fight Hoku described had made them cautious. *Good.* She didn't want any more Kampii risking their lives because of her.

"What's that?" Hoku said, pointing up ahead. Aluna squinted. The beach was littered with silvery-gray bodies.

"Dolphins!" she said, and took off running. Maybe some were still alive. If they'd beached themselves by accident, she and Hoku could push them back out to sea.

As she approached, the thick stench of blood clogged her nose. The sand under the creatures was stained dark, like a great crimson cloak dragged out of the ocean. A web of ropes lay over their bodies. The creatures hadn't beached themselves. They'd been pulled from the sea and slaughtered.

"The dragonflier-people," Aluna said. "They must have come this way after destroying the Human village. But why would they kill dolphins?"

She looked at the closest animal. It was long and sleek and gray, much like a slender shark. A dorsal fin jutted out of its back. But instead of flippers, it had arms. Instead of a wide, pointed snout, it had a hairless human head, great bulging black eyes, and tiny holes for ears. Its mouth, slightly open, contained rows of pointed, razor-sharp teeth.

"By the tides," she hissed, and took a step back. Hoku ran up beside her, breathing hard.

"Are those—?"

"Yes," Aluna said. She looked at the two dozen other bodies lying torn and bleeding on the sand and gripped the knife belted to her leg.

"Deepfell."

CHAPTER 12

"ARE THEY DEAD?" Hoku asked. None of the Deepfell demons were moving. They lay tangled in big nets, like a school of caught fish. "They're probably dead. Come on, let's keep going."

"Wait. Some of them are missing . . . *parts,*" Aluna said.

"Parts?" he echoed weakly. He scanned the bodies and saw one without a dorsal fin, another with half of its tail cut off. "Oh. Parts. I guess that's what the patchwork people are after. And why they killed the Humans, too. Parts are like tech to them." He tried not to think about the pit of dead Humans back at the village.

Aluna gripped her dagger in one hand and knelt beside a Deepfell to check for a pulse. "This one's gone," she said, standing back up. "I'll go check the others."

He watched her hop from one Deepfell to the next, checking for signs of life. Grandma Nani had been telling him stories about the Deepfell his whole life. "They gave up their humanity to live in deep ocean," his grandma had said. "But if we were meant to live there, the price wouldn't be so high."

The water in the deep-dark was ice-cold, the pressure so intense it would snap the bones of a Kampii in the flick of a tail. Strange creatures lived down there — monsters out of nightmares. Things with tentacles and teeth and no memory of the sun. And on those things, the Deepfell preyed.

He'd been a youngling during the last Deepfell raid on the colony, but his uncle had been a hunter and one of the first to die. The Deepfell had ripped chunks out of him until there was nothing left for the sharks. His grandfather — Grandma Nani's husband — had died trying to save him.

"Hoku, quick! This one's alive."

Aluna crouched by a Deepfell, her dagger hovering in the air between them. It didn't look like the demon was going anywhere, not with that huge gash in its neck. It just lay there, quivering. Hoku hurried toward

Aluna, giving the dead a wide berth and doing his best to step around the patches of red sand.

"Look," she said as he approached. "It's trying to talk."

Hoku stared down at the creature's face. Its lidless black eyes bulged like domes from its sockets. He'd seen other fish with eyes like that. The Deepfell needed to absorb every speck of light in the darkness of the deep. They never truly slept; there were far too many enemies lurking beyond their range of sight. But eyes weren't enough, not in the deep ocean. He'd heard them at night, their high-pitched keening echoing through the colony as they hunted kilometers away.

This demon lay before him, its mouth moving ever so slightly, its eyes aware and watching. Aluna dropped to her knee near the creature and lowered her ear toward its mouth.

"Be careful," Hoku said. "You know how fast they can kill."

She waved him into silence. Hoku saw the Deepfell pull in a shuddering breath and try to speak. He saw Aluna's knife, still tight in her hand, its point aimed directly at the back of the monster's neck.

"I can't understand you," Aluna said. "What are you trying to tell me?" She lowered her ear even closer to its mouth.

"We should go," Hoku said quietly. He thought of

his mother, and all the months she had mourned her father and her brother. Every year, she covered their family shrine with offerings on the anniversary of the attack. She remembered them, and she cursed the Deepfell. "We should swim away," he said again.

"It can't breathe," Aluna said, finally looking at him. Her face, normally bright with energy, seemed drained. Her brown skin had paled to the color of wet sand, and her knife hand began to shake. "He's suffocating," she said. "Just like Makina."

Hoku looked away quickly. He'd watched Humans get killed today, and he'd stumbled upon a pit filled with their dead. Now he stood on a beach covered with the slick gray bodies of the Kampii's mortal enemies. But the worst thing he'd seen today by far was that knife wobbling in Aluna's hand.

"I don't understand," Aluna said. She was looking back down at the demon. Her knife lay useless in the sand as she gently pressed the rubbery skin around the Deepfell's wounded throat. "They don't wear breathing shells," she said. "How do they get air from the water?"

"They don't have shells the same way we do," Hoku said. "Their ancestors modified the inside of their bodies instead. They pull in air through those slits in their throats."

"See him gasping?" she said. "The slits are above

his wound, so the air isn't making it to his lungs. He's not getting enough oxygen."

Hoku shrugged. "Even if we wanted to save it, there's nothing we can do."

"But he's going to die."

"You say that like it's a bad thing," Hoku said. "If that monster had been able to fight, it would have tried to kill us!" He wished they'd never found these Deepfell, or found them an hour later, when the decision had been made for them.

Aluna said nothing. For a minute, she just stared at him. He recognized that look: the furrow of her brow, the slight closing of her right eye, and the almost imperceptible twitching of her lips. Aluna was thinking, and there wasn't a more dangerous activity in all the world.

"I couldn't save Makina or the other Kampii," Aluna said. "I couldn't do anything. In the City of Shifting Tides, I was useless."

"That's not true," he said. "You're brave and funny, and—"

"Useless," she interrupted. "I can't fix their necklaces or stop any of them from dying."

Her hand gripped the small pouch around her neck. He knew her mother's ring lay nestled inside, and that she never touched it unless her thoughts were dark.

"Aluna, what are you—?"

"I'm going to save someone," she said. "I'm going to save the only person I can."

He watched her suck in a huge breath of air, filling her lungs. Both her hands went to the breathing shell at the base of her throat.

"No! Stop! You don't even know if it will work!"

Hoku fell to his knees. He grabbed Aluna's wrist with both his hands and yanked. Her body jerked, but she was strong. Much stronger than he was. Her hands stayed on the shell as she tugged and twisted, trying to dislodge it from its rightful place in her flesh.

"No!" he yelled again, but it was no use. With a sudden pop, the breathing shell came loose. As she pulled it away from her throat, the shell trailed two long, thin metallic tendrils with a sickening slurp.

Aluna had just ruined her chance of ever returning to the ocean.

CHAPTER 13

HOKU WATCHED, horrified, as the tendrils of Aluna's breathing shell retracted into the device. She wasted no time. Still holding her breath, she slapped the necklace against the Deepfell's throat below its wound.

Nothing happened at first. She pushed and twisted it. Her face started to turn an unhealthy shade of purple.

"Stop!" Hoku said. "Put it back on. It's not too late!"

Aluna shook her head. She twisted the breathing shell again. This time it glowed and whirred. The Deepfell's eyes — those ludicrous black orbs — widened even more.

"The shell's tails are burrowing to your lungs, demon," Hoku said. "Lie still. Struggling will make them lose their way." He'd never seen a shell affixed to an adult before. Kampii received their shells within a few days of birth, once their mothers were sure they were healthy enough to journey beneath the waves. He had no idea how the Deepfell's body would react.

Beside him, Aluna gasped. She'd held her breath as long as she could. Now she toppled forward, onto her hands and knees, and choked.

The demon choked, too. And gurgled. And tried to claw at its own throat. *Let it,* Hoku thought. Aluna was his only concern. He grabbed her by the shoulders and tried to steady her as she coughed and hacked.

"What's . . . happening . . . to me?" she managed between choking sobs.

"The shell does more than burrow. I don't know what. But it does something to your lungs and your breathing and eating tubes. I . . ." Her face was red, her eyes bulging. Her body was trying to expel something, and it wouldn't leave.

"I don't know exactly," he said, frustrated. He held her shoulders tighter. That's all he could think to do. The Deepfell squirmed nearby, and if the demon wanted to, it could grab Aluna's knife and murder them both.

"Don't fight it," Hoku said. "Your body knows what it needs. Don't fight it."

Her coughing eased slightly. He saw her take in a shuddering breath, and then another. She looked at him just as another spasm shook her body. She fell out of his grip and curled into a ball on the sand.

Behind him, the demon had stopped clawing at the breathing shell and had started wriggling toward the surf. It was heading back to the deep—*with Aluna's shell.*

He glanced at the sand where the Deepfell had been. Aluna's knife was still there, where she had dropped it. The demon was a dozen drags from the water. Hoku had time to get the necklace back. He could take the knife and . . . what? He'd never deliberately hurt anyone in his whole life.

"'Ku, 'Ku," Aluna said, wincing. "My insides burn."

The Deepfell was only a few drags from the sea now. Hoku should stop the demon, but how? Even if he were strong enough to strike, he could never be a killer. He watched the Deepfell pull itself the last few meters. Once it reached the surf, it disappeared quickly into the waves.

Maybe he couldn't be a killer, but he could be a best friend.

"I'm here," he said.

"Oh, no," Aluna gasped. "Not again." And she was off on another coughing bout. He winced and held her. He couldn't look at her face, so he stared at the knife, his water safe, the dead bodies on the beach. Anything but her pain.

And that's when he noticed the birds. A dozen winged shadows glided across the sand. It took him a moment to realize that they were getting larger, and another long moment to find the courage to look up.

The birds weren't birds. They had wings — vast feathered wings — but their bodies and faces were Human. Not only Human, but *female*. They wore sleek silvery armor around their chests and elaborate metallic bands around their arms and necks. They gripped their spears and harpoons with warriors' ease.

"Tides' teeth," he hissed. "Aviars!"

According to his grandfather, an Aviar warrior could kill a Kampii in one thrust of her spear, but needed a full day to cook and eat her prey afterward. "Sharks," he whispered to Aluna's shuddering body. "Sharks in the sky."

Two Aviars drifted to the beach and landed near one of the dead Deepfell. They stood over the creature and pointed to something in the sand. Another pair dropped behind him, and another. Were they assessing the battle scene or planning for their next feast?

Hoku reached for their bags and pulled them close. He wrapped his body over Aluna's, trying to hide her from their view.

What was she always saying—*still as a starfish, calm as a . . . jellyfish?* That didn't sound right. And how was a silly phrase going to help, anyway? Here they were, out in plain sight, not a single hidey-hole within crawling distance, and he was acting like it mattered if he stayed calm or not. Did a shark care if your heart was racing when it bit your head off? No, the only reason they hadn't been plucked from the beach already was that the dead Deepfell probably smelled more like food than they did.

The bird-women called to one another. He understood "too late" and "food." Their language was more similar to the Kampiis' than the Humans' had been. Only the Aviars' accents made it difficult to figure out their words.

"To pull so many Deepfell from the water would take a great beast. Or a machine," an Aviar with orange-and-red-feathered wings said.

"Agreed," the other said. Her white feathers were covered with strange symbols painted in blue and black. "Upgraders did this. The bodies have been desecrated. Fathom's minions always take pieces for their master."

"This far north? We must inform the president immediately," Redfeather said. "Perhaps he is planning another attack."

Whitefeather turned and spat on the sand. "Go. Scout east. You know the signs to look for. Be back by dawn."

Redfeather pounded her fist to her chest, then leaped into the sky.

"Aluna, what should I do?" Hoku whispered. She was the tactician. She was the fighter.

And she was unconscious.

Hoku lowered his ear toward her mouth and listened for her breathing. Her heartbeat was there, weak and ragged, but growing steady. His own breath came a little easier. Maybe the worst was over. Her lungs were figuring out how to work on their own again.

Whitefeather let loose a high-pitched screech, and two Aviars flew over. "Bring the two Human children," she said. "They may have witnessed the attack. The president will wish to question them."

"Yes, Sister," they said.

Heavy ropes fell across his shoulders and back. Hoku lunged for the knife, but it was out of reach. Three Aviars swooped to the sand. Rough hands grabbed him, tumbled him back. He smelled dead meat and sweat. Feathers brushed his legs and face.

In no time at all, he and Aluna were tangled tight

together. Two Aviars vaulted into the air, and the net jerked into the sky.

The ground fell away. The sand became a yellow ribbon between the blue of the ocean and the green of the trees. They rose fast. The frantic flapping of giant bird wings resolved into a steady rhythm. His hair flattened against his face with each downswing.

The sea spread out to the horizon, seemingly endless. As vast as the ocean had always seemed, he'd never seen this much of it at once. If they flew high enough, could he see around the entire world? Trees, mountains, birds, clouds . . . his eyes couldn't take it all in fast enough.

He should have been planning their escape. He should have been trying to wake Aluna or negotiate with their captors. At the very least, he should have been panicked or frozen with fear.

But as the Above World sprawled out below him, all he could do was stare.

CHAPTER 14

ALUNA'S THROAT BURNED. Something was on top of her, crushing her cheek against a web of coarse ropes. And, as if that weren't enough, she was adrift in a choppy current.

No, wait. It wasn't water buffeting her skin, but air. She opened her eyes.

The world swam below her, all blue ocean and trees and chiseled gray rocks. She wanted to scream, but her throat hurt too much. She was in a net—mashed under Hoku and his bag—dozens of meters above the ground. She twisted her head to see what was holding the net and caught sight of wing tips.

Hoku's words came back to her: *sharks in the sky*. Her brothers had spoken about the Aviars often, usually speculating about who would win in a fight. Even underwater, the bird-people's warrior skills and tactics were renowned.

The net surged upward and the landscape changed. The trees dotting the mountainside were replaced by row after row of black squares tilted toward the sky. Hundreds of them hugged the ground, obscuring the natural contours of the rock. They sparkled like waves in the sunlight.

"What are they?" came Hoku's voice in her ear. She tried to whisper back, but her throat refused to function. She tried again, and a third time, until it obeyed.

"Hoku," she said. "Are . . . ?" She swallowed, closed her eyes, tried again. "Are you okay?"

"Aluna!" came his voice. She wished she could see his face. "I'm fine," he whispered. "The Aviars captured us—"

"Really? Are you sure?"

"Yes! They came with a net—oh. Ha ha."

She smiled. Above them, the Aviars' wings whooshed as they continued to rise. She felt pressure building in the back of her head and the dull throb of an oncoming headache.

"You know what you did," Hoku said in his serious voice. "You can't go back to the ocean now."

"I know."

"Then . . . why did you do it?" Hoku asked.

She could hear his real question, unspoken but loud as waves crashing in her mind: *Why did you leave me?*

Staring into that Deepfell's eyes, those glossy black bubbles, it had felt so right. Deepfell came from the same ancestors as the Kampii. They changed their bodies more drastically, but they still had the same capacity to love and hate, the same right to live. Most Kampii called them demons, forgetting that three generations ago, it was a group of Kampii hunters that initiated the first raid. Daphine knew. As the city's Voice, she had urged tolerance and tried to negotiate a peace treaty. No one ever listened. Not the Kampii, not the Deepfell, and not even Aluna.

But seeing that Deepfell's pain and fear, his helplessness . . . she imagined she was seeing Makina's last minutes. Would her friend's panic have been any different? Aluna couldn't bear the thought of letting a Deepfell, a *person,* die when she had the chance to save him.

"I had to," she said. That was all the answer she had. "I'll find another necklace, or some other way to go back. HydroTek will have the answers. This is just one more reason to find it." She wished she felt as brave and confident as she sounded. "Besides, we have other things to worry about right now, like the Aviars."

"They're going to question us," he said. "And I think eating us is under consideration, too."

She answered brightly, trying to ignore the growing pain in her skull. "See? That's definitely a more immediate problem."

One of the Aviars shifted, and the net spun slightly. Their captors were headed for a small tunnel carved into the mountain. She didn't think they'd all fit—two winged women carrying a couple of Kampii in a net took up a lot of space. But the opening seemed to get bigger and bigger the closer they came. By the time they arrived at the passage, Aluna was convinced that Big Blue himself could have swum right through.

The tunnel curved up and down and around. They left the warmth of the sun, and Aluna's eyes instantly adjusted to the dark. Glow stripes had been painted along the tunnel's stone walls, no doubt to help the Aviars navigate if they came home at night. Maybe they'd been so excited to give themselves wings, that they'd forgotten to give themselves dark sight. The Aviars swooped down and up one last time, and then they plunged back into the sun.

Aluna gasped. It looked as if someone had scooped a huge bowl out of the mountaintop. They emerged halfway up the side. Aluna could see tunnels and caves carved into the walls, making it look as pockmarked and pitted as the coral in the City of Shifting Tides. She imagined a network of passages and family nests and secret meeting rooms, like the ones the Kampii had back home.

In the center of the bowl, a huge tower jutted hundreds of meters into the air. Aviars flew in and out of the spire's countless windows and perched on the resting sticks integrated into the architecture.

The City of Shifting Tides was probably as big, but you could never see all of it at once through the murkiness of the water. In the clean, crisp air of the mountain, she could make out details for kilometers in every direction. The flurry of brightly colored wings and a constant breeze made the whole place feel perched on the edge of chaos.

She heard Hoku suck in his breath. She imagined him trying to look in every direction at once, his eyes wide. She didn't blame him.

"Hoku," she whispered.

"Yes?"

"Do you think they'll let us explore before they eat us?"

He chuckled. "They'll need more than wings and pointy spears to stop us."

Aluna watched a blue-winged Aviar fly straight up and out of the colony's open roof.

"Did you see the pulleys?" Hoku said. "Over there,

where the water runs down the wall. They can lift things from the ground all the way to the sky! I wonder where they get the power."

Aluna wasn't entirely sure what a pulley was, but she loved the way the water fell from the edge, splashed hundreds of meters down the side of the bowl, and pooled in a glistening circle around the center spire. A variety of four-legged animals stood drinking from its edges.

The Aviars carrying them flew toward the central building. The pain in Aluna's head pulsed with each wing flap. She shut her eyes and swallowed, trying not to be sick. In the ocean you had to be careful how fast you went up to the surface or back down to the city. Was the same true for the sky?

She kept her mouth shut as the Aviar flew into one of the tower's wider windows and dropped the net to the floor. Hoku's bag slammed into her shoulder, followed by Hoku himself. She yelped, more from the pounding in her head than from their weight.

Winged women with spears surrounded them and yanked them to their feet. Aluna gasped again. Without her breathing shell, she just couldn't get enough air.

"Welcome to Skyfeather's Landing," a tall Aviar said. "You are in the Palace of Wings, and I am High Senator Electra." She stood like a leader, relaxed and strong at the same time. The gold bands wrapped around her muscled arms were more elaborate than the bands the other Aviars wore. Her brown-and-tan feathers reminded Aluna of the hawks that flew over the coral reef, but her face was much like a Kampii's. If she'd had a tail instead of wings, she could have been one of the Elders.

"Quickly, are either of you feeling ill?" High Senator Electra asked.

Aluna ground her teeth together and refused to answer. *Never let your opponent see your weaknesses,* Anadar always said. Usually right before he knocked the weapon out of her hands.

"Answer me!" the Aviar yelled.

Aluna clutched her head from the pain. Black spots swam in her eyes. Anadar would be so disappointed.

"Fetch a breather," Electra said to one of the Aviars. Then to Aluna she said, "Listen to me carefully. You have sky sickness. The air here is thin, and your body is not adjusting. You need more oxygen."

Aluna could hear her words, but only partially understand them. The whole world felt blurry, like the moon when viewed from beneath the waves. She breathed faster, but her lungs never seemed satisfied.

An Aviar with white feathers covered in symbols spoke. "I'm sorry, High Senator. We rose too quickly. I wasn't thinking."

"No, you weren't," Electra said. "We'll discuss it later."

"Help her," Hoku said. Even through her haze, Aluna could hear the panic in his voice. Why was he worried? "You did this to her. You have to save her!"

With a rustle of wings, the Aviar who had been sent for the breather returned. A moment later, High Senator Electra shoved something into Aluna's mouth. She tried to resist, but her body felt heavy, as if her arms were filled with sand instead of muscle. The artifact was the size of a clam and covered in tubes and blinking lights. It emitted a low hum that she found strangely soothing.

"Breathe through the device," the high senator said.

Aluna shook her head and tried to spit the machine out of her mouth. Another hand grabbed her arm. A smaller one. She looked over and saw freckles.

"Do it, Aluna," Hoku said quietly. "If you don't trust them, at least trust me."

She inhaled. Air rushed into her body. The invisible hand crushing her chest released its grip slightly. She breathed again, and again.

"Good," Electra said. "Now I'm going to stick something to your skin. Do not pull it off. It will instruct your body to adapt faster to the altitude."

"How?" Hoku asked.

"There are messengers in our blood that carry oxygen from the lungs to the rest of the body. We will tell the girl's body to make more messengers."

High Senator Electra gripped Aluna's shoulder and clipped something to her earlobe. It stung, but no more so than pricking a finger on a sea urchin. She disliked earrings, but then again, the City of Shifting Tides didn't have any that could save your life.

Her headache receded. She fisted her hand, relieved to feel its strength returning.

"The worst has passed," Electra said. "Continue using the breather until you can do twenty push-ups without straining."

Aluna had no idea what a push-up was, but she understood all the same. *Keep it on until you're ready to fight.*

The Aviar whistled and four guards stepped forward, their spears clutched at their sides.

"Escort our guests to their chambers on the prison level," Electra said. She turned to Aluna and Hoku. "I have saved you, but only for now. I will inform Her Royal Greatness, President Iolanthe, of your presence. It is she who will decide whether you ever leave this place alive."

CHAPTER 15

ALUNA'S PRISON CELL had walls of stone and a door of metal bars. She wrapped her hands around two of the bars and shook them once, then again, then again with all her strength. Nothing. No sign of weakness. She leaned forward and rested her forehead against the coolness of the metal.

"I can't see you," she whispered to Hoku.

"No," he said quickly, "but we can still talk. And we don't even have to yell. The artifacts in our ears still work up here."

"Unless they separate us," she said. "This place is huge."

She released her grip on the bars and turned around to survey her new home. The room was small, but still bigger than her nest at the colony. The pile of rags in the corner was probably her bed. She walked to the other corner and lifted a small hatch. It hid a hole and, farther down, some running water. The smell tipped her off as to its use.

"I don't even have a window," she whispered to Hoku. "I would have liked to watch them flying." Hoku didn't respond, so she kept talking. "And this is supposed to be a palace? If these prison cells are any indication, it isn't a very nice one."

Still nothing.

"Hoku?"

"Hm?"

"What are you doing?"

"Combinations," he said, as if that explained everything. She waited. "The water safe," he added. "I'm trying more number sequences on the lock."

"Are you almost done trying them all?"

Hoku snorted. She didn't ask again.

Her hand went to the small pouch she wore around her neck. She longed to take her mother's ring out, to roll it in her palm and admire how it shone. She tucked the pouch back into her shirt to keep it safe and hidden, along with the Ocean Seed.

Her hand drifted up to the earring High Senator Electra had clipped to her earlobe, then down to the base of her neck. The holes where her breathing shell had burrowed its tails were closed, as if the necklace had sewn her back up on its way out of her flesh. The skin there was sensitive, like a bruise, and her throat felt raw and angry. Aluna pulled out the breather device that had saved her life. Could she use it to return to the water?

"What kind of food do you think they gave us?" Hoku asked. He must have gotten frustrated with his water safe. Aluna walked over and picked up the pouch of water the Aviars had tossed in her cell. She took a long swig while eyeing the meat at her feet.

"It's probably not one of the Deepfell," she said, trying to keep the smile from her voice. "It smells cooked, and they didn't have time to do that."

"Barnacles!" Hoku said. "I didn't even think of that. Maybe I'm not hungry after all."

"Don't be silly. You have to eat." She picked up the meat by its protruding bone and sniffed it. "Mmm," she said, pretending her mouth was full. "Tastes great!"

"Ha ha," came Hoku's dry reply. "I'm not a youngling anymore, you know."

She laughed. "I'm starting to figure that out." The meat's aroma tickled her nose. She took a tentative bite and then another, much bigger, bite. "Hoku, you have to try this. I've never tasted anything like it." She finished her piece and gnawed on the bone to get every last scrap of food from it. "If you don't want yours, I'll take it!"

"Keep your fins to yourself," Hoku said with his mouth full. "I may be small, but I'm scrappy."

They dozed and talked while they waited, alternating their conversation between praise for the food they'd just eaten and plans for their imminent escape.

"Okay, so we kill a few Aviars and make wings from their feathers," Hoku said. "I'll handle the wing making," he said, "and you'll take care of the . . . feather procurement."

"The killing, you mean," Aluna said. "Killing Deepfell and Aviars isn't like trapping crabs or collecting mussels. I'd rather find another way." Her sister, Daphine, would be able to talk them out of captivity. She'd probably get them all a free ride back to the ocean, too.

Hoku sighed. "Well, it's not like we have a lot of options."

Something moved in the hallway. Aluna and Hoku became still as starfish. Someone was shuffling down the corridor.

"Don't be scared," a voice said. "I'm not here to hurt you."

Hoku whispered, "And there's a pearl in every oyster."

Aluna stood up and walked over to the bars of her

cell. A girl Aviar about Hoku's age slouched in the hallway, gripping a strange rectangular object in both hands. She had long dull-brown hair and tawny wings painted black at the tips. She wore one of the intricate gold necklaces Aluna had seen on every bird-woman so far.

"Who are you?" Aluna said. She didn't see much purpose for courtesy when she was being forced to eat meat off the ground and pee into a hole in the floor. Of course, she didn't see much purpose for courtesy in general.

"I'm Calli," the girl said.

"Did you come here to torture us?" Hoku asked.

"No, don't be silly," Calli said with a nervous laugh. "I was just listening to you, and you sounded nice. I particularly liked the part about not wanting to kill us." She held up the strange box in her hands. Knobs and buttons protruded from the surface, each surrounded by strange markings.

"What do you mean, you were listening to us?" Aluna asked. "Were you hiding around the corner?" Even then, the girl shouldn't have been able to hear. They'd been whispering, letting their voices sound in each other's ears the way they did back in the ocean.

The girl put her box on the ground and fiddled with its buttons. Then she turned it so the front faced their cells. The box crackled.

"Say something," Calli said. "Anything."

"Is that an artifact?" Hoku asked. As he was saying it, Aluna heard his voice in her ears and from the box at the same time.

"Magic!" she said. And the box said, "Magic!" too—in her voice!

"It's a radio," Calli said, grinning. "I check all the frequencies every day, just in case." She blushed, but continued, "This is the first time I've ever heard anything."

"That's amazing," Hoku said, his surly mood instantly forgotten. "A radio! I've heard about them, but I've never seen one. Well, except for the ones in our throats and ears."

"These things are in our ears?" Aluna asked, trying to keep up.

"Yes," Hoku and Calli answered together, then laughed. Calli's cheeks reddened, and Aluna imagined Hoku's cheeks were doing the same.

Oh, ink it all! This was not the time for another one of his hopeless crushes.

"Are you Humans?" Calli asked.

Aluna snorted. "Of course not. Do we look like barbarians to you?"

"No, I didn't mean—"

"We're Kampii," Hoku said quickly. "You know, from the ocean?"

"Oh! That explains your necklace," Calli said to Hoku. She ran a finger along the elaborate golden links around her throat. "The tech that allows you to breathe underwater helps you get more oxygen up here, too."

"That's why Aluna got sky sickness and I didn't," Hoku said brightly. "Because she doesn't have a breathing shell anymore."

Why would he say that to a stranger? To an enemy? He may as well just stab her in the back and be done with it.

"We were designed for high altitudes," Calli said, ignoring Hoku's comment but avoiding Aluna's gaze all the same. "But we can fly hundreds of meters higher than this, and then we need the oxygen the necklaces give us. Down here, at Skyfeather's Landing, they're mostly just pretty."

"Pretty," Hoku said. "Yeah, the necklaces are pretty."

Calli blushed and fiddled with a knob on her radio.

"What about the ocean?" Aluna asked. "Could an Aviar necklace help me breathe underwater?"

Her heart thudded in her chest. *Please say yes.*

But Calli shook her head. "The water makes things complicated. . . ."

"Our shells don't just give us air," Hoku said. "They change our lungs to deal with the pressure. They do a lot more than just—"

"Fine," Aluna said. "I understand." She'd done this to herself. Her choice, her sacrifice, her price. There was no easy fix.

Suddenly Calli's gaze darted down the hallway, her eyes wide. She twisted a knob on the radio and the crackling stopped.

"Someone's coming," she said. She hugged the radio to her chest, looking ever so much like Hoku cradling his water safe, except with wings. She backed farther into the hallway and hid in a shadowy alcove.

Four Aviars walked up to their cells, led by High Senator Electra. She thumped the bottom of her spear on the stone floor with all the ceremony and arrogance of Elder Peleke.

"The president will see you now."

CHAPTER 16

IS THIS HOW you will present yourselves to President Iolanthe? Have you no pride?" High Senator Electra said.

Hoku ran his hand through his hair and smoothed the pockets on his shirt. Without the ocean, he had no way to wash the sand and grime off his skin. Feeling dirty was a new sensation, and he didn't enjoy it.

"It's no use," the Aviar snapped. "We'd need a platoon of groomers to make you presentable, and the president will not be kept waiting. Senators Hypatia and Niobe will now release you from your cells. Do not attempt an escape. Do not fight. Show proper respect for the president and you will be afforded the prisoner's right to a quick and merciful death . . . should the president decide your lives are no longer necessary."

Hoku glanced back at the alcove where Calli was hiding, but couldn't see her in the shadows. *Good.* She'd been the first even remotely nice Aviar they'd met so far. Also, he wanted another look at her radio.

Senator Hypatia—Whitefeather from the beach— opened Aluna's cell first, and Hoku heard, "Get your feathers off me. I can walk all by myself."

Hoku sucked in a breath. As much as he admired her bravery, sometimes he wished she'd choose the coward's path of flinching and silence. *His* path. It made certain predicaments much easier to survive.

Senator Electra chuckled. "I see you have recovered from the sky sickness, child. I think I liked you better when you were closer to death."

Redfeather, Senator Niobe, opened his door and motioned for him to exit. He went without a struggle. As she shoved him down the corridor, Hoku glanced back at Calli's alcove. The winged girl was gone.

During their first trip through the Palace of Wings, he'd been too worried about Aluna to concentrate on their surroundings. Now, as they walked to their probable death, he couldn't take his eyes off the murals covering the walls. Back home, pictures were created by pressing different colored shells and stones into a soft surface to make patterns and images. Mosaics, his teachers had called them. But here, the images were painted in vivid colors directly on the walls. Aviars fought Humans. Aviars flew in a great flock through the sky. Aviars sat together eating, playing instruments, and making things with their hands. The Kampii treasured secrecy, but the Aviars seemed just the opposite: they shouted everything they did and everything they were in vivid color and detail.

After being pushed and prodded down a series of passages, they all stepped through an opening into a small, square room. Four huge ropes ran through holes in the ceiling, passed vertically through the room, and exited through worn holes in the floor.

Niobe and Hypatia propped their spears against the wall and started pulling on the ropes. The floor lurched.

"A shifting room?" Aluna asked, reaching for the wall.

But the floor wasn't shifting; it was *dropping*. Hoku's heart beat faster. What wonderful new tech was this? The holes in the ceiling were larger, so he could see the mechanism. "Pulleys?" he asked.

"Yes! It's called an elevator," Senator Hypatia said in between pulls of the rope, her face suddenly open and animated. "It runs up through the center of the Palace of Wings. This used to be a standard descent and ascent column, until the president—"

"Enough!" Electra said. Hypatia clamped her mouth shut and actually seemed to blush.

"Before the president did what?" Aluna asked.

"Nothing, prisoner," High Senator Electra said, visibly tightening the grip on her spear. "Remain silent." Even Aluna got the hint that time.

Down, down, down they went. Through the one open wall, they could see the other levels in the palace whoosh by in a blur. Hoku enjoyed the falling sensation much more than the lifting one he'd experienced when they were first captured. His stomach felt like it was scrambling to catch up, but he didn't care. Part of him wanted to yell and laugh. A bigger part of him wanted to figure out how it all worked. It must go up as well as down, since it was called an "elevator."

A few moments later, a *thump* shook the tiny room. Then a *thump-thump-thump*. The senators on the ropes stopped pulling, and the thumping slowed.

"Those bumps — they let you know that you're getting close to the bottom so you can slow down," Hoku said. "Brilliant!"

High Senator Electra scowled at him, but Hypatia snuck him a quick nod behind her back. The Aviars braced themselves against the walls, so Hoku did the same. Aluna followed his example, just in time. The room shuddered to a stop. His teeth knocked together, but he didn't lose his balance.

They filed out into yet another corridor. This one

was wider and higher than the others. Bits of the color-ful murals along the walls glinted in gold and silver.

"Wait here," High Senator Electra said. She strode forward, to the end of the corridor. Hoku heard her yell, "The High Senator wishes to present the pris-oners to Her Royalness, President Iolanthe. May she enter the Oval Chamber?"

After a moment, Electra turned around and motioned to the other guards. "Bring them."

Hoku stopped at the threshold of the Oval Chamber and stared. The room was big. Bigger than the ritual dome, bigger than the old broken stadium dome. It was more of a mangled circle than an oval. They'd clearly been going for oval but hadn't quite hit their mark. He looked up, and a thousand glittering, golden Aviars stared back at him. The winged women had been carved right into the ceiling and lit from all sides by a ring of high windows lining the room. They shimmered, forever in flight.

Next to him, he heard Aluna suck in her breath.

"Tides' teeth," she whispered.

"Exactly," he agreed. Why hadn't he known more about this city? Why hadn't the Kampii been sharing tech with the Aviars all along? Together, their peoples would be so much stronger than they were alone.

President Iolanthe sat on a throne at the far end of

the Oval Chamber. Most of the Aviars kept their wings folded against their backs when they weren't flying, but the president kept hers spread out to the sides, as wide as the wings of a giant manta ray. He felt insignificant in her presence, which was probably the point.

As they got closer, Hoku noticed that the president's right wing wasn't a wing at all, but a mechanical device attached to the throne itself and painted to look like a wing.

Aluna nudged him. "Do you see—?"

"Yes," he whispered.

"I bet she can't—"

"No," he agreed.

He wanted to study the fake wing, but he forced himself to look at the president's face instead. Aluna managed to do the same. President Iolanthe wasn't as old as the Kampii Elders, but she was still old—at least thirty or forty. Hoku liked the way her short black hair stood up in all directions, like ruffled feathers. She wasn't a big Aviar, not compared to High Senator Electra and the other warriors, but she looked wiry and strong, and not an ounce of her body wasn't muscle or skin. Unlike the other Aviars, she wore only two pieces of jewelry: her breathing necklace and a thin golden cord encircling her brow.

The senators escorted them down a long dusty-red carpet and deposited them within a few meters of the throne. When Senator Niobe bowed, she gave Hoku a shove. He took the hint and bobbed a quick bow of his own.

"First things first," President Iolanthe said. "My loyal senators tell me you are Humans, but you don't carry yourselves like those barbarians." She leaned forward slightly in her throne, her icy-blue eyes piercing in their intensity. "So tell me . . . exactly who and what are you?"

CHAPTER 17

HOKU HAD NEVER SEEN a woman with eyes like that. They were bright but hard, like glittering scales on a poisonous fish.

"I'm Aluna, and this is Hoku," Aluna said. "We're Coral Kampii from the City of Shifting Tides."

"Mermaids!" the president said. Feathers rustled as the senators shifted in their stances at her side.

Hoku frowned. No one used the *M*-word anymore.

"No," Aluna said through gritted teeth. "We're Kampii."

The president seemed to recover herself. She leaned back into her chair and smiled. Her real wing gave a little flutter, but the mechanical one remained still.

"Yes, yes," she said. "My apologies, young ones. You are indeed children of the Kampii splinter. And from the hidden city, no less! Though"—she lifted an eyebrow artfully—"not yet old enough to have earned your tails?"

Hoku saw Aluna grind her teeth. He was positive that she was sifting through insults in her head, trying to find the best one. He closed his eyes and begged their ancestors to grant her patience. A rash decision could turn them into bird food.

Luckily, a guard interrupted them. "Her Future Royalness, Vice President Calliope!"

Everyone turned at the sound of shuffling wings and feet. Hoku's mouth dropped open. The Aviar shuffling toward them was none other than the radio girl they had met by their cells.

Calliope was dressed in more traditional warriors' clothes now, a shimmering silver breastplate hanging awkwardly from her hunched shoulders. She kept her gaze on the floor as she hurried down the carpet. Her hands, now bereft of her beloved radio, twisted around and around each other like coiling eels. He'd never seen anyone look so out of place in his life.

"Daughter," the president said, "I'm glad you could finally join us."

Calliope blushed and dropped her head even

lower. She rushed to the small throne at Iolanthe's side and tried to disappear into it.

If the president was embarrassed by her daughter's behavior, she hid the disappointment well under a heavy veneer of disgust. Hoku balled his hand into a clumsy fist. He'd never hit anyone before, but for the first time, he wanted to.

President Iolanthe glared at her daughter for another long moment before turning back to Aluna and Hoku, a dangerous new spark in her eyes.

"And so tell me, children," the president said. "What brings our ocean cousins so far from their watery sanctuary?" She leaned closer. "We found you amid the slaughtered bodies of your foes. Have the mermaids joined forces with Fathom and his army of Upgraders?"

"No!" Hoku blurted out. "Those other people killed the Humans. They flew across the water on a dragonflier. They tried to kill Daphine, too, but she got away. We didn't have anything to do with the Deepfell. Except that Aluna saved one of them. That's what happened to her necklace."

"Hoku, stop!" Aluna's dark face was tense and pinched. "Don't say another word."

He ignored her and continued to babble. She'd be mad later, but right now, he wanted the Aviars as allies, not enemies. "The Upgraders—is that your name for those people? For the people who change their bodies with tech? We're not on their side. And we've never even heard of Fathom."

"We'll trade with you," Aluna said, cutting him off. "We have information you want, and we need help. We're looking for HydroTek—our people's safety depends on us finding it. If you help, we'll tell you everything we know about what happened on the beach and the Upgraders we saw."

No one said anything. Aluna stared at the president, and the president stared back at her. For a brief, wonderful moment, Hoku thought the Aviars might actually be willing to help them.

President Iolanthe laughed. Not a nervous giggle, like he was prone to, but a full-throated belly laugh so loud that it filled the entire Oval Chamber and echoed off the carved Aviars watching from the ceiling.

"Our people are dying, and you think it's funny?" Aluna said quietly. Hoku recognized the look in her eyes. He grabbed for her arm, but she shook him off as if he were a stray strand of kelp. "Stop laughing!" she yelled, and launched herself at President Iolanthe.

High Senator Electra intercepted her halfway to the throne. The Aviar held her spear sideways, creating a barrier. She was trying to stop Aluna, not kill her.

Aluna didn't even break her stride. She just jumped, used Electra's arm and spear as a launching pad, vaulted over the Aviar's shoulder, and kept running for the president.

The other Aviars started to move, but they were so much slower than Aluna, who had grown strong in the ocean's dense waters. Hoku watched her heading for the president, who had, thankfully, finally stopped laughing.

Aluna sprang for Iolanthe, arms outstretched, fingers curved like claws.

The president moved in a blur. She raised an arm and swatted Aluna in midair. Aluna crashed to the stone floor, rolled, and came up in a crouch. Her cheek blossomed red from the hit, and blood dotted the corner of her mouth.

Four guards surrounded her, their spears set to kill. High Senator Electra positioned herself between Aluna and the president, a murderous look in her eye. Aluna studied them all like a trapped animal waiting for its chance to strike.

Hoku couldn't breathe. He couldn't blink. If anyone moved, people would get hurt. People would die. He couldn't bear the thought.

"Enough!" President Iolanthe yelled. "Stand down, Senators. Release the warrior."

Reluctantly, the senators raised their spear tips and stepped back. Electra was the last. She moved ever so slightly to the side, still trying to keep herself in between Aluna and the president.

Aluna stayed crouched and wary.

"Well done, Aluna of the Kampii," President Iolanthe said, smiling. "I am greatly impressed." High Senator Electra looked as if she'd swallowed a stinkfish.

The president continued, "If only our own children exhibited such bravery and resourcefulness." All eyes turned to Calliope, who squirmed in her throne and kept her eyes down. "Yes, we are quite impressed with the gift our waterlogged brethren have sent us. We are impressed, and we accept."

"Gift?" Hoku ventured. "Gift" didn't sound good. Not good at all.

"Gift," the president said. "The Kampii girl Aluna will be appointed aide to the vice president. She will instruct my daughter in the ways of the warrior spirit and help prepare her for her future rulership."

"But—" Hoku and Aluna said together.

"Men are not permitted to stay at Skyfeather's Landing," the president continued, "but we will make an exception for the boy Kampii—"

"Well, that's something," Hoku muttered.

"The boy will be kept as our honored guest, to ensure the continued loyalty of his friend," the president finished.

"Mother, no!" Calliope said. "You can't do this!"

Everyone in the room stared at Calliope. Her defiant pose wilted immediately.

"I see my plan is working already," President Iolanthe said, clearly pleased with her daughter's brief outburst. "Yes, yes. This will work nicely. Guards! Take the boy back to his cell."

"Wait!" Aluna said. "I'll agree to stay and help your daughter, but only if you promise to keep Hoku safe, and if you give us what we want in return."

President Iolanthe waved her hand. "Now, this is a bargain I can understand, Aluna of the Kampii. Very well. No harm will come to the boy while you remain at my daughter's side," she said.

Aluna finally stood up from her fighting stance. "And you'll tell us how to find HydroTek."

The president looked at Aluna for a moment, then nodded. "I will tell you what we know, although I don't think you'll enjoy hearing it."

CHAPTER 18

PRESIDENT IOLANTHE leaned back, her real wing rustling. "History is not a fixed truth. It changes with the speaker, just as no two feathers will ever find the same path in the wind. So first, our story."

Aluna shifted her weight to a more comfortable standing position. History may be different, but Elders were the same everywhere.

"Hundreds of years ago, when we were all Human, the world started to run out of space," Iolanthe began. She spoke loudly, her voice filling the Oval Chamber and echoing off the Aviars carved into the ceiling. "Humans were spread across the land, crammed into every niche and nook that could support life.

They were using up the world, and their time was running out."

"So they changed," Calliope said. She blushed when everyone looked at her, but stammered on. "They looked at the places that couldn't support Humans, and they made themselves fit anyway."

"Like the Kampii and the Deepfell, and the Aviars," Hoku said. "We live in the oceans and you live in the skies."

Calli grinned at him, and that silly fish grinned back at her.

"Yes, boy," President Iolanthe said. "And like the Equians and the Serpentis in the deserts, and like all the splinters whose names have been lost to us. Some Humans even made skyships and left the world altogether."

"The legends say they wanted to go to the stars," Calliope said.

"In order to live in these places, the LegendaryTek companies—HydroTek, SkyTek, SandTek, and the others—gave us wings or tails, or four fast hooves to cross the endless sands. They became our saviors. Do you see? Once we agreed to modify ourselves and rely on the tech they created, they exerted complete power over us from their domes. They kept us weak."

"Yes, weak," Aluna said. "And helpless. That's how

I felt in the City of Shifting Tides. That's why we need to find HydroTek."

"You don't need to *find* HydroTek," President Iolanthe said. "You need to *take* it."

"Take it?" Hoku asked. "How?"

"We were lazy at first," High Senator Electra said. "We did nothing to protect ourselves until it was almost too late." She looked at President Iolanthe with admiration, and maybe something more. "It took a young leader to show us the way."

Iolanthe waved off her praise. "A man came," she said. "His name was Tempest, and he called himself Master of the Sky. He'd been Human once, but born from some process that twisted his body almost as much as it twisted his mind. He and his warriors—Upgraders more metal than flesh—assaulted the SkyTek dome and claimed it for their own." She leaned forward on her throne. "They thought we wouldn't fight. They were wrong."

"The battle was bloody and we lost many warriors," High Senator Electra said, glancing at the president's missing wing, "but now all Aviar strongholds that were once beholden to SkyTek are self-sufficient. We don't need anybody but ourselves anymore."

"The SkyTek dome has been broken, rendered useless. No one will ever use it again," President Iolanthe said. "We earned our freedom on that day."

"Could Tempest have gone to HydroTek next?" Aluna said.

"No, Tempest did not live past the Battle of the Dome," President Iolanthe said. "But during the battle, Tempest sent word to his brother Fathom, asking for reinforcements. Fathom calls himself the Master of the Sea, and it is he who has taken control of the HydroTek dome."

Electra nodded. "The journey from HydroTek must be a long one. Fathom's forces arrived too late, after we'd defeated Tempest and his minions. Since then, Fathom has continued to attack us, seeking revenge for his brother's death and killing everything else in his path."

"Fathom," Aluna said, feeling the shape of the word, letting it settle into her mind. Finally, her enemy had a name. Whatever was happening to the Kampii, Fathom must be the key. "How do we get there? To HydroTek?"

President Iolanthe shook her head. "I don't know. Our scouts fly a few days in all directions from Skyfeather's Landing, but they have never seen HydroTek. Someday we may follow Fathom's warriors back to their home, but not until our numbers are greater. Not until we are ready to fight." She sat back in her throne with a sigh. "I think there has been enough talk of battle for one day."

"But—" Aluna said.

"Enough," the president repeated, her eyes tired but holding the promise of wrath should she be disobeyed. Aluna's father had used the same look almost every time he spoke. "I have honored our part of the bargain, and now I have other matters to attend to."

Aluna glowered. She saw Hoku clamp his mouth shut, clearly biting back another question, and reluctantly followed his lead.

She looked at Calliope. The girl was barely able to sit up straight on her throne. Did she hold the answers they sought about HydroTek? President Iolanthe wanted Aluna to teach the girl bravery. Well, one of her first lessons was going to be "When to defy your parents."

"This audience is now over," the president said. "High Senator Electra, give our guests quarters near my daughter. I'll expect you and your senators to . . . *ensure their safety* . . . during their stay."

"We're prisoners," Aluna said. "You can just say it."

President Iolanthe smiled, but her eyes lost none of their dangerous promise. "You say tomato, I say watermelon," she said.

Aluna had no idea what she meant, but it didn't sound good.

Two of the senators escorted her and Hoku to their new rooms but made them wait outside while the previous occupants vacated. A pair of very irritated Aviar girls, their arms full of clothes and other personal items, shoved past them not long after.

Don't shoot your ink, she thought at them. *You'll have your rooms back as soon as I can get us out of this place.*

Aluna's room was huge, bigger than her family's whole nest. Six Kampii could have slept on the bed all at once. She gulped it all in: the desk, the sitting stools, the mirrors, the colorful pictures covering the walls. And everything was designed for feet! She glanced up at the high ceiling and saw perches high above her head. Okay, so everything was designed for feet and wings. Still, it was a nice change from the tail-centric City of Shifting Tides. She couldn't wait to explore. But first, she longed to throw herself on the bed and sleep for a hundred days.

"Don't get comfortable," Senator Niobe said. "Vice President Calliope has warrior training now, which means that you do as well."

Aluna stood in the doorway of her new room and stared at the bed.

"Warrior training?" she asked.

"Yes," the senator replied. "The vice president must train for several hours every day. The boy is not invited.

He will remain here." She nodded to Senator Hypatia, who took up a guard position outside Hoku's door.

"I'll be okay," Hoku called. "Fins and flippers, did you see all this food?"

"Food?" So that explained the glorious smell wafting through the hallway.

Senator Niobe said, "You and the vice president will dine with the president tonight, after warrior training, bathing, and a lesson in etiquette."

Aluna scowled at the mention of etiquette, but didn't fuss. She'd put up with far more than social humiliation in order to train with the hunters back home. Warrior training! Suddenly, being a prisoner didn't seem like such a bad fate after all.

CHAPTER 19

NIOBE ESCORTED ALUNA through passageway after passageway until they emerged in the bright afternoon sun at the base of Skyfeather's Landing. Aluna blinked up into the sky and gaped at the flocks of winged women swooping and darting through the air. Even higher still, Aviars no bigger than dots drifted in wide circles on invisible currents. *Watchers,* Aluna thought. From way up there, they could probably see for forever.

Senator Niobe pointed to a series of platforms jutting out from the basin wall almost a hundred meters above the ground. "That is the training area." She pointed below it. Aluna had to squint to see a steep staircase cut into the wall. "Use the breather as you climb, and stop if your vision blurs or the headache returns. But hurry. It's not respectful to keep your instructors waiting, even for sky sickness. I'll be watching, so attempt no escape."

Aluna grunted. "Why would I try to escape *before* warrior training?"

The senator crouched and sprang into the air. Her wings unfolded and caught the wind. She rose fast as air bubbles in the deep. Wings, Aluna had to admit, were almost as wonderful as tails.

She jogged over to the base of the great basin wall and started up the stairs. She took them two at a time at first, eager not to miss a single moment of practice. Halfway up, her head started to spin and her lungs demanded more air. She puffed on the breather and kept going. By the time she'd made it to the top, she had to drag herself up the final stairs, one at a time, with a rest between steps. Sweat clung to her skin, a sensation she despised. The ocean kept you clean and cool.

The first platform seemed to be a preparation and resting area. Long benches lined the rim around neat stacks of equipment, jugs of water, and piles of towels for wiping away sweat. Water flowed inside three alcoves nestled into the cliff face for Aviars who wanted a more thorough cleaning.

The warriors on the platform pretended to ignore her, but she caught more than one stealing a look. Those beginning their training donned padded armor, then leaped off the platform and flew to another. Aviars finished with their exercise jumped off the edge and drifted out of sight.

Aluna was wiping sweat off her face when Calliope landed next to her in a flutter of wings and a gush of air.

"I'm so sorry!" Calli blurted. "I didn't want you and Hoku to get stuck here because of me. You don't really have to be my friend."

Aluna opened her mouth to speak, but her lungs needed more air. She popped the breather in her mouth and inhaled. Even with the steep climb, she was beginning to need the artifact less and less. After she'd gotten a few good puffs, she secured the breather in her waist pouch.

"We all have to obey my mother," Calli continued. "But you don't have to pretend to like me or anything." Her face was red, and her arms crossed and uncrossed and crossed again in front of her. "I'll understand."

"Calli—"

"I don't even want to be a fighter," the girl said nervously. "If I hadn't been born the daughter of the president, I'd be a tailor, just like everyone else born that month. Can you imagine? Me, making clothes! If I got to pick, I'd be a technician or a doctor. I like figuring out how things work. But those jobs weren't scheduled to come up for ages."

"Wait. You don't pick your job based on what you're good at?" Aluna asked. "What if you don't have the skills you need?"

"Oh, we're designed to be good at everything," Calli said. "We've analyzed all our eggs and only the best ones are grown into Aviars."

"Aviars lay eggs?" Aluna asked, astonished.

"Not that kind of egg, silly," Calli said. She sounded just like Hoku. "Let's go — we'll get in trouble if we're late." She swooped up toward one of the training platforms, leaving Aluna to scramble for the next set of stairs.

When she got to the top, High Senator Electra was waiting, a sharp gleam in her eyes. "Where's your gear? You should always arrive at practice on time and properly attired for the workout."

Aluna hauled herself up the last stair and stood at attention as best she could. Now it made sense why their lesson had to take place on the highest of all the platforms. *To inflict maximum pain and suffering.*

"I'll practice without it," Aluna said. She'd rather be covered in bruises than have to climb back down and up those stairs again.

"Never mind," Electra said. She motioned to a pile of armor. "I brought an extra set. Put it on."

For once, Aluna did as she was told. She pulled padded leg guards over her shins and wrapped thick foam around her forearms. The chest guard was tight—Aviars were thin as eels compared to Kampii—but she managed to squirm into it. Electra tossed her a padded hat. It fit snugly around her head, even without the straps tied beneath her chin.

Calli watched but said nothing.

"Spears first," Electra said.

She and Calliope plucked long spears from the rack affixed to the basin wall. Aluna hefted the weapon in her right hand. The spear was thin and light, even a little wobbly. Kampii spears were short and sturdy. Underwater, the Aviar spears would snap in half.

"Ready positions!"

Calli stood opposite Aluna, both hands on the wooden shaft of her spear. Aluna took a traditional hunter pose, with some frustration. A hunter never stood on the ocean floor if he could help it. You wanted the ability to swim in any direction during a fight, so you swam or hovered in the water, ready to move any way you wanted. Fighting on land made her feel cornered before she even started.

High Senator Electra stood between them, her own spear gripped firmly in one hand.

"Let me see what you know, but slowly!" she said. "I don't want to see any blood."

Aluna darted forward and drove her spear toward Calliope's gut, a very basic but useful maneuver. She hadn't intended to go so fast, but without the ocean's thick embrace, her moves blurred with speed.

Calli let out a squeak and dropped her spear. Aluna's weapon was batted off target at the last possible moment. Electra followed up her first hit with a shove that sent Aluna careening across the platform.

"It seems our waterlogged cousins can't understand simple instructions," Electra said. "Let me try a different approach." She beckoned to Aluna. "Get up and stand ready."

Calli tried to protest, but Electra cut her off.

"Quiet," the high senator said. "Stand over there and make sure the wingless girl doesn't fall to her death prematurely."

Aluna stood up and wiped the dirt off her cheek. She was fast as a shark up here! She took up a ready stance across from Electra and grinned.

The high senator attacked.

Aluna dodged. She jumped left and right, nimbly avoiding lightning-fast pokes from Electra's staff. Electra held the staff in the middle, but when she lunged, the shaft slid forward between her hands, gaining a full meter of length. The first two times, the spearhead almost nicked Aluna in the arms.

Aluna countered with a forward roll into a strike. Rolling on solid ground hurt a whole lot more than flipping in the ocean, but the effect was similar. Electra seemed surprised to find Aluna at her feet and backed up hastily to get out of range.

Aluna pressed her attack. She spun and struck, spun and struck. Electra regained her composure and parried the blows with increasing speed. Then she did something Aluna had never seen before. She spun her spear in a wide arc, faster and faster. So fast that it whirred in the air.

Aluna stumbled backward. She couldn't see where the spear was. It looked as if it were everywhere at once! No weapon moved like that in the ocean. Water was thick and clung to everything. But air—air seemed to exult in velocity. Electra loosened her grip and the arc of the spear increased, creating a great whirling blade of air that she moved from side to side.

Electra advanced, one corner of her mouth twisted into a smile.

"Stop!" Calli yelled. Aluna could barely hear her over the whir of Electra's weapon and the thundering of her own heart.

She looked left and right. No hidey-holes. She looked up and down, but without wings, there was nowhere she could go. She was running out of options.

Electra's stance changed. Her spear thwacked into the padding on Aluna's ribs and sent her tumbling to the right. A second knock to the head, and she went rolling back to the left. And still, she couldn't even see the spear for all its deadly spinning.

But Electra had developed a rhythm, and Aluna dodged before the next blow struck. This time instead of getting out of range, she slid between Electra's feet and rolled onto her back. She brought her own spear through Electra's legs, then thrust it lengthwise against the back of her opponent's knees, forcing them to bend.

Electra toppled backward and they tangled in an awkward pile. Both of them scrambled to their feet, but the high senator was faster. The sharp, cold point of Electra's spear dug painfully into the soft skin of Aluna's throat, exactly where her breathing shell used to be.

The senator took three deep breaths in through her nose, and three quick breaths out through her mouth.

"Not bad, girl," she said. "You've obviously had some training, and you think well under pressure. You'll never be a decent warrior without wings, but you have the potential to be better than horrible."

Aluna pushed Electra's spear point away from her throat, took a step back, and returned to her ready stance. Her head throbbed, her ribs ached, and she was ready to push as much as she needed to to learn everything the senator could teach her.

She looked Electra full in the eyes. "Again."

CHAPTER 20

Hoku HUNCHED over his desk, his legs wrapped around the bottom rung of his stool, and slowly unscrewed another piece of the artifact. Somewhere in the distance, he heard knocking. No time for that, he thought. It wouldn't be long before Aluna found some way for them to escape, and he intended to learn as much as possible about Aviar tech before they left.

Louder knocking. Definitely his door. One more screw . . .

"Hoku?"

He pulled himself away from his project and saw Calli standing in the doorway. She wore the same kind of loose leggings and billowy shirt as she had when they'd been in their prison cells, only this time her clothes were bright green instead of blue. The soft fabrics suited her far more than the silvery armor she'd been trapped in during their audience with the president.

"Calli—er, I mean, Vice President," he said. Reluctantly, he unwound his legs from the stool and stood up.

"Just Calli," she said. "May I . . . can I come in?"

"You can probably do whatever you want, you know?" He hoped he didn't sound bitter. He actually didn't mind being a prisoner. Captivity was a lot more fun than cowering in a Human village or hiking along the beach.

Calli stepped into the room and closed the door behind her. She nodded toward the tray of fruit and bread and meat sitting by the bed. "You didn't eat? I thought you were hungry."

He looked at the food. His stomach whined. He'd forgotten all about it.

"I guess I got a little distracted," he said. He felt heat on his cheeks and turned quickly back to his desk.

"You took apart the lamp!" Calli said.

"It started to get dark, and this torch started to glow all by itself," Hoku said. "I want to see how it works. Don't worry, I can put it back together."

Calli joined him at the desk. "Electricity," she said, and touched one of the pieces. "This is the power receptor. It takes energy from the air and uses it to run the lamp."

He touched the receptor, an inch away from where she was touching it. "But where does the energy come from? I couldn't find a power source."

"From our generators," she said. "They're like really big batteries that store and transmit energy."

"But where—?"

"From the sun," she said, talking fast. "Did you see all the sun traps on the cliffs when you flew in? All those black panels? Those are like nets we use to gather energy from the sun."

"You store the sun's light so you can use it to make other light later?" Hoku said. He touched the round glass bubble jar that had been emitting the glow.

Calli nodded. "To make light, and to do other things, too. Like run our necklaces. Filtering oxygen from the air takes power, and they're far too small and light to contain generators themselves. I'm sure your breathing shells work the same way."

He ran his finger over the seahorse imprint on his necklace. He'd always assumed the power for their shells came from somewhere inside the City of Shifting Tides. But President Iolanthe had said that LegendaryTek wanted to control them. They must have kept the power source at HydroTek, far away from the Kampii, who actually needed it. He swallowed.

"Our shells are failing," he said quietly. "The generator must have been damaged or destroyed. That means all our shells are going to stop functioning when they run out of power." He fell back onto his stool. "There's so much we don't know. I'll never be able to learn it all in time."

"Then we'd better get started," Calli said, pressing her lips into a thin, determined line. She handed him a stack of items from her other hand. "Here. I brought you some books."

He held out his hands and she put three books in them. Actual, real books. Grandma Nani had taught him to read, but the City of Shifting Tides didn't have a big collection. Before he turned twelve, he'd read all the books that weren't hidden by the Elders.

"Before the Battle of the Dome, we got all of our energy from SkyTek," Calli said. "But now we use the sun traps and wind traps, and sometimes waterfalls, for our energy."

"And when something breaks, you fix it yourselves," Hoku said.

"Exactly! We make our own babies now, and grow our own wings. Of course, my mother made a lot of enemies when she defeated Tempest and his Upgrader army. Word travels. A lot of people want our tech. We have to keep it hidden, and we're not allowed to talk about it."

He smiled. "Except you told me."

"I guess I did," Calli said, smiling back.

Hoku walked over and placed the books in a neat row on the bed. He ran his fingertips over the cover of the first one.

"That one explains the basics of electricity," she said. "We aren't supposed to read it until next season, but I couldn't wait." She picked up the book and flipped through the pages until she found the one she wanted. "Look," she said. "This whole chapter is on using energy from the sun."

She held it open for him. On the first page was a picture of the sun, with lines indicating its light hitting an artifact like the Aviars' sun traps. He had to know how it worked! The Kampii lived underwater but had ample access to sunlight. Maybe he could float a web of sun traps on the surface of the ocean. They'd have plenty of their own power then!

He opened the book, admiring the clear print and silky pages. Skimming the list of contents at the beginning made his heart trip over itself.

"Are you going to read that right now?" Calli said with an odd tone in her voice.

"Huh?" He looked up, suddenly remembering where he was. And who he was with.

Calli laughed. "It's okay, I've seen that look

before. I'd be the same way if I got to read books about Kampii tech."

"Not that you could find any," Hoku said bitterly. "The Elders don't really encourage this sort of education. They think we're better off forgetting the past. Every generation, we lose a little more knowledge. We're getting dumber instead of smarter."

He sat on the edge of his bed, leaving plenty of room for Calli to sit next to him, or to sit far away. She chose somewhere in the middle.

"Wait," he said. "Where's Aluna? I thought she was with you."

Calli rolled her eyes. "She's probably still up there practicing. I left after the first hour, and they didn't even notice."

Hoku tried to keep his smile small, but failed. "I know exactly how you feel," he said. "One day she was four hours late for our exploring trip because her brother decided to show her how to throw a harpoon. And then all she did was talk about it for the rest of the day."

"Is she a great warrior in your culture?"

Hoku shook his head. "Girls can't be hunters. The Elders say we don't have as many people as we should, so the girls are supposed to do safer things. So they can have babies."

"Your females actually carry the babies inside them? Like in ancient times?"

"Of course," he said. "How do you do it?"

"Little food beds," Calli said, as if it were the most normal thing in the world. "After we choose which eggs to use, a special machine combines them. We take the final seed and plant it in a tank filled with all the nutrients the baby needs to grow."

Hoku shook his head. "So you really don't need men in the colony."

"There are other Aviar colonies that grow boys," she said. "Far to the north is Talon's Peak, and I've heard that the president there even has a male consort. Niobe and Hypatia gossip about it all the time."

Hoku laughed, and he told her about his parents.

Calli sat there, stunned. "I can't even imagine what your world is like."

"You should visit sometime," Hoku blurted. "If you want, I mean. I'm sure I could modify your breathing device, assuming I haven't made us a bunch of new breathing shells by then. But how could we protect your wings? I wonder if your bones are too thin and light because of the flying. Maybe if we . . ."

She looked at him and smiled, and his insides turned to jellyfish. He would build her anything she wanted. Anything at all.

CHAPTER 21

ALUNA SAT WITH CALLI on the rim above Skyfeather's Landing and studied the landscape. She'd been here more than three weeks, and she still hadn't figured out how to get herself and Hoku off the mountain and away from the Aviars.

She looked down the mountainside, toward the sea. Far below, jagged rocks gave way to scrubby green trees, then bigger trees, then suddenly the vast shimmering blanket of blue ocean. There was no beach, no gentle transition between the Above World and her home.

If she could only find a way to the cliffs. She pictured herself scrambling down the rocks, dodging between trees, and diving a hundred meters into the water. Too bad the Aviars would probably catch her before she made it ten meters down the mountain. Wings were so unfair.

Aluna picked a stone from the pile in her left hand and threw it as far as she could. It bounced three times on the rocks and disappeared.

"You're amazing with the spear," Calli said. She tossed one of her own stones, and it fell not far from where they were sitting. "I can't believe how fast you're learning. If you had wings, they'd beg you to be a warrior."

"But I don't have wings, do I? This isn't my home, and it never will be," Aluna snapped, with more anger than she'd intended. She took a slow breath, then continued more calmly. "Calli, you know I have to leave."

She'd been trying to bring up the subject most of the day. It shouldn't have been that hard, but she genuinely liked Calli and the girl so desperately wanted a friend. Aluna threw another rock and watched it ricochet out of sight. "I have to save my people. You understand that, right?" She said it to remind Calli, but also to remind herself. She had a place here with the Aviar, a useful place. In many ways, she fit in with the bird women far better than she did with her own people. But she'd never truly belong.

Besides, the Coral Kampii needed her. She couldn't

bear the thought that more Kampii might have died while she'd been stuck in this place.

Calli didn't say anything. She didn't throw another rock, either.

"Oh, fins and flippers!" Aluna said.

"It's just . . . I know you're being forced to stay here and all, but the last few weeks have been . . . *nice,*" Calli said. "I like spending time with you and Hoku."

She gave Calli credit for not stumbling over Hoku's name this time, though the girl still turned red as a shrimp. Young love looked so incredibly messy, with all the mumbling and smiling and saying ridiculous things. Good thing Aluna had never fallen into that trap. None of the boys back in the City of Shifting Tides had ever inspired her to embarrass herself like that. Life was easier without the complication. Taking care of Hoku was enough work without throwing another boy into the mix.

Calli stammered on. "I was hoping that you might want to stay. You seem to like the fighting, and I know Hoku has a lot more books to read. And, well, I've always dreamed of having a sister. . . ."

As Calli's words trailed off, Aluna thought about Daphine and how her older sister had practically raised her from birth. Fed her, dressed her, held her when she cried . . . mocked her gently, before their brothers could jump in with harsher words. Without Daphine, what would have happened to her? As frustrating as her sister's perfection was, she couldn't imagine life without her. By comparison, Calli's life seemed so lonely—full of women and politics and important things, but no real friends.

"I promised to help you escape, and I will," Calli added hastily. She dropped her handful of rocks into a pile by her side. "I was just hoping you'd stop wanting to leave. I was dumb to even think it."

Aluna shifted to her feet and dropped her remaining rocks back to the earth.

"I wish it were different. I like you—I really do," Aluna said, and she meant it. Calli smiled. "But we're captives here. We can't leave, and we can't truly be ourselves. If you and I got in a fight, you could probably have me punished, maybe even killed." She looked at the girl, the so-called vice president of the Aviar, and felt a surge of pity. "We can't truly be sisters like this."

Calli stood up suddenly, but kept her eyes on the ground. "We're supposed to be practicing. I don't want to get in trouble." She grabbed her spear off the ground and readied it. Aluna didn't have the heart to tell her it was upside down.

She pulled out the weapons she'd been learning, a pair of tiny, sleek talons. She held a silver canister in the palm of each hand. With a flick of her wrist, the tips of the canisters opened and two sharp claws attached to long, slender chains flew out. She spun the chains in the patterns High Senator Electra had taught her. Not only could she stab someone's eye out, she could use the talons to wrap around her opponent's leg or neck or weapon. She did that to Calli now. One of her talons shot out and wound itself around the grip of Calli's spear. Aluna yanked. Calli's spear jerked out of the girl's hands and landed straight into Aluna's.

"Wow," Calli said. "That was fast."

Aluna dropped the spear to the ground, pressed a button on her talons, and watched the long chains retract back into their canisters.

"There. We practiced. Now I'm going for a walk."

Calli didn't argue.

High above, a group of senators circled. They drifted in calculated patterns, watching for enemies. Aluna never went anywhere without feeling their gaze prickling on the back of her neck. Still, she turned her back on Calli and started to walk. She needed privacy, even if it was an illusion.

She gave the basin that housed Skyfeather's Landing a wide berth. There was too much activity— scavenging parties were always leaving or returning, Aviars with their beautiful wings fluttering everywhere. Aluna hugged the lip of the mountain and walked away from the ocean. On days like today, it hurt to see so much blue.

Traveling this direction, the scrubby green covering the mountain slope turned into forest, then into an even bigger and scarier forest. The trees crowded so close together that it was impossible to see the ground. She suspected that not even the Aviars' enhanced eyesight could penetrate the thick layers of green. It would be difficult to fly through the dense trunks and branches. With wings, it would be hard to even walk through the brush without losing feathers. All of which made it the perfect direction for her escape . . . if only she could figure out how to survive several hundred meters of an almost sheer drop to make it to the tree line.

The Above World felt lonely. She missed the water's embrace, the sound of dolphins laughing, the month-long soliloquies of dying whales. She missed Daphine and practicing with Anadar. She even missed Ehu and Pilipo, despite the fact that they annoyed her most of the time. Her father, now, he was a fish of a different color. She didn't exactly miss him, but she did wonder sometimes if he'd be proud of her, of everything she was trying to do.

Far below, the trees began to move. Strange, since there was almost no breeze; even the Aviars had to flap to stay in their positions. Aluna looked closer. Only a few of the trees shook, a small cluster that seemed to be moving closer and closer up the mountain. Something was cutting through the forest like a harpoon through the water. Something big. And it was headed straight for Skyfeather's Landing.

The Aviars were under attack.

CHAPTER 22

ALUNA WAVED HER ARMS above her head, trying to get the guards' attention, but the Aviars had already changed formation. An alarm screeched inside the basin, and then another.

She ran, legs and arms pumping, wishing she had a tail and that the world was made of water. She made it halfway back to the ocean side of the mountain rim before she saw Calli flying straight at her.

"Attack!" Calli said. "Upgraders!"

"Is it Fathom?" Aluna panted.

"Fathom never leaves HydroTek," Calli said. "But the Upgraders are bad enough on their own. They're here to steal our tech and kill as many of us as they can. Killing is the part they like most." She tugged Aluna's arm. "Come on, we have to get inside!"

Aluna hesitated. Calli was safe, as safe as any of them. Now was her chance. She could escape right now, while Skyfeather's Landing was enveloped in chaos. Maybe Calli could help her scale down the side of the cliff.

Then she saw the look on Calli's face. Wide-eyed panic. *Fear.* Aluna needed Calli calm—or at least as calm as the girl could manage—before they could attempt the escape. And it's not like Aluna could leave without Hoku.

"Let's go," Aluna said, and took off in a sprint toward Skyfeather's Landing. Calli flew by her side, easily keeping pace. "Will they be able to scale the slope?"

"Yes, they have creatures with spiked hooves and machines with special treads," Calli said. "We've tried different barriers and traps, but they always find a way around them."

They reached the lip of the city. Normally, Aluna could see Aviars fluttering to and fro, filling the space with a frenetic and lively energy. But a shark had entered their waters. Now the Aviars flew in tight formations, looking larger than their individual selves.

Aluna headed for the thin, crumbly stairway carved into the side of the bowl and forced herself to slow down. This was no time to take the stairs two at a time, slip, and find herself plunging to her death. Calli's wings twitched and fluttered anxiously as she hovered nearby. All around them, alarms screeched and Aviars called out orders.

"My mother—" Calli said.

"I'm going as fast as I can," Aluna grumbled. She couldn't risk taking her eyes off the narrow steps in front of her.

"No, I think you can go a little faster."

High Senator Electra plucked Aluna off the stairway the way a pelican plucks a fish out of the ocean. In a flash of wings, Aluna was flying. The three of them plunged toward the Palace of Wings at a terrifying speed.

Aluna looked everywhere but the ground. She saw dozens of Aviars fighting around a tunnel opening to the right. She couldn't see what they were fighting, but she could feel its growls in her bones. An Aviar screamed. A spray of red hit the other Aviars, and Aluna averted her gaze before she saw any more.

All the other Aviars had fled into the city's catacombed walls. The farmers had abandoned their cliffside crops, and the chickens and pigs that normally milled around the bottom of the basin had been herded to safety. Only the senators remained.

Above them, a creature made of metal screeched into view. No, it was a Human sitting in a flying metal artifact. She recognized it from Hoku's description: a dragonflier! Just like the ones that had attacked her sister and brothers on the Trade Rock. The Human controlling the device directed streams of green liquid at any Aviar brave enough to get within range.

"Insectoid," Electra said. "We're not safe out here. Calli, keep up with me."

Electra folded her wings and they plummeted. Air flew past Aluna's face so fast that it stung. She wanted to scream. She opened her mouth and air rushed in, billowing her cheeks out like bubbles in the deep ocean. The Palace of Wings surged toward them. They'd never be able to stop in time.

Electra opened her wings and swung her legs under them both. Air whooshed by Aluna's ears. They landed on a platform near the point of the spire and jarred to a stop. Calli wasn't as lucky. She hit the stone too fast and fell to one knee with a sharp cry.

"Calli!" Aluna said.

Electra dropped her and bent by Calli. "Can you stand? Is it broken?"

All Aluna could see was wings. All she could hear was a tiny sob.

"I don't know. I don't think so," Calli said.

"You have to get inside," the high senator said, motioning to the palace entrance behind them. "Aluna, help Calli walk—there isn't room in the passage for her to fly. Take her to the president. I'll take care of anyone who tries to stop you."

Aluna nodded. She'd rather be on guard duty herself, but she knew what Electra was capable of. They'd been training together for weeks, and there wasn't anyone alive she'd trust more to watch her back. Not even her brothers.

"Come on," she said to Calli. The girl's ankle was already swollen and an angry red. Calli winced with each step, but kept moving.

When they made it inside the palace entranceway, Calli stopped. She turned to Aluna, her eyes wide and intense.

"We have to do it now, while there's so much confusion," Calli said. "I'm going to help you escape."

CHAPTER 23

HOKU TOOK ANOTHER huge bite of his sandwich — a delicious Aviar concoction with different types of food layered between two pieces of a spongy substance called bread. Senator Niobe had recommended this combination of foods, including a bright-yellow substance called mustard that he was learning to love almost as much as his artifacts.

Oh, the City of Shifting Tides had good cooks, too. His own mother could work miracles with a net full of clams. But there was no escaping the frigid salt water that soaked every meal and surrounded every taste bud. Kampii ate out of necessity, not pleasure.

But so many different animals and crops grew in the Above World! You could grill food over a fire, or boil it, or steam it. And the spices! Little specks of orange or red or black that brought whole new sensations to his mouth and stomach. Senator Niobe ordered him something different every day and seemed to delight in watching his reaction as he ate. The way she talked about it, Hoku suspected that she'd rather have been born a cook than a warrior. The two had equal status in Aviar society, and a cook was a lot less likely to get impaled on her enemy's spear.

Hoku licked the mustard off his fingers and tried a few more combinations on his water safe. He found the repetition relaxing: advance a number, try to open the box, and advance the number again. In some ways, he didn't even care what was inside. The safe itself was enough of a joy. He'd gotten in the habit of tracing the mermaid design on the lid while he was reading.

Although Aluna had the freedom to roam Skyfeather's Landing, Hoku was restricted to his room and an exercise chamber they foolishly thought he'd want to use. He didn't mind the confinement. Calli found time to spend with him almost every day. Sometimes she stopped by late at night, when the senator guarding his room was napping by the door. Those were his favorite visits. They kept their voices low so even Aluna couldn't hear them. He'd already learned more about technology than he would have if he'd spent his whole life under Elder Peleke's tutelage.

And being with Calli made him feel good. He liked her more than he ever liked Jessia back in the City of Shifting Tides. Jessia was nice, but Calli was *special.* She was smart and clever and teased him, but not in a mean way. He loved the way she bit her lip and stared into the distance when she was thinking really hard.

A bell clanged somewhere higher up in the Palace of Wings. Another bell joined it, then another.

Hoku hopped over to the window. The sun burned low near the rim of the mountain, its light dotted with the normal flurry of winged women in the sky.

An Aviar shouted somewhere above him. He twisted his neck to see her and almost missed the squad of senators that shot up past his window, flying in a tight pack.

He saw another group fly up to the right, and two more to the left, their spears glinting and ready. He'd been at Skyfeather's Landing for weeks, but he'd never seen the Aviars perform drills like this.

He ran to the door and flung it open. Senator Niobe stood outside in the hallway, clearly agitated.

"Get back in the room," she said.

"Not until you tell me what's going on."

Her hand tightened around the shaft of her spear. "Get back in there before I put you back in there myself."

"What's going on? Are we under attack?" he said.

"If we're under attack, then who's attacking? What do they want? Is it Fathom?"

Niobe glared at him, but then softened. She always did.

"Fathom's Upgraders, here for raiding and revenge." She spat on the floor. "But we're ready for them, and for whatever warped tech they use against us. We'll stain the clouds with their blood."

Hoku could tell she was angry. Angry at the Upgraders and angry at being stuck guarding him when the colony was under attack.

"Go," he said to her. "I'll stay in my room with my books."

"I have to guard you," she said, but he could tell she was wavering.

"I'll be safest here," he said. "If anyone comes looking for me, I'll hide under the bed."

She narrowed her eyes. "You won't try to escape?"

"When there's a war going on? Tides' teeth, I'm not stupid! And besides, I still have half my sandwich left."

"Okay, then," she said, nodding. "Stay here. But if the Upgraders penetrate this deeply, do yourself a favor and jump out the window or fall on your spear. Better death than to let them harvest your parts."

"Uh . . ." Hoku said, not at all certain he wanted her to leave now.

"Good luck, boy," Niobe said. She bolted down

the corridor toward the yelling and was out of sight in three flashes of a tail.

Hoku waited another flash or two before he was convinced the good senator wasn't going to change her mind and come back.

"Aluna!" he said. "Can you hear me?"

No answer. She wasn't close enough to hear. She was probably with Calli. That gave Calli a much better chance at survival . . . but also a better chance of being in the middle of whatever chaos was occurring up in the skies.

He looked back into his room. The bed was covered with open books, crumbs, and the silvery water safe. The desk held the designs he'd been working on — his ideas for mechanical wings that might someday allow him to fly. He didn't want to leave Skyfeather's Landing. Not now, and maybe not ever. But Aluna and Calli could be in trouble.

Hoku pulled an Extra Ear out of its pouch and secured it in place. He had a much better chance of finding Aluna and Calli if he could hear them, and the device would increase his range. Then he took a deep breath, shut the door, and sprinted down the corridor to find his friends.

CHAPTER 24

ALUNA LOOKED AT CALLI, uncertain what she'd heard.

"You're helping me?"

Calli nodded, her face pale, her lips pressed into a thin line. "I want you to *want* to stay, but you don't. Does that make any sense? If you go now, no one will blame the high senator and no one will blame me. It's the perfect chance."

For the first time, Aluna saw a hint of President Iolanthe's power and charisma deep in Calli's eyes.

"But what about your mother's safety?"

"She'll be surrounded by senators," Calli said quickly. "And directing our forces. And screaming at people. And cursing her inability to get out there and fight herself."

Aluna nodded. Her father would have been the same way.

"So where do we go? Your water and waste must be funneled somewhere. It sounds gross, but maybe we can find one of those chutes and follow it."

"No, all of our water and sewage is recycled," Calli said. She took a step and collapsed. She would have fallen to her knees if Aluna hadn't caught her. "This way," she said, brushing the tears away from her eyes. "There's a secret tunnel under the palace that leads to an old escape passage. It goes all the way down to the bottom of the mountain. They installed it all after my mother lost her wing."

Calli had never mentioned the passage before, not in all of their discussions about her escape. But she was mentioning it now, and that had to be good enough.

"Now is not the time for stiff wings," Calli said. "Let's go!"

Aluna nodded and helped Calli hobble down the corridor. Twice they hid in alcoves—Aluna's sweaty back pressed against cool stone—as messengers ran by. And still, the alarms screamed and screeched, adding to the growing chaos.

"A few more passages," Calli said, huffing. The girl winced with each step. Aluna shifted her shoulder to take more of her weight.

"Hoku!" Aluna said suddenly. "We need to go back!"

"We'd never make it," Calli said. "We'll find another way to get him out. Hoku is smart. I am, too. We'll find a way."

Aluna closed her eyes and nodded. Calli was right. She could help Hoku more from the outside, even if it meant raising an army of Kampii to come rescue him. The Aviars were fierce but honorable. They'd treat him fairly. Still, her stomach clenched at the thought of leaving him behind.

They rounded the last corner and heard metal clank against metal. Senator Niobe stood in the hallway, struggling with an Upgrader who had clearly emerged from the hidden door in the wall. At first, Aluna thought the man was a Human. Then she caught the glint of metal where his eyes should have been. Instead of fingers on his right hand, five thin metal blades dripped a mixture of blood and green fluid. Niobe had the man's wrists gripped in her hands and was trying to fend him off. Four parallel cuts in her shoulder told Aluna that she'd already been hit . . . and possibly poisoned.

"The passage is already open. You can make it out," Calli whispered. "Now, while they're both fighting!"

Escaping was the right thing to do. Aluna's people needed her. The Aviars weren't her people; they were her captors. She owed them nothing. If she didn't leave now, she might never get another chance.

The Upgrader's bladed hand inched closer to Senator Niobe's face. The Aviar gritted her teeth as she struggled to keep its poison tips away from her eyes.

Aluna edged toward the passage. Neither Niobe nor the Upgrader appeared to notice her. She kept her body low and crept steadily along the wall. And it was from that vantage point that she saw the needles coming out of the Upgrader's boot. One swift kick and he'd pump vile green fluid into the senator's body.

She was almost there. A crisp breeze blew out from the open passage, promising fresh air and sunlight and freedom. *Focus,* she told herself. *Keep your head in the hunt.*

The Upgrader pulled back his foot to kick.

Instead of diving for the passage, Aluna dropped onto her back and kicked her own legs out in front of her. She trapped the Upgrader's swinging leg between her own, like using a crab's claws to trap a fish. Her legs were thick and strong from a lifetime of swimming. Despite his size, he couldn't budge his leg.

Aluna couldn't watch Niobe die, not when she had the power to save her.

With the Upgrader suddenly off balance, Niobe swung both his wrists to the left. Together, they swept him off his feet. Aluna kept her eyes on the needles sticking out of his foot. One wrong move and she'd get whatever venom they held. Niobe slammed her knee into the man's chest, but couldn't afford to let go of his wrists.

Aluna grunted, trying to break the man's leg between her own. "Break," she said. "Break!" But his leg wouldn't snap. Was it even made of bone and flesh?

"Surrender!" Niobe screamed, but the man continued fighting.

The sound of metal thwacking bone pierced the cacophony of battle noise, and the Upgrader's body fell limp.

"It's over, child," Niobe said, her breath coming hard and fast. The senator untangled herself from the Upgrader and stood up, pressing her right hand against the gashes in her shoulder. "The boy took care of him."

"The boy?" Aluna untangled her legs from the Upgrader's and sat up. Hoku stood by the man's head, shaking. He held a dented metal lantern in his hand. A lantern he'd clearly used to bludgeon the Upgrader's skull. As she watched, the lantern fell from his hand and clanked to the floor.

Hoku's voice cracked. "Is he . . . ?"

"Unconscious," Niobe said. "Good work, boy, even though I told you to stay in your room."

Hoku looked pale as a milkfish. Aluna opened her mouth to tell him it was okay, to tell him he'd just done what needed to be done for their survival, but she didn't get a chance. Before she could speak, Calli hobbled into his arms.

"You saved us," Calli said. She hugged him and kissed his cheek.

And Hoku kissed her back.

CHAPTER 25

Hoku STOOD next to Aluna on the red carpet of the Oval Chamber and fidgeted. The Upgrader attack had been repelled, the dead had been counted, and the prisoners had been "taken care of," according to Senator Niobe. But now President Iolanthe wanted to speak with them, and he didn't know why.

Unless it was the incident in the hallway. Not the part with the Upgrader, but the part where he kissed the president's daughter right on the lips in front of everyone.

His insides warmed at the thought. It was difficult to even remember the whole head-bashing aspect of the fight in light of the kiss. His first kiss. Calli had kissed him. He had kissed Calli. They had kissed. He was now a person who had kissed another person, and been kissed by them in return. He would never be the same as he was before. Kissing changed everything.

He looked over at Calli, his face hot. She sat on her throne and smiled and blushed and lowered her eyes. Hoku grinned back, and blushed some more, and lowered his eyes, too. Yes, yes. Kissing changed everything. He hoped to be kissing again very soon. And very often. He was highly in favor of kissing.

Beside him, Aluna crossed her arms in front of her chest and shifted her weight. He could practically hear her frustration. She'd had the chance to escape, and she hadn't taken it. It had been her choice, and now she was beating herself up over it.

The senator by the entrance yelled, "All rise for Her Royal Highness, President Iolanthe!"

An odd thing to say, Hoku thought, since they were standing already. But he tried to straighten up anyway.

The president strode down the red carpet looking off balance with only one wing behind her. She nodded to Calliope and took her seat, unfurling her wing to match the metal wing built into the throne. He had no idea why they bothered with the pretense. Two wings, one wing, no wings—President Iolanthe scared the ink out of him.

"The Upgraders have been repelled with minimal losses to our people," the president began. "A prisoner has been released with a message for Fathom: we will never bend. We will never break. Skyfeather's Landing will never be his!"

The Aviars cheered and clanged their weapons against their armor. Hoku was surprised to find himself cheering right along with them. When the noise died, the president continued.

"We are especially pleased that the vice president came to no harm during the skirmish. For this, we have High Senator Electra, Senator Niobe, and our ocean cousins to thank."

Hoku stood even taller. For once, he'd actually done something brave.

"The warriors Aluna and Hoku will approach the throne."

Warrior! Him? He glanced at Aluna, and she gave him a quick grin. They walked forward and stopped a meter from the throne.

The president spoke to Aluna. "A few weeks ago, when you first stood before us in this hallowed chamber, I appointed you aide to the vice president. It was my intention that you would teach my daughter about bravery." She looked at her daughter, then back at Aluna. "I did not expect that you would also teach her about honor."

Hoku heard wings rustle behind him as the Aviars reacted to their president's words.

"You had the opportunity to leave," Iolanthe continued. "Calliope informed me of your plan—*after* the battle, of course. I'm not surprised. I would have schemed similarly in your place."

And then the president smiled. The harsh lines of her face melted smooth, and Hoku saw, for one fragile moment, what she would have looked like had she been born a Kampii. Or a Human. Or anything except the ruler of a war-torn people.

The president reached for the clip at her waist and unhooked something. It looked like a pair of the talon weapons that Aluna had been training with for the last few weeks.

"Aluna of the City of Shifting Tides, I hereby grant you your freedom. You are henceforth to be considered an honored friend and ally of Skyfeather's Landing, and you may call on us for assistance in times of need. We share the same sky."

At the president's last words, all of the other Aviars in the room echoed, "We share the same sky." Their words rang in the vast chamber, and it seemed as if all the golden Aviars carved into the ceiling were speaking them, too.

Iolanthe held out her talons. "*Spirit* and *Spite* have been in my family for generations. Take them and use them well."

Aluna glanced at Calliope.

The president waved a hand. "My daughter does not desire my talons, and my days as First Wing are long over." She held out her hand until Aluna was forced to accept the gift. "They are yours."

"I . . . thank you," Aluna said.

Hoku had never seen her so surprised, or so humbled. For all her bravery, the Kampii back home had never treated her as anything more than a troublemaker. He felt ashamed of his people.

The president turned to him. "To you, Hoku of the City of Shifting Tides, we also grant freedom."

Hoku swallowed. He'd been dreading this moment for so long. He tried to choose his words carefully.

"Does that also mean the freedom to return one day . . . and stay?"

He didn't dare look at Aluna. He could picture her face, a mix of anger and astonishment. But he wanted this. He *needed* this. Even without Calli's friendship, Skyfeather's Landing offered him books and tech to study, and the opportunity to experiment that he'd never get underwater. If he was going to help the Kampii, it would be with his brain, not his spear arm.

President Iolanthe smiled gently, then shook her head. "No, child, you cannot live here."

Hoku dropped his gaze to the floor and studied the dusty-red rug. He couldn't bear to look in Calli's direction. Or Aluna's.

"Skyfeather's Landing is open only to girls and women," the president continued. "There are other Aviar strongholds that welcome men. We can arrange transportation to Talon's Peak if—"

"No," Hoku said, the word choking in his throat. "That's okay. Never mind."

"Child, look at me," the president said.

Child, thought Hoku. No more *warrior.* Tides' teeth, respectability had been short-lived. Still, he did as he was told.

President Iolanthe knew better than to smile, knew better than to show pity. She said simply, "You may not live here, child, but you may visit."

"Visit?"

He looked at Calli, suddenly hopeful. She grinned back at him.

"Visiting would be, ah, good," he said stiffly. "Very good."

Calli smothered a laugh, but the president made no attempt to hide hers. "Now that you are free, where may we take you? High Senator Electra and Senator Niobe have volunteered to fly you wherever you desire. We don't know where HydroTek is, but we do think it is located in a dome on the ocean's surface somewhere to the south. Farther than we can travel safely from here."

"Then take us to the SkyTek dome, please," Aluna

said. "That's the only place I can think of that might have a clue for us to follow."

"There is nothing but devastation and danger there now," President Iolanthe said. "But I suspect that will not deter you?"

Aluna grinned. "How soon can we leave?"

He wanted to kick her. Why was she in such a rush? They'd been here for weeks. Would another few nights make any difference? He looked at Calli. However much time, it just wouldn't be enough.

"Pack your things," Iolanthe said. "Our sisters are ready to fly."

CHAPTER 26

AN OCEAN OF GREEN FOREST bobbed below Hoku, in time with the flap of Senator Niobe's wings. She held him close to her body as they flew. Her shoulder was freshly bandaged from the Upgrader fight, and he could smell the antiseptic the Aviar medic had slathered under the dressing in hopes of neutralizing the poison from the Upgrader's finger blades. But Niobe had insisted on taking him despite her wound, and he was glad for her company.

Up ahead, High Senator Electra carried Aluna, and the two chatted about the battle. He tried to follow their conversation, but he could only hear what Aluna was saying. He had no interest in tactics or strategy, but he wanted to think about something, anything, other than Calli . . . and the fact that every wing beat took him farther away from her.

He hadn't gotten even one last kiss before they'd left. He'd barely had time to shove his water safe and two of the smaller books Calli had given him into his satchel before Aluna had hustled him back to the Oval Chamber for their formal good-bye. He'd lingered as long as he could, trying to urge Calli off her throne with his mind. She hadn't budged. He didn't blame her. Kissing in front of all those people before they'd had time to practice more could have been a disaster.

Still. One more kiss. It wouldn't have been that bad.

Calli wasn't like Aluna. She understood what it felt like to be shy, to be bad at hunting and good at fiddling with tech. She made him feel like it was okay to like the things he liked.

Grudgingly, he knew they needed to keep moving. He believed in their quest, and as much as he loved living with the Aviars, he hated the thought of more Kampii dying. He pictured his mother and father and his grandma Nani going out for their evening swim, and a familiar knot twisted in his stomach.

Aluna was right. They had to keep looking for HydroTek. He had to fix their breathing shells' power source and figure out how to make more of the necklaces. There was no way Aluna could do it without him.

The mountains became forest. The Aviars dropped into small wooded clearings three separate times to rest their wings. Aluna practiced with her talons while Electra and Niobe called out tips and critiqued her form. Hoku used the privacy to examine the books he'd brought: one on microengineering, with lots of detailed diagrams, and another containing overviews of all sorts of science topics.

He took the second book and flipped open the cover. Under the title, Calli had written him a secret note:

Dear Hoku,

May this book help you to save your people so you can come back and visit me soon. I wish you strong wind under your wings.

Your friend always,

Calli

He read it again. And a third time. It was so like her, so sweet and thoughtful. But . . . what did she mean by "friend"? Weren't they more than friends? Friends didn't kiss like that, not even when they'd saved each other's lives. Or did they? He read her note a fourth time. She mentioned him visiting, which was definitely a good sign. But the friend thing . . . was she trying to let him down easy? Was she saying, "Hey, about that kiss . . . I was just grateful that you saved us, but it didn't mean anything more than that."

He slammed the book shut and shoved it back in his bag, careful not to break the collection of tiny, waterproof spice jars Niobe had insisted he pack. Over by their camp, Aluna and High Senator Electra were laughing at something Niobe had said. *Girls,* he thought, and shook his head.

During the next part of the journey, he pondered every single word in Calli's note until Niobe woke him up from his girl-induced stupor.

"We're here," she said.

A plateau jutted out of the green forest, twice as tall as the highest tree. Atop the plateau stood a massive dome, big enough to enclose the remains of a sprawling city the size of the entire Kampii colony. One side of the dome remained intact, but most of the dome's surface had been shattered. Even from high above, he could see dark things moving amid the city's broken buildings and detritus.

"The dome used to house SkyTek and all the people who worked there," Niobe said. "It was a thriving metropolis in its time. Now it's all bones and memories, refugees and thieves."

"Sounds wonderful," Hoku grumbled, and Niobe chuckled.

The dome felt even bigger as they got closer. A wide path circled the outside of the dome and spiraled down around the plateau to the forest below. Instead of dirt, it was paved with a slick black coating, cracked and crumbling in places. Old buildings jutted up inside the dome, creating a landscape of silver and brown and gray that looked more like a forest of metal than a city. Black smoke billowed up in dozens of places. He wondered how many people lived there, or if the smoke came from old fires that refused to die.

The Aviars landed inside the dome, in the hollowed-out shell of an old building.

"This is our base of operations for our scavenging runs," High Senator Electra said. "You can sleep here if you have to, but without lookouts flying overhead and an arsenal of weapons, it's not much safer than the rest of the dome."

"Find what you need, and find it fast," Niobe added. "Every day you stay here reduces the chance that you'll ever leave."

"I wish you would change your mind," Electra said. "However brave, you are still children, and this is no place for you. If I had not been ordered to return immediately . . ." Her words trailed off, and she pulled Aluna into a gruff hug.

Niobe dropped to one knee in front of Hoku so she could look him in the eye.

"Take this, Hoku," she said quietly. She took his hand and pressed a small, smooth cylinder against his palm. "Use this flare if you need us. Aim high. We don't fly far from home that often, but there's always a chance we might see it."

"Thank you," he said, putting the artifact carefully into his satchel. "I hope I don't have to use it."

He could see in her eyes that there was more she wanted to say. Her mouth twitched, but stayed closed. After staring at him a few more seconds, she said, "Be safe, my ocean brother."

He nodded and forced his mouth into a smile. "Swift currents."

This good-bye was taking too long. When he'd left his family, he hadn't even seen his mother or father. Saying farewell like this was worse than swimming into a nest of stinger crabs. He felt battered from the inside out. Niobe must have understood. She stood quickly and nodded to High Senator Electra.

He and Aluna thanked them both again. Niobe and Electra vaulted into the air. Their wings unfurled and caught the currents. Within three blinks of his eye, they were so deep into the sky that he couldn't tell them apart. He continued to watch anyway, until they were specks, until they had disappeared.

CHAPTER 27

STANDING INSIDE the ruins of what had once been a tall, shimmering Human building reminded Hoku of swimming through the bones of Big Blue on the ocean floor. When a whale died, all its adventures died with it. No one would ever know what treasures it had seen in the Great Ravine, or what strange melodies it had heard the night all the dolphins decided to sing at once. But a whale's ancient bones quickly became a thriving colony of skittering crabs and shadowy eels, of bright sponges and schools of darting fish. Life went on, changed. New stories were written on top of the old.

The same was true of this building. Humans had lived here, some only a few decades ago. What food had they eaten? What games had they played? What tech had they used? No one would ever hear their stories now. But the dome was far from desolate. Up close, the signs of new life were everywhere. Birds darted back and forth, making their nests in the building's framework and hunting for vermin in the garbage. Rats and strange patchwork mice scampered around the fringes of the building's interior. To them, these ruins must seem like a vast banquet of opportunity. Once they had been chased and killed by the people who lived here. Now they were kings.

"Move your tail," Aluna said, breaking his mood. She pulled at a pile of rocks and plastic barricading a hole in the building's rim. "We should have had the Aviars drop us on the outside. Little good this place does us without wings."

Hoku rushed to help her, and they had a small passage cleared within a few minutes. Aluna clambered through the opening, and he scrambled after her. He barely avoided twisting his ankle two separate times, and a jagged piece of glass gave him a shallow slash on his left forearm. By the time he climbed through to the other side, his skin had already stitched itself back together—thanks to the Kampii ancients and their gift of fast healing.

"Good thing we're not in the ocean, or the sharks would be all over you," she said. She'd meant it to be cheerful, but it made him miss the water.

Outside the building, he got a better sense of the city's shape. The debris-filled valleys between the shattered buildings must have been roads. Scorch marks stained everything, big sooty smears marring what had once been shiny silver and glass. The Battle of the Dome had killed more than Aviars and Upgraders; it had killed the city itself.

"Hoku, look," Aluna said quietly.

He followed her gaze. In the distance, he saw a Human-shaped creature climbing a pile of rubble on eight hairy spider legs. When it got to the top of the pile, it picked up a boulder with its two Human hands, and another with two of its spindly spider legs, then scampered out of sight.

"It could be a Dome Mek," Hoku whispered, even though the creature seemed far away. "Niobe told me they were created to defend and maintain the dome. She said most of them died in the battle, when Tempest tried to use them as a shield."

"I wonder if they're still trying to protect the dome," Aluna said.

"I don't want to find out," Hoku said. "Let's give it some space."

She snorted. "Did you think I would take us *closer* to that thing?"

And then she was off again, weaving through the garbage jungle, leaving him to keep up or get left behind. He followed her as fast as he could, barely getting a chance to study their surroundings. Nothing looked like it might hold the secret to HydroTek's location. Just trash, rubble, and debris, with a bit of spiky, dangerous trash thrown in for variety.

If he'd had more time, he would have loved to explore more slowly. Maybe one day he and Calli could sort through the piles, looking for bits of technology. He'd be good at that. Or maybe they could approach the Dome Mek and talk to it. Convince it they were friends and ask it some questions.

He caught sight of four more Meks as they traveled, saw the smoke from three separate fires. Birds zoomed overhead, and tiny furred squirrels and chipmunks clambered atop the ruins. A mottled gray cat and a striped brown dog sat together in a doorway, a dead rat between them, and he would have bet anything that they were discussing how to split their spoils.

After what felt like hours, he couldn't keep up with Aluna's pace. The distance between them went from five meters to ten to twenty, until he couldn't even see her anymore. She would notice he was gone sooner or later. Until then, what would it hurt to rest his legs for a few minutes? Kampii were never meant to run around like this, anyway. Tails were so much more practical for crossing large distances.

He looked around for someplace safe to sit and

settled on a fragment of smooth plastic that may once have been a chair. His legs throbbed, the cut on his arm itched, and his breath came out ragged. He flopped into the plastic and closed his eyes.

Metal clanged behind him. His eyes shot open.

Another clang. And a voice—a Human! He couldn't make out the words, but the tone was angry.

Hoku stayed perfectly still. *Please go the other way. Please go the other way.*

"Aluna," he whispered, "are you there?"

No answer. She must be too far away to hear him.

Glass shattered. The Human cursed.

Hoku stared in the direction of the voice, afraid to move.

Suddenly, a small creature bolted around the corner of a broken building and smacked straight into Hoku's chest. Tiny claws gripped his shirt, and he fell sideways onto the ground. Hoku grabbed the animal, trying to keep its teeth away from his neck. His fingers dug into soft fur.

But the creature wasn't going for his jugular; it was trying to burrow under his shirt! The scared little thing was trying to hide.

He heard the Human voice again. It was male and angry, and way too close.

"You will die swiftly," the voice said. "And you will die by my hands."

CHAPTER 28

ALUNA HAD BEEN HOPING to find clues about HydroTek, not kilometer after kilometer of desolation. Garbage clung to everything, drifted up against the shattered building walls like sand dunes. Tempest's army must have had massive weapons to cause such havoc. If Fathom's were similar, they had a tough fight ahead of them. The Kampii had nothing so powerful underwater. Harpoons and spears and nets were like toys compared to the Above World's methods of destruction. Sarah Jennings and the other Kampii ancients had been wise to hide the colony. They could never survive a war with the Upgraders by themselves.

She'd been walking and climbing for maybe two hours, maintaining a brisk pace. She kept track of Hoku by listening to his huffing in her ear. When she heard him sigh and stop walking, she took a break herself. Sitting down would only stiffen her leg muscles, so she decided to stretch until he felt like catching up again.

Just as she was finishing her first round of back twists, she heard the yelling.

Aluna bolted back the way she had come. She vaulted over jagged metal scraps on the ground and ducked under strange overhangs of concrete. She hadn't realized how far ahead she'd gotten. As she rounded the last corner, her talons were already unclipped and waiting in her hands.

A Human stood over Hoku. The attacker wasn't big, but almost everyone towered over Hoku. She didn't wait to see what he was going to do next.

Aluna swung her arm forward, releasing Spirit, her right-hand talon. The sharp tip sped toward the villain, trailing the thin silvery chain that kept it connected to her hand. It swung under the man's raised arm and wrapped itself around his wrist several times.

She yanked, hard. The attacker's arm snapped, and he howled in pain. She whipped out Spite, her left-hand talon, and wrapped it around the man's leg. She yanked again, and he fell hard with another yelp of pain.

"Stop! Stop!" he yelled. "I do not wish to fight!"

Hoku scrambled back, out of the Human's reach.

Something bulged and squirmed under his shirt. He reached in and pulled out a fuzzy gray-and-black creature, no bigger than a lobster. It had four legs ending in tiny, delicate paws, a long, poofy striped tail, and a black band of fur over both its eyes that made it look like a masked bandit. Hoku held it by the scruff of its neck and glared at it.

"Hoku, get back," Aluna said. He was already more focused on the creature than on his assailant. What was wrong with that boy?

She walked toward their fallen foe, careful to keep Spirit's chain taut. One hint of a fight, and she could yank on the man's broken arm again.

Only he wasn't a man. He was a boy. His skin was brown. Not as dark as hers, but far more tan and sun worn than Hoku's. His long black hair was gathered by a cord at the nape of his neck. She snorted. Long hair still seemed like too much trouble, even out of the ocean's currents. She couldn't tell how old he was, but she guessed a few years older than she was, if he was older at all.

He watched her stalk closer with brown, unblinking eyes. She gave him credit for his lack of whining or crying. The talon was still wrapped tightly around his arm, but he didn't struggle against it. He wasn't just a trapped animal; he was smart. And that made him all the more dangerous.

"What are your intentions?" the boy asked. His accent was thick and unfamiliar. His tongue seemed to linger over the words, giving them more flavor than she was used to hearing. "I do not wish to harm you, but I will defend myself if I must."

"Why were you trying to kill my friend?" she asked.

He looked confused. Maybe her accent was as strange to him.

"I am not after the boy," her prisoner said finally. "I am after the creature. The little *novsh* stole my food."

She looked over at Hoku. He had the furry thing cradled against his chest and was scratching it behind its oversized furry ears. It looked up at him with big eyes. Then she saw the pale-red apple in its paws, nibbled on one side. She'd grown fond of the fruit during their stay with the Aviars. She imagined taking a big, crisp bite out of its side, and her mouth watered.

"Hoku, make it give the apple back," Aluna said.

"And how am I supposed to do that?" Hoku said. He tried to pull the fruit from the animal's paws, but it held on tightly, then rubbed its cheek against Hoku's chin. He gave up and resumed petting it.

She turned back to her prisoner and shrugged. He didn't seem nearly so threatening now that he was flat on his back with a broken arm. And if that animal had stolen her last scrap of food, she'd probably hunt it down and cook it up for dinner. Hard to fault someone for trying to survive.

"If I let you go, are you going to attack us?" she asked the stranger.

He thought a moment. "I will not attack you or the boy, but I must eat," he said finally. "I don't care if it is the apple or the animal."

Aluna couldn't help herself. She laughed.

"I am serious," the boy said, clearly offended. He pushed himself up into a sitting position with his good hand.

"Oh, she would have said the same thing," Hoku said. "That's probably what she finds so funny."

"I'm Aluna. He's Hoku," she said, and began to unwind her talons from the stranger's limbs. "We have some food we can share."

"Dashiyn," he said, "but I am also known as Dash."

She freed his leg first, then started to work on his wrist. She tried not to move it any more than she had to.

"Dash is good," she said, "because I'm not sure I can pronounce *Dasheeyan* anyway."

His chuckle was cut off with a hiss as she finished unwinding Spirit.

"Sorry," she said, surprised that she actually meant it. "I thought you were going to kill Hoku."

"I understand," Dash said simply. "Sometimes

we must act before all the facts can be examined. Unfortunately, I am going to need a splint."

She nodded. "I saw a piece of plastic that might work. If I hear any fighting while I'm gone, I'll be back to break your other arm." She said it with a smile, but she meant it.

As she jogged up the path, she heard Dash ask, "Is she always like this?" Hoku's answer rang loud in her ears. "You have no idea."

She wandered through the rubble until she found a smooth, flat piece of plastic as long as her forearm. She remembered jumping over it during her race to save Hoku. When she got back to the clearing, she crouched by Dash and measured the plastic against the length of his arm.

Up close, the boy smelled strange. Wild. He smelled of places she'd never been. Her heart beat faster, and she struggled to steady her arm.

"That will serve well," Dash said. His accent sounded thicker, his voice deeper. "I have twine in my satchel. Can you . . . ? Do you mind . . . ?"

Aluna looked for his pack and saw it half crushed under his back. He leaned to the side and helped her retrieve it. She was careful not to touch him more than was absolutely necessary, and he seemed to be taking the same precautions.

Dash opened the sack with his good hand, dug around, and pulled out a length of thick twine.

"We've got to set the break first," she said.

The boy nodded, grim. She took his forearm gently in her hands and felt around near his wrist. His arm was wiry but muscled, his hand callused. He knew work, and he probably knew how to fight. He didn't seem like the type to slit your throat in the middle of the night or to stab you in the back when you weren't looking, but High Senator Electra had warned her that such men existed. She'd have to be careful.

Luckily for him, only the smaller arm bone was broken, not the larger one, and none of the tiny ones in the wrist. Without warning, she used her thumb to push the bone back into place.

Dash uttered a short stream of curses in a strange language, but didn't move. Not even a twitch. She grabbed the splint and twine and set to work immobilizing his arm as fast as she could.

"So, you're a Human?" she asked, trying to distract him from the pain.

"No!" Dash said. He jerked back as if she'd struck him.

"Stop moving," she commanded. "Tides' teeth, it was only a question."

The boy scowled. His eyebrows pulled into one flat line under his furrowed brow. "I am not a Human."

"Then what are you?" she pressed. "You don't have wings, so you're not an Aviar. And you're certainly no Kampii. I've heard the Equians have legs like a horse, but—"

"Never mind what I am," Dash blurted. "Tell me about you and Hoku. I would like to know your story. You are Humans, yes?"

Now it was her turn to be insulted. "Of course not! We're Kampii from the City of Shifting Tides."

Dash looked suspicious. "If you are Kampii, then where are your tails? You are supposed to be frolicking in the water, braiding each other's hair, and singing love songs to the sea."

"What?" Aluna dropped his arm none too gently and stood up. "Those are stupid old stories. None of that is true!"

From behind her, Hoku said, "Well, your sister does spend a lot of time playing with her hair, and we do actually sing a lot of songs about the sea."

She scowled at him. "Stop messing with that animal and bring over some food and water. And don't pick on Daphine."

At least Hoku tried to hide his smirk as he dug through their rations.

"I apologize for the offense," Dash said. "I have never met a Kampii before. I thought . . . well, I believed you breathed water and never left the sea."

"We don't," Aluna said, her hand going to her throat and the breathing shell that should have been lodged there. "Not usually. But our people are dying. Hoku and I left home so we could find a way to save them."

Dash nodded. "This is a brave plan."

Aluna felt heat flood into her face.

"So where are you from?" Hoku asked. "Only thieves and cutthroats could call this place home."

Dash managed to pull himself upright and shifted to lean against the remains of a concrete wall. His shoulders looked stiff, and he held his chin high.

He said, "I have been exiled from my people. I no longer have a home."

CHAPTER 29

EXILED?" Aluna said. Hoku winced, probably at her lack of decorum, but she ignored him. "Meaning, you can't ever go back?" The thought of never returning to the City of Shifting Tides, of never hearing Daphine make fun of her clothes or her hair, of never seeing her brothers fight over the last scrap of fish at dinner was too horrible to imagine—and all too real. Unless she found HydroTek and another breathing shell.

Dash kept his face devoid of emotion, but it looked like it was taking every muscle in his body to do it.

"I will never return," he said.

"Where?" asked Hoku.

"To the Equians," Dash said, and for a moment, she could see the pain in his eyes. He smoothed it away quickly. "My herd . . . my *old* herd . . . they live in the desert east of here."

"The Equians!" Aluna said. Like the Kampii and Aviars, they had altered themselves to live in harsh climates that no one else wanted. "The Equians are horse folk," she said. "But you're not part horse."

"Yes? And where is your tail, mermaid?"

She scowled.

Hoku snorted. "That's a fair point."

She touched the tiny pouch hanging under her shirt. She still had a tail if she wanted one. But Hoku didn't know that. No one knew that except her.

"Our tails are none of your concern," she said.

"And my lack of hooves is none of yours," Dash retorted.

"Fine," she said. "Let's leave it at that."

"Good."

"Fine."

"I'm fine with that, too," Hoku said brightly.

She and Dash looked over at him, but he seemed oblivious to anything but his new best friend. The animal had curled up in his lap and was happily munching on the apple.

"Raccoons!" Dash said. "Insufferable creatures, every last one."

"There's a little tag attached to his collar," Hoku said. "I think his name is Zorro TM. It also says WILD

BUDDIES PROGRAMMABLE PETS. I wonder what that means."

"I have no idea," she said, "but Zorro TM is definitely a strange name."

"Not really," Dash said. "The Equians have many groomer monkeys named Bananas TM. Possibly they are related."

"Groomer monkeys?" Aluna and Hoku said at the same time.

Dash shrugged. "When you are part horse, it is difficult to reach your tail or to clean out stones from your hooves. We—*they*—train the monkeys to comb out tangles. The creatures are very useful." He glared at the raccoon. "And they never stole our apples."

Hoku scratched Zorro behind the ears. "What tricks can you do, little thing?" Zorro licked his nose with a tiny pink tongue.

Glass shattered in the distance, followed by a guttural laugh.

They all stopped, looked, listened.

Upgraders, or just thieves? She wouldn't welcome either right now.

"We should keep moving," she said. "We're like fish in a tide pool here."

Hoku stood up. Zorro dropped the apple core, climbed up his arm, and balanced on his shoulder.

"Well, it was sort of nice to meet you, Dash, despite

all the fighting and cursing," Hoku said. "But Aluna and I have to keep moving. Swift currents, safe travels, and may the spirits guide you on your journey."

"Dash is coming with us," Aluna said.

"He is?"

"I am?"

"Yes." She squinted at the sun, her heart beating fast. *Why did she say that? Why was she doing this?* "We don't have many hours of daylight left. Let's get moving. If we can find a clue that points us toward HydroTek, we can be out of this place by dawn."

"What if I do not wish to join you?" Dash said. His stiff shoulders and raised chin were back.

"You have a broken arm, and I'm the one who gave it to you," she said. "You're my responsibility, at least until we're out of danger."

"I can take care of myself," Dash said. "I am not without defenses."

He'd kept his satchel close to his body ever since the fight. What kind of weapons was he hiding?

The people in the distance were getting closer. There were at least three distinct voices now, but no dragonfliers in the air. Maybe they still had time.

"Look, I have no doubt that you're good in a fight," she said, trying to be polite. "But we're all better off if we stick together while we're in this dome." She could see him wavering. She decided to make it easier for him. "Besides, Hoku and I could use a hand if things get nasty. You'd be doing us a favor."

Dash studied her, thinking. He looked wiry strong, but thin. His once-white shirt looked soaked with sweat and dirt, and even a little blood. He'd been out here for a while, she guessed. Even with two good arms it would be hard to survive in this place.

"Fins and flippers, we don't have all day!" Hoku said. "I've already been attacked once. I don't want to make it a habit."

Dash sighed and nodded.

"Follow me," he said. "I know a place that might hold the answers you seek."

He looked at Aluna, his eyes challenging her to contradict him. She smiled and motioned for him to take the lead. Hoku scrambled after Dash, and Aluna took her place at the back of the line, closest to the sounds of the approaching men.

They quickly fell into a rhythm. Slower than the one she'd set earlier, but quicker than what Hoku seemed to want. The creature on his shoulder squeaked whenever he tripped or stumbled.

For the most part, she watched Dash. The horse folk intrigued her, and she burned to know Dash's story. An Equian who wasn't a horse from the waist down. How did something like that happen? Was that why he'd been exiled? His long hair swished across his back when he walked. She imagined it looked a lot like a horse's tail.

The sun sank lower. After an hour or so of hiking, Dash stopped and pointed. "There," he said.

The building stood several stories tall, a silvery monolith with a space at the bottom where an opening hatch used to be. Its walls shimmered and reflected the debris all around, making it almost invisible.

"What is it?" Hoku asked.

"It stands at the exact center of the dome," Dash said solemnly. "It must be important."

"I don't understand," Aluna said. "Why is it still here? Why haven't the Aviars or the Upgraders scavenged it for parts? It must be a trap."

"Trap or no, it might hold the answers you seek," Dash said. "If we can save your people, is any price too high to pay?"

She was here, wasn't she? She'd given up everything for the crazy idea that she could make a difference.

"What are you waiting for? Let's go," Aluna said.

CHAPTER 30

HOKU HATED to admit it, but he felt safer now that Dash was with them. Without him, Hoku would either have to go first into the strange building or go last when there were possibly murderous thugs coming up behind them. The middle was a vast improvement.

As they walked through the narrow entrance corridor, he saw evenly spaced holes in the walls. They used to hold security cameras, he guessed, like the kind he read about at Skyfeather's Landing. The cameras must have been easy pickings for the early tech scavengers. Too bad. He would have loved to take one apart.

The corridor opened into a huge room the size of the whole first floor. The room seemed hollowed out except for a clear tube in the center. He expected to see stairs, but there were none. Maybe it once held an "elevator," like the one the Aviars had. Dead video displays lined the walls from the ceiling down to the smooth, molded work spaces that ringed the whole room.

Everything had once been shiny and silvery-slick. Despite the intrusion of garbage and the attempts to break everything breakable, very little damage had been done. He ran his fingers over the nearest workstation. Scratches and dings marred the surface . . . the result of hundreds of people trying to get inside the computer or destroy it for everyone else.

"Do you have torches?" Dash said. "It is too dark to see much."

Hoku hadn't even noticed the darkness. His eyes had adjusted. Dash's people were probably more used to the sun.

"We can see just fine," Aluna said absently.

Hoku heard Dash mumble something about mermaids, but Aluna, staring up the plastic tube in the center of the room, was too far away to hear.

"Can we get to the other levels?" she asked.

"I believe so," Dash said. "That shaft goes all the way up, though whatever mechanism it used to house is long gone. I have scouted up five more levels. They all look like this. The top floor contains only tables and chairs and is overrun by squatters." He wrinkled his nose. "Judging from the smell, they are not concerned with infiltrating the computer so much as drinking themselves into sickness."

Zorro wiggled down Hoku's arm and clambered onto the work surface. Hoku started to walk a circuit around the room, trailing his hand along the massive desk. It stayed dark and cold and silent, oblivious to his touch. Zorro hopped after him, pausing to sniff the wall or the desk at random spots.

"If this is the brain of SkyTek, then I'd say this dome is dead," Aluna said.

Hoku paused in his exploration to look at her. She picked up a piece of trash from the floor, turned it over in her hands, then threw it back down. She looked as out of place here as she did in the ritual dome back home. Dash was no better. The horse-boy couldn't even see. He was cradling his broken arm and sticking his face a few centimeters away from the wall, squinting. Hoku would have to figure this out on his own.

If all the floors looked the same, where was the access point? He'd been half expecting to see a big machine with glowing knobs emitting, "Get your answers here!" in some mechanical voice. Instead, everything looked the same. All the workstations were the same size. If this SkyTek had an Elder, she'd have to sit at a regular old desk like everyone else.

He kept walking, kept scanning the walls and the desk surfaces for clues. Zorro kept pace, his little claws clattering on the smooth surface as he trotted along. Hoku stopped when they reached a small pile of rags on one of the workstations.

Zorro squeaked and jumped onto the pile. He turned around three times, then plopped down in the center.

"Zorro, is that your bed?" he asked.

The raccoon's eyes pulsed green.

Hoku jumped back, surprised. He glanced back at Aluna. Dash was showing her how to shimmy up the elevator shaft. Neither one of them was paying him any attention.

"Did . . . did you just answer me?" he asked quietly.

Zorro tilted his head to the side, but his eyes stayed unremarkably black.

"Can you talk?"

Zorro started to lick his paw.

"Zorro, can you understand me?" he tried again.

The raccoon snapped to attention. His eyes glowed green once, then fell dark again.

"By the tides," Hoku hissed.

Zorro tilted his head again—in exactly the same way as before. Did that mean he was listening but didn't understand? And why hadn't he acted like this before?

Hoku stared at the raccoon. The raccoon stared back at him.

"Zorro, can you speak?"

The raccoon's eyes pulsed red.

"Well, it was worth a try," he said. He gave Zorro a little scratch on the head. The animal's fur was warm—much warmer than it had been before.

"Hey!" Hoku said. "What are you hiding?" He started to pull away the rags that made up Zorro's bed. The creature didn't complain; he sat there staring. Hoku petted the raccoon a few times to keep him mollified, and he nuzzled his arm in response. When all the rags were gone, Hoku ran his hands slowly over Zorro's body, feeling for . . . well, for anything weird.

Nothing on his head except the collar. Nothing on his ribs. Nothing on his four dainty black paws. He ran his hand over the raccoon's fluffy ringed tail, and . . . the tip was stuck to the desk! Hoku pulled at it gently, but nothing happened. He pulled a little harder, and Zorro's tail popped off the surface. But what had it been stuck to? The desk was as smooth as ever, no sign of glue or a clip or a plug. No little tail-devouring mouth had been built by the ancients to nibble unsuspecting animals. At least, he couldn't *see* any such mouth.

He lowered Zorro's tail toward the desk. At a few centimeters away, it suddenly snapped out of his hand and back into place exactly as it had been before.

"Magnets!" Hoku said. They used magnets back at

the colony to keep things from floating away—in fact, his own sticky plate was actually a magnet. He pulled Zorro's tail off the desk and put it back three more times. "Magnets," he repeated.

Somehow, Zorro had plugged himself into the building.

"What's going on?" Aluna asked. She was halfway up the elevator shaft, her back pressed against one side and her feet braced against the other.

"Nothing," Hoku said quickly. He didn't have anything to share with them. Not yet. For now, the secret belonged to him and Zorro.

"Okay, boy, let's see how this works," he whispered, and plugged Zorro's tail back into the desk. "Zorro, can you talk to the brain?"

The animal tilted his head. This time, its eyes flashed yellow.

"Zorro, can you talk to the ancients?"

His head tilted to the other side with another flash of yellow. Cute, but not helpful.

Hoku unzipped his backpack and pulled out his books, looking for words that might trigger some response from the SkyTek brain. He tried "Internet," "CPU," "computer," "network," and even "SkyTek," which he'd thought was particularly ingenious. More head tilts, more red or yellow eyes, more scratches behind the ears, but no luck.

"Maybe 'talk' is the wrong word." He tapped his cheek with one of his fingers, a habit he developed at Skyfeather's Landing. "Zorro," he said finally, "can you turn it on?"

Zorro's eyes glowed green. Hoku felt warmth emanating from his tiny body, along with a low-pitched whirring.

Suddenly, the huge video screen in front of Hoku came to life, and a strange voice said, "Welcome to SkyTek, our dream for the future!"

CHAPTER 31

HOKU GASPED. Images appeared on the screen—bright, beautiful images in full color. It was as if he were flying toward the SkyTek dome again, only this time the landscape was full of Humans. And the dome wasn't cracked, but glittering in the sun!

He barely noticed when Dash and Aluna joined him. He reached out to touch one of the tiny trees on the screen, expecting to feel leaves, but the surface was as flat and smooth as it had been before.

"With the world's population growing past the point of sustainability . . ." the voice said, and images fluttered on the screen. Masses of people crammed in landscapes of metal and glass. Grime-covered children, too skinny, begging for food. Huge machines covering the side of a hill like a swarm of glittering beetles.

". . . SkyTek and its sister LegendaryTek corporations are prepared to bring you the future . . . in the form of the past!"

The picture changed, and suddenly they were soaring over the ocean to the sound of flapping wings. It reminded him of flying with Senator Niobe, and his heart lifted.

"Fly with the birds!" the voice exclaimed. "Our sustainable high-altitude communities of winged Aviars offer freedom from crowded cities, pollution, rationing, and even freedom from the earth itself! The ancient Greeks gave us the idea of winged women, and now we give you the skies!"

The image pulled back to reveal a beautiful winged woman hovering in midair, a huge smile on her face. Her wings were pristine and perfect white, and her long hair fluttered in the wind, like shifting golden kelp. She didn't much look like a real Aviar—she didn't have muscles and scars and painted symbols all over her wings—but they got the general idea right.

"Please see your local sales office for more details, or apply online at LegendaryTek dot com, where you can preview some of our other exciting new communities."

Another flash of images: A half horse, half Human racing across a sandy plain on four hooves; a beautiful Kampii woman with long, silly hair swimming through the ocean wearing shells on her chest instead of a shirt; a man with the long, sinuous body of a snake slithering in an underground chamber full of gemstones; and a Deepfell swimming between two sharks in the dark ocean.

"Many more communities are in development," said the voice. "It's time to take evolution into your own hands!"

The final image—a lone figure silhouetted on top of a mountain and breathing fire from his mouth—was covered up in a stream of tiny text that Hoku had no hope of reading. After that, the screen went dark.

"Play it again," Dash said. "Please."

"Yes," Aluna said, similarly dazed. She reached out and touched the screen, just as he had done earlier.

"Zorro, play it again," Hoku said. The little raccoon's eyes glowed green, and the screen lit up. They watched the images again, and a third time, and then a fourth.

"Did you see that?" Hoku said. "In the picture with the Kampii—there was a dome in the background!"

"Really?" Aluna said. "I missed it. I kept waiting for those ridiculous shells to fall off that Kampii's chest. How could she possibly swim like that?"

Hoku laughed. "I know!"

"Can we regain focus, please?" Dash said. "Can you make the animal stop the image in that spot?"

"Um . . . I don't know. Let me try."

They replayed the images again. This time Hoku said, "Zorro, stop!" when the Kampii appeared. Zorro's eyes glowed green, and the screen fell dark.

"Well, that didn't work," Aluna said.

"Apparently not," Hoku grumbled.

They heard glass shattering from outside the building, and distant laughter.

"We need to leave before they get here," Dash said.

"Why don't you two find us a place to hide while I figure this out?" Hoku said.

Aluna nodded. "Or maybe we can find some weapons."

"I would prefer to find an escape route," Dash said.

Hoku focused his attention back on Zorro. He could hear Aluna and Dash enter a heated discussion behind him, but he didn't care. It was easy to tune out their words, even though Aluna's echoed from inside his ears. He had work to do.

He was starting to figure out how Zorro worked, or at least how he was supposed to interact with him. If he didn't say Zorro's name first, the animal didn't acknowledge being spoken to. And the exact words he picked were important. "Stopping" the image hadn't worked, but what other word could he use?

"Zorro, play it again," he said.

The screen exploded back to life. He tried telling

Zorro to "wait," but nothing happened. When he said, "Zorro, freeze!" the flow of images halted on the picture of the crowded metal city. "Zorro, play it slow," he said. The picture resumed its progress, but at half the speed. The voice slowed down, too, sounding much more like someone talking underwater. He found it strangely comforting.

When the images returned to the silly Kampii with the shells, Hoku told Zorro to "freeze" again. The image stood still on the screen, perfectly clear. He could almost feel the ocean current, could almost taste the salt.

The smiling Kampii was there, tail gleaming, one arm waving. This time he pulled his eyes away from her to study the background. And there it was, plain as Big Blue. Behind her, in the distance, a huge dome sat on the water like a giant jellyfish filled with glittering spires.

"I've got it!" he yelled.

Dash came over, holding a long, sleek metal sword in his good hand.

"Where did you find that?" Hoku asked, amazed that the scavengers had missed something so shiny.

"I did not find it. I had it with me. In my bag," Dash said. He pressed a button on the sword's hilt and its blade retracted with a series of *snikt*s. Another button press, and the blade extended, looking as sharp and deadly as ever. Hoku thought about their first encounter with Dash in the dome and how differently it could have ended.

"Aluna went outside to scout," Dash said. He looked up at the picture. "That shoreline looks a bit familiar." The horse-boy squinted. "I may have walked along that beach a few weeks ago. I did not see the dome, but I believe I remember that cliff."

"Can you take us there?" Hoku asked, his breathing necklace pulsing fast to keep up with the jittering of his heart.

"I am not certain," Dash said, "but I think so. It was a long journey, and I traveled mostly by night."

"Good enough for me," Aluna said from the doorway of the building. She was breathing hard, her cheeks flushed. Both of her talons were unsheathed and waiting in her hands. "If we don't leave now, the Upgraders will be adding fresh Kampii and Equian to their list of parts."

CHAPTER 32

THEY'RE RIGHT BEHIND ME," Aluna said, glancing over her shoulder. "I don't think they saw me, but they're heading for the building."

"How many?" asked Dash.

She shook her head. "Not sure. Maybe four. And another one in the sky."

Dash cursed. She didn't understand the words, but she understood his meaning.

"We're trapped in here," she said. "Going up another level or two will only make us more trapped."

"I will distract them," Dash said. "You and Hoku try to escape."

She opened her mouth but didn't say anything. She'd broken his arm, and now he was volunteering to sacrifice himself for them? The Equians, wherever they were, must be an honorable people.

"No," Hoku said. "You're the only one who knows how to get to the dome, Dash."

"Then I'll stay," Aluna said. Besides, if anyone was going to sacrifice herself for the greater good, it was going to be her.

"How about none of us stay," said Hoku. He turned back to that weird pet of his and said, "Zorro, can you access the other workstations?"

The animal's eyes glowed green.

"Hide under the desks by the entrance," Hoku said to Aluna. He hugged the raccoon and whispered something to it. Inside her ear, Aluna heard him say, "I'll miss you, boy. We would have been good friends."

She blinked and swallowed. Dash retracted his sword and was trying to crawl under the desk without using his bad arm, so she focused on helping him. A moment later, Hoku squeezed in next to her and Dash with his backpack.

They were all still as starfish. She could hear her own heart beating, could feel the sweat on Dash's arm where he was pressed up against her. Hoku seemed impossibly small crouched in front of her.

The Upgraders' voices got louder.

"Better find us some true wired sparklies or we'll

be missing more than a few parts when we's get back," one of them said.

"I say we go for the harpy witches after this. Heard the tech they got is true wired! We'd eat like Fathom himself if we bring those generators back in flash and glory," another said. "Imagine! New bits of shiny to play and sell. Been needing a new nose since my last one got blasted to bolts."

A third uttered some words about the Aviars that made Aluna blush, and the other Upgraders chuckled and grunted with appreciation.

Hoku shifted his weight. Aluna could feel anxiety rolling off him in waves.

"Wait," she whispered. "Not yet."

His shoulders relaxed slightly. She tried to calm her own heart as well. Any fear she showed would amplify his, and Dash's. Their lives were her responsibility, and she couldn't afford weakness. At least not when the enemies were less than a spear's throw away.

The Upgraders shuffled through the entrance corridor and into the room. From below the desk, all she could see were their dust-covered pants. One of them sported hidden-needle boots, like the man she'd fought at Skyfeather's Landing. Another seemed to have bare feet, but they were made of dull-black metal. Even the toenails! If the Upgraders were Humans once, they'd left that legacy behind them, as sure as the Kampii had left the dry land.

Aluna cast a quick glance over at Zorro. The animal had burrowed into its pile of rags. She wouldn't have seen him if she didn't know where to look.

She held her breath. If any of the Upgraders decided to look down, they'd be discovered. And captured. And probably killed. But the Upgraders seemed more focused on their crowbars and their greed. They wandered deeper into the room. One of them smashed his crowbar into the desk a meter from Dash's head. It bounced off harmlessly, and the Upgrader moved on.

Another man was getting closer and closer to Zorro. He seemed smarter than the rest, less focused on smashing things. She felt Hoku tense. She wanted to calm him, but didn't dare speak. When the Upgrader reached for the top rag in Zorro's pile, it was already too late.

"Zorro, play!" Hoku yelled.

The Upgraders looked over at their hiding place. At the same time, every screen in the whole room erupted with sound and color and motion.

"Welcome to SkyTek, our dream for the future!" four dozen voices said at once.

The Upgraders spun around, holding their tools

like weapons. Lights flashed as images flickered from every direction.

"Now!" Dash said.

Aluna shoved Hoku toward the entrance and pulled Dash behind her. The Upgraders would see them, no question about it. But would they recognize them as enemies, or just part of the whirlwind of images and sounds filling the room?

Four dozen voices said, "With the world's population growing past the point of sustainability . . ."

They darted through the corridor and burst into a courtyard outside the building. The day's light was fading fast. They didn't have much time before Dash's poor eyesight would render him useless in a fight.

"The Upgraders came from this direction," she said. "Maybe we can find the creatures they rode to get to the dome."

"Good thought," Dash said. "I have never seen them without mounts."

She had to yank Hoku's hand to get him moving. He was staring back at the building, and for a moment she thought he was looking for the Upgraders. Then she remembered Zorro and pulled him a little more gently.

They ran through the dome's debris, following the Upgrader's trail toward the rim of the dome. Hoku sniffled as he ran. Dash followed after him and made no noise at all. She checked up on him a few times to see if he was keeping up. He was. And the look of determination on his face told her that she needn't worry about him again.

They made fast progress toward the edge of the dome. She had no idea if the Upgraders were right behind them. It was safer to assume that they were—safer to keep pushing until they found safety.

"We're almost there," she said. She didn't know if that was true or not, but it seemed like something a leader should say. Her brothers were always telling her how important good morale was on their hunting expeditions.

They reached a towering wall of debris as the last of the sun's light fled the sky. She tried to find a place to climb it, but the wall was too steep.

"Spread out and look for a way over," she said.

She made it four meters up in one spot, but she couldn't find another handhold and tumbled back to the ground. Dash was more tentative as he moved the other way, poking at the pile with his good hand and squinting to see in the darkness. Hoku stood where she had left him.

"Here!" Dash said.

She jogged over. He was kneeling by a filthy rag draped over some garbage at the base of the wall. With his good hand, he pulled the rag aside.

"A tunnel!" she said.

Dash nodded. "You go first. Then the boy. It will take me longer to crawl."

Aluna's talons would be useless in the tunnel. She pulled the knife from the sheath on her thigh and clamped the blade between her teeth. Dash and Hoku said nothing. She dropped to all fours and crawled into the darkness.

CHAPTER 33

THE GARBAGE BENEATH Aluna's hands and feet had been packed and smoothed. Unfortunately, the walls of the tunnel were less groomed. She bumped her head on a metal pipe and felt a sliver of plastic scratch her arm as she wriggled forward. The knife blade in her mouth made it impossible to talk, so she stopped and pointed at the obstacles for Hoku.

The tunnel had obviously been carved for bigger people. There was enough room for her to avoid dangerous-looking debris, now that she knew to look for it. They'd certainly swum through tighter holes and hidden in smaller spots than this back in the ocean.

She heard a whimper from behind her and paused. Behind Hoku, she could see Dash clambering on his three good limbs. But he didn't look good. Even in the darkness, her eyes picked up the beads of sweat on his face. He jerked his head from left to right. His breath came out in ragged, uneven gasps. Apparently, the horse folk didn't do well in confined spaces.

She pulled the knife out of her mouth and said, "Keep moving. Don't stop. Focus on Hoku's feet in front of you. Nothing else. Just Hoku's feet."

She kept the knife hilt in her fist and crawled forward, faster. Hoku kept pace with her—he'd always been agile, like a crab scurrying over a coral reef. He shifted from side to side, just as she did, trusting her to avoid the worst of the dangers.

They moved fast, but it wasn't fast enough. They were losing Dash. His breathing had become labored, and Hoku had been forced to grab him by the hair and pull in order to keep him moving.

"Tell me about the horse folk, Dash," she said.

No answer. Hoku looked at her, his brow furrowed with worry.

"Tell me about your mother," she tried. "Or your father."

Dash gulped and shook his head.

Too personal. He had some pain there, and now was not the right time to stir it up. She kept them moving while she tried to think of something else to ask.

"Tell us about running across the desert," Hoku said. "Tell us about sunsets."

They crawled another few meters before Dash started to speak.

"The sun," he said, his voice cracking, "she commands the sky. She is our great mother, gifting life and granting death as she wishes. At night, she abandons us to darkness so that we may understand the world without her. We make bonfires and let our bodies become one with the cold. Our word-weavers tell stories to lure her back into our sky. They take turns sleeping so that their stories last the whole night, until the great mother returns and again grants us her gifts."

His voice was not only stronger; it was *beautiful.*

"Were you a word-weaver?" she asked.

Silence, and then, "No, though I would have liked to be," Dash said. "Many things would have been different had that path been open to me. But it was not meant to be."

Meant to be, she thought. So many things were *meant to be.* She shouldn't have been creeping through some tunnel of garbage trying to escape from an ancient, broken-down dome full of once-Human scoundrels. She was *meant to be* in the ocean, swimming around with her grown-up tail.

"I smell fresh air," Dash said.

She hadn't noticed, but he was right.

"Quiet now," she said. "If the Upgraders came this way, they probably left someone behind to guard the exit."

They crawled the rest of the way silent as sharks. Ahead of them, a rag hung across the tunnel, flickering firelight haloed around its ragged edges. Aluna crept slowly to the exit, sheathed her knife at her waist, and pulled aside the cloth.

A few meters from the tunnel exit, a monstrous animal stood grazing on scrawny tufts of grass sticking out of the packed brown dirt of the plateau. She'd seen animals like it in a picture book Hoku and Calli had shown her back at Skyfeather's Landing. Its thick, armored body was striped black and white like a zebra. But unlike that slender animal, its legs were stout and muscled, more like tree stumps. And instead of a horse's head, it had the round skull of an ancient rhino, complete with wicked metal-tipped horns.

Hoku and Dash crouched behind her. When the fresh air hit Dash, he sighed.

"What is it?" Hoku asked.

"No idea," she whispered.

"It is a rhinebra," Dash said. "A beast of burden. They can carry and pull great weights and are more aggressive than smaller pack animals."

"Great weights?" she said. "It's got a saddle. Do you think it can hold all three of us?"

Dash snorted. "It could carry ten of us and not even notice."

"Okay," she said, "then we've got a plan. Follow me."

She stepped out of the tunnel before either of them could protest and snuck toward the rhinebra.

"Better be heading home after this smash and grab," a woman's voice said from the other side of the animal. "I need a fix-up. My skin's itching fierce."

Aluna froze.

"There's no medtek in the wide world with skills wired enough for fixin' you," a male voice said with a laugh.

"Shut it," the female Upgrader said. "No unmarked noob gets to high-talk me about tech."

As long as they kept talking, everything would be fine. Aluna beckoned to Dash and Hoku. They tiptoed out of the tunnel toward her. She held a finger up to her lips, and they nodded.

"You hear something?" the woman said.

The man grunted. "You're the Gizmo with the full-gold ear. You tell me if I'm supposed to hear something."

None of them moved. None of them even breathed.

"Probably Pebbles chewin'," the woman said finally. "Stupid striped cow."

Aluna shared looks of relief with Dash and Hoku. Dash took another step forward and reached for the rhinebra's reins.

Behind them, something squeaked.

A small gray streak of fur galloped out of the tunnel, raced across the ground, and launched itself into Hoku's arms, chittering happily.

Hoku hugged Zorro to his chest and tried to cover the little creature's mouth with his hand. "Zorro, quiet!" he whispered.

Aluna cursed under her breath. The animal had fallen silent immediately, but so had the Upgraders. She crouched low and readied her talons. The smooth metal weapons warmed quickly in her palms.

"Get on the animal! Both of you!" she said. "I'll hold them off and catch up when I can."

CHAPTER 34

Hoku hugged the raccoon tight. He never thought the little guy would escape the Upgraders in the dome. *What a good boy!* Zorro licked his chin.

But now, thanks to Zorro's noisy entrance, they had a whole new set of problems to solve.

The first Upgrader jumped out from behind the rhinebra. She was huge. Her arms bulged muscles, and tattoos covered every inch of her exposed skin, including her slick, bald head. One of her hands had been replaced with a sleek black blade. In the other, she held a gun that dripped fire.

"Look out!" Dash yelled.

Hoku ducked, sheltering Zorro with his body. A short spear whizzed over the top of his head. The male Upgrader had climbed up the other side of the rhinebra and was using it as a shield.

"Aluna's right!" Hoku yelled. "Let's get out of here!"

Aluna's talons were already spinning. The female Upgrader spewed fire at her. Aluna rolled left, her thin talon chains cutting through the gout of fire as if it weren't there. A slash of blood appeared on the Upgrader's cheek, and she stumbled back, surprised.

Hoku scurried under the rhinebra's belly. The man shooting spears switched targets to Dash. Hoku heard the horse-boy say something to the rhinebra, and the massive animal started grunting and shifting its weight. The Upgrader had to stop shooting in order to hold on.

Zorro scampered up Hoku's arm and clung to his shoulders while he danced between the rhinebra's tree-trunk legs. Something bopped Hoku in the head. A rope ladder! He grabbed the bottom of it and looked up. A half-dozen rungs higher was the male Upgrader's foot.

The rope ladder was attached to a saddle, and the saddle was attached to the rhinebra with straps . . . straps that were fastened right in front of Hoku.

He grabbed the first of three straps and yanked. Nothing happened. He tugged harder. The strap budged ever so slightly.

"I don't suppose you've got superstrength," he whispered to Zorro. The raccoon tilted his head. "Didn't think so."

Dash was still talking to the creature, commanding it to keep hopping around. But Hoku knew that as soon as the creature tired, the Upgrader clinging to its side would recover his balance and shoot Dash and Aluna.

Hoku grabbed the strap with both hands, took a deep breath, and pulled as hard as he could. The fastener wiggled. He widened his stance, using his feet to push against the earth for more power. He never could have done that in the ocean, but up here, gravity had its uses. He pulled again. The rhinebra jerked up suddenly, and the strap popped free.

He used the creature's erratic movements to help loosen the next fastener. As soon as it popped open, the third strap snapped. The thick leather whipped across his face. He reached up to touch the bridge of his nose and found it slick with blood.

Zorro squeaked. Hoku looked up and saw the saddle twisting off the rhinebra. In a second, he'd be face-to-face with that horrible Upgrader. Unless . . .

He jumped and tried to grab the flailing straps, hoping they would pull him up the rhinebra's flank as the saddle slid off the other side. The straps slapped him in the face instead.

The Upgrader grunted as he hit the ground, then yelped as the immense saddle fell on top of him. Hoku scrambled to the rhinebra's head and found Dash guiding it by the reins.

"The Upgrader is down, but only for a flash!" he said.

Dash nodded and said something to the rhinebra. The huge creature bent its foreleg. Dash hopped up onto its knee and clambered onto its back, the reins still clutched in the hand of his good arm. Hoku scrambled up after him.

"Wow," Hoku said. Had Dash really told this animal what to do — and it had listened?

"Sit behind me and hold on," Dash said.

"No, we can't leave Aluna," Hoku said firmly.

"I have no intention of leaving without her," Dash said. "Hold on, or you will find yourself on the ground again."

The rhinebra's striped fur was too short, and everything worth clinging to had gone overboard with the saddle. Hoku had no choice but to grab Dash around the waist.

"Here we go!" Dash said some strange words to the rhinebra and jangled the reins toward the left. The creature reacted instantly.

Aluna and the tattooed Upgrader woman were still fighting. Hoku watched her send a searing cone of fire toward Aluna. Aluna dropped and rolled forward. She tried to kick the flame shooter out of the Upgrader's hand, but it didn't budge. It was attached! The Upgrader swung her bladed hand down, but Aluna dodged. The black sword plunged into the earth right where Aluna's head had been.

"Hurry," Hoku said to Dash. His heart stuttered so fast that he could barely catch his breath. *Don't get skewered,* he thought at Aluna. *Don't get skewered!*

Dash turned the animal around and whispered to it again. The rhinebra threw back its head and roared. It wasn't the high-pitched giggle of a dolphin or the distant weeping dirge of a whale. Its bellow crashed over them like a tidal wave.

Aluna and the female Upgrader both looked up, dazed.

"Now!" Dash yelled.

Aluna jumped to her feet. She whipped one of her talons through the air and sent it flying toward the rhinebra. The thin chain wrapped around the biggest horn jutting out of the creature's forehead.

"Go!" she shouted back.

Dash urged the rhinebra into a trot. The ground thundered with each of its steps. Aluna ran beside it, stumbling, but using the talon chain to keep her balance.

Flames licked Aluna and the rhinebra as the female

Upgrader recovered her senses. The creature bellowed again and launched into a full gallop. Hoku grabbed Dash tighter. Zorro seemed safe enough clinging to the creature's mane. How Dash was staying upright using only his legs was a mystery.

A spear whizzed by the rhinebra's flank. Another nicked Dash in the ear. Both the Upgraders were up and chasing them now. Aluna ran and tried to jump onto the rhinebra's head. She got one hand around its horn. Her legs dangled off the side as the creature galloped.

"Hold on!" Dash yelled.

The horse-boy urged the rhinebra even faster. Hoku could feel the animal's muscles bunching and springing. He could barely keep his hold on Dash.

Aluna's legs dragged along the ground. She tried to pull herself up, but kept slipping even farther down the rhinebra's horn.

"Can't make it," Aluna panted. "Go . . . without me!"

"No! We will not leave you here," Dash said.

"You're strong. You can do it!" Hoku urged. If he could barely keep his own seat, how was he going to help Aluna?

"Do you have any ideas?" Dash said to him. "We are running out of time."

Hoku looked back toward the dome and saw the

Upgraders racing straight at them on another rhinebra and a terrifying black creature with eight legs. They were far behind, but gaining ground.

"Surrender," Hoku said. "Maybe we can reason—"

"No!" Aluna screamed. "Do it, and I'll . . . kill you both . . . myself!"

Hoku caught a flash of tawny wings in the sky.

An Aviar!

The Aviar dove faster than he believed possible. So fast, all he saw were feathers and a streak of brown hair. A moment later, she was lifting Aluna to the rhinebra's back, tucking her wings, and grinning at him.

"Calli!"

"Hi," she said, panting. Her cheeks glowed lobster red and her smile made his heart somersault in his chest.

"Go!" Aluna yelled.

Dash directed the rhinebra toward the path that wound around the outside of the plateau and led to the forest far below. They barreled down it in the near dark, and the two trailing Upgraders were quickly out of sight.

Hoku burned with questions for Calli but didn't speak. None of them did. Not until they'd reached the ground and the rhinebra plunged into the thick foliage of the forest. Only then did his words come tumbling out.

"Calli! But what about your mother? How did you get away?"

"Logic," Calli said, her eyes sparkling. "I pointed out to my mother that her grand plan had actually worked. Aluna *did* teach me about courage and honor, and I felt it was my duty to aid you in your quest. Mother tried to object, but I think it was mostly for show. She was so proud, she practically kicked me out of the palace."

"Well, I'm grateful she let you go," Aluna said. "You saved my life!"

Calli lowered her eyes, embarrassed, then looked up again. "I kind of did, didn't I?"

Hoku laughed. And if he hadn't been holding on to the rhinebra with every ounce of muscle he possessed, he would have leaned over and kissed her.

CHAPTER 35

ALUNA COULD SEE through the nighttime forest, but the rhinebra's eyesight wasn't much better than Dash's. The third time the massive creature stumbled, she said, "We should make camp." Dash seemed intent on getting as far away from the SkyTek dome as possible. Good instinct, but they were all exhausted.

Dash nodded. "I agree. Do you see a good place to claim for the night?"

She directed him to a small, tree-covered clearing and he pulled the rhinebra to a stop.

Aluna jumped down first, eager to get her feet on solid ground, and collapsed in a messy heap. The long ride had not only bruised her backside but rendered her legs useless. Hoku landed next to her with even less grace and an "Oof."

Calli drifted down and landed gently on one foot.

"How is your ankle?" Aluna asked.

"Better," Calli said. "It's only a sprain. We need light bones for flying, so SkyTek gave us superfast healing to compensate. It was a good trade."

Behind her, Dash slid easily off the rhinebra, even with just one good arm, and looped the animal's reins around a tree branch. He moved with such grace and fluidity. If he had a tail, he'd fit right in with the Kampii.

"I will go back and misdirect our trail," Dash said. "Build a fire while I am gone. It will be cold tonight."

"Cold?" Hoku said, pushing himself to his feet. "It's not like this is deep ocean."

"We don't need a fire," Aluna said. Aside from the fact that she had no idea how to build a fire, they hadn't been cold once since they came to the Above World. Not even a little. Thick Kampii skin kept them warm in the frigid ocean and kept them sweltering in the Above World sun.

"You never need torches?" Dash asked.

Hoku snorted. "Why would we need torches when we have glowfish? Besides, fire doesn't work that well underwater."

Dash's shoulders seemed to deflate. "Well, I will need a fire. Both for warmth and to see."

"And to honor the sun," Aluna said, remembering

what Dash had said about the Equian word-weavers keeping a fire blazing all night.

Dash looked at her strangely. "Yes," he said quietly. "And to honor the sun."

"I'd like a fire, too," Calli said. "We're built for the cold of high altitudes, but I can't see in the dark."

Dash walked into the clearing and squinted in the darkness. "Can you please clear a spot here? And fetch some twigs and small branches?"

"I can do that!" Aluna said. She jumped up and limped toward the forest, picking up sticks as she walked. She had no idea what would burn, so she grabbed everything she could find and piled it next to the fire spot. Her legs threatened to stiffen whenever she stopped walking, so she kept at it, bringing armful after armful. She would have brought the rhinebra some food, but it seemed content to munch on the nearby bushes.

"Hey, fish breath!" she called to Hoku. "You want to help gather twigs?"

"Not really," Hoku replied. He was sitting with his back against a tree, talking to Calli and fiddling with his water safe. "Calli and I are teaching Zorro how to try combinations."

"That sounds useful."

"It is! He can test numbers much faster than I can. His paws are like little hands."

She glanced over and saw Zorro pressing numbers with blurring speed. But Hoku and Calli weren't even watching him — they were staring at each other instead. Aluna shook her head and headed back into the forest.

By the time Dash stumbled back into camp, the forest was dark as deep ocean, and Aluna had made a little ring of stones around some of the twigs she'd collected. She remembered the configuration from the Human village they'd stumbled on back when they'd first come to the Above World.

"Good," Dash said, sounding surprised. "You are sure you have never done this before?"

"Not even once," she said, feeling a bit too proud for someone who had merely pushed some stones around and picked up some sticks.

Dash knelt by the circle — looking a little less graceful and more tired than before — and motioned to her. "Come, sit here. I will show you the rest. And besides, I need your eyes until we get the flames started."

She hobbled over and sat a foot or so away from Dash, close enough but not too close. At least that's what she hoped he would think. Had he wanted her to sit closer?

Barnacles, she thought, *I'm turning into a gibbering mermaid.* In her mind, mermaids spent the whole day combing their hair and thinking about boys, two things that normally bored her beyond reason. Aluna ran a nervous hand through her hair. When *was* the last time she'd bothered to untangle it? Good thing the Aviars' chief groomer had chopped off most of it for her before they'd left.

Dash plopped his satchel in the space between them—the perfect amount, Aluna decided—and dug around inside it.

"Aha!" he said, pulling out two unimpressive pieces of stone. "Here is my flint. We are going to scrape these together until we get a spark."

He did it once to show her how, then handed her the stones. It took her twelve tries. She knew the exact number because Hoku and Calli counted them aloud.

"Excellent," Dash said. "Now we will use the spark to ignite some of our dried leaves and tiny sticks."

She followed his instructions and even let him reposition her hand for a better angle. Eventually, one of the leaves started to smolder.

"Now blow gently on your tiny fire," Dash said. "It is your way of asking the flames to grow."

The flames surged briefly when she blew, but quickly shrank back to embers.

"Softer," Dash replied. "Let me show you." He blew, and within a minute, they had a real fire blazing.

She didn't need the warmth, but she loved the fire anyway. It crackled and sizzled, dancing wildly to some unheard rhythm. And the smell! So unlike the stench of the Human village. A fire didn't just warm your outsides; it warmed your insides, too.

The wind changed, and the smoke blew in her face. She coughed and tried to blink away the soot. Her face stung, as if the fire were trying to burn out the orbs of her eyes.

"This way," Dash said, and pulled her to the other side. "Never sit downwind."

Her lungs cleared. She stared at the fire again, a little more warily.

"This really is your first fire," Dash whispered. He motioned to Hoku, Calli, and Zorro, who had curled up by their tree and fallen asleep.

Aluna nodded. The firelight flickered off Dash's face. He looked strange and wild—and unlike any of the Kampii boys back in the city. Some Kampii shared his coloring, but none had the same eyes. What were the girls like where he came from? she wondered. In her mind, they were tall, strong girls with the bodies of horses who could run for miles and miles and never get tired. Their hair streamed behind them as they ran, much like their horsey tails, and they laughed in the sun.

"When do the Equians grow their horse legs?" she asked. "Do you have a ceremony, like we do, and swallow a seed that makes them grow? Or does half a horse sprout out of you one day when you're not expecting it?"

Dash's brow furrowed, but only for a moment before he regained control of himself. He finished chewing a bit of jerky the Aviars had supplied them with and swallowed slowly.

"It's not a difficult question," she pushed.

Dash looked down at the strip of dried meat gripped in his hand. "Equians do not *grow* their horse legs," he said. "When everything . . . goes correctly . . . they are born with them."

She looked at his legs, legs not much different from her own.

"Was that why you were exiled?"

"I was born without a horse heart, or four hooves, or a tail. I am a mistake," he said quietly. "I am . . . I am only half a person."

She didn't know what to say. "I'm sorry" seemed so . . . *useless.* Dash was kicked out of his family because he was different, because he didn't fit in. She didn't fit in with her family, either, but they'd never make her leave—not the family nest, and certainly not the City of Shifting Tides.

"I'm sorry," she said finally. Because, really, there was nothing better to say.

CHAPTER 36

DASH, ALUNA, AND CALLI were already awake when Hoku finally managed to open his eyes. Sunlight streamed through the treetops in slender rays. For a moment, he thought he'd fallen asleep atop the old broken dome back home. Light used to refract through the ocean in much the same way. He'd spent dozens of tides there, trying to figure out how the light's path was altered when it hit the surface of the water. Zorro's small pink tongue on his cheek washed away the memory.

"Time to wake up, sleepy-bones," Aluna said. "Dash found some nuts and leaves for us to eat."

"Nuts? Leaves? Are those even food?" Hoku mumbled. Then he made the mistake of trying to stand up. His legs and back felt pulverized, as if a shark had munched on him for a while then spat him back out. He tried to walk, but his legs would barely obey. The best he could manage was a slow hobble, and even that required moaning. Cutting the rhinebra's saddle off had been a very bad idea after all.

"Can I use some of the spices that Senator Niobe gave you?" Calli asked him. She looked far too happy to be awake and stranded in the middle of a scary forest. "I think I can make something a bit more tasty from our ingredients if we can spare a few minutes."

Aluna spat out the leaf she'd been chewing. "If you can make this stuff taste good, you'll save my life a second time."

Calli laughed. "Well, I'm not really that good at it, but I learned a few tricks while I was hiding in the kitchens when I was young. And besides, cooking is a lot like science."

Hoku hobbled over, handed her the spices from his bag, and collapsed near the glowing embers of the fire. If anything could distract him from the pain, it was a certain winged girl with bright brown eyes. He watched her clean a piece of her armor and use it to toast the nuts and tubers Dash had found. She sprinkled spices on the food and hummed while she worked. Soon the sizzle and the smell had his mouth watering and everyone gathering around the fire to eat.

"This is truly amazing," Dash said with his mouth full. "Spices are highly valued in the desert. My people would trade generously for even a small vial."

"Let's try the mustard tomorrow," Hoku said, grabbing another leaf and stuffing it with nut mash. "Everything tastes better with a smear of that stuff."

Aluna licked her fingers. "Dash and I will be on hunting-and-gathering duty if you two share the cooking."

Hoku looked at Calli just as she looked at him. They both grinned.

"Let's go," Aluna said. "We have a lot of distance to cross."

Amid groans and curses, they put out the fire, wrapped up their leftover food, and managed to get back on the rhinebra. Dash started them at a walk, but even the slow pace felt like torture. Hoku distracted himself by discussing the angle of light refraction with Calli and by teaching Zorro to balance on his hind legs.

The next few days blurred together. Physically, Hoku suffered almost every minute from the rhinebra's unforgiving back and the soreness it created. Even so, he'd never been happier. His conversations with Calli ranged from pulleys and aerodynamics to electronics and cooking. When they set Zorro to work on water safe combinations, he and Calli had fun modifying one of his Extra Ears to work on the radio she'd brought. The radio was already stronger than the Kampii internal ear artifacts. With the added reception boost, there was no telling how far away the radio could receive a signal. They vowed to test it out as soon as they got a chance.

Hoku still hadn't found the courage to ask about the note Calli had written in his book. Were they friends, and nothing more? Is that what she wanted? He understood his own feelings, at least. He wanted more kissing, true, but he wanted more of everything else as well. Talking, laughing, fiddling with tech . . . If he ruined all that just because he wanted something that Calli didn't, he'd never forgive himself.

At night, they cooked and ate around their campfire. He loved the flames. Not just the flickering light, but the way it drew them together around its circumference. Fire had a gravity all its own.

He sat next to Calli, grateful that she never seemed to mind. Her hand rested on the ground just a few millimeters from his. And yet . . . those millimeters meant everything. Would he ever be brave enough to cross that distance?

They sang at night. He was surprised to find that in the Above World, Aluna's voice was strong and true. Not refined or really beautiful, but full of passion. She sang her heart in every note. Calli's songs were sweeter and softer, usually ballads about Aviars fighting and dying in heroic ways. He liked the love songs, too, although they almost always ended unhappily.

Dash refused to sing at first, but Aluna and Calli worked away at him until finally, after several nights, he relented. He began not with melody, but with ritual. A series of hand motions and stomping around the fire, clearly intended to be performed by someone with horse hooves. And the song, when he finally started to sing it, came low out of his throat. It had rhythm and power, but no words.

When he had finished, no one spoke. Hoku stole a glance at Aluna and saw that her eyes were wet. He looked away quickly. Then, without even thinking about it, he reached out and took Calli's hand. Her fingers wrapped around his hand immediately, as if they'd been waiting all night for the chance. His heart thundered in his chest, but he didn't dare look at her. He stared at the fire, pretending to be mesmerized, when all he could think about was how warm and light her hand felt in his.

He fell asleep each night listening to Aluna and Dash on watch. The truth was, they mostly sat together in silence. Sometimes they'd talk about hunting rabbits and squirrels, but since neither of them could walk easily, those plans never amounted to much. Aluna filled Dash in on the Upgrader attack at Skyfeather's

Landing, and they debated strategies for handling their enemies with greater efficiency. Hoku found the conversations boring, the perfect way to lull himself to sleep at night despite all the excitement.

On the seventh day of travel, the trees thinned. More sunlight speared through the branches as they rode, and the rhinebra was able to galumph in straighter lines.

"We made good distance," Dash said. "I would have bet both sand and sky that the Upgraders would have caught us by now."

"Will we reach the shoreline soon?" Aluna asked.

Dash shrugged. He seemed more comfortable with her questions now, although she could still catch him off guard with her enthusiasm. Hoku knew the feeling.

Not long after, the trees thinned even more, and they spied gold and blue through the green and brown trunks.

"Sand!" Aluna yelled. "Ocean!"

Hoku grinned at Aluna and they both cheered. Calli cheered, too, in support.

The rhinebra hurtled toward shore. Dirt changed to sand, and blue once again filled the sky. They were finally free from all that suffocating foliage. Hoku heard the waves crash against the beach and laughed. It was like hearing his heartbeat after weeks of silence.

He wanted to leap from the rhinebra's back, flop into the water, and dive down as deep as he could go. He wanted to feel the water around him like a hug.

And if he hadn't been wearing his satchel strapped across his back, and if it hadn't been full of books, he would have jumped in right then. As he started to remove it, he heard Calli gasp.

"Over there!" Aluna yelled, pointing up the shore.

Hoku followed her gaze, and the wave of joy swelling inside him dissolved into now-familiar fear.

"Six of them," Dash said. "And two flying devices. They must have been waiting for us. That is why they did not follow. I should have anticipated this!"

"We can't handle eight," Aluna said. "Four maybe, but not eight."

Hoku could hear fear creeping into her voice, and it scared him.

A cry went up among the Upgraders. Six huge beasts—two rhinebras and four massive insects—thundered toward them, with the two dragonfliers in the lead. They were far away, but moving fast.

"Into the ocean," Hoku said. "Now!"

"But—"

"He's right," Aluna said. "It's our only hope."

Dash kicked the rhinebra, hard, and the huge animal lumbered into a gallop, straight into the waves.

CHAPTER 37

WHEN THE FIRST drop of salt water touched her lips, Aluna shivered. The taste unleashed a flood of feelings inside her. It was as if the ocean itself were speaking to her: *You never should have left. You never should have abandoned the sea.*

The Upgraders charged down the beach toward them. Dash urged the rhinebra forward, but the creature refused to go farther into the water. Dash raised his voice and yelled something in a stange language. The rhinebra bucked.

There was nothing to grab. Aluna flew into the air and, a second later, smacked full force into a cresting wave. The initial sting along her legs and back dissolved quickly into pain. Hoku plunged headfirst into the same wave and surfaced with a sputter. Calli floated above them, flapping her wings.

"Help!" a distant voice called.

"Dash!" Aluna yelled. He must have landed on the other side of the rhinebra. "His arm," she said to Hoku. "He can't swim!"

"I'll get him!" Calli called. She flew just above the whitecaps and hovered over Dash's location. He grabbed for her leg, but with only one good hand, he couldn't hold on when she tried to pull him out. "I'm not strong enough," she cried. "I don't have him!"

"On my way!" Aluna dove under the water and started to swim. On her second stroke, she took a deep breath.

Cold seawater poured into her mouth and nose. It should have filled her throat and lungs easily and helped balance in the surrounding water pressure, allowing her breathing shell to deliver all the oxygen she needed to her body.

But of course her breathing shell was gone. Instead of relaxing, her body fought for air, and she choked. It felt as if an icy hand were reaching down her throat and trying to rip out her lungs. She gagged and more water rushed into her mouth. She kicked for the surface, her hands scrabbling along her neck.

The world turned black. The icy hand made a fist in her breathing passage. Someone had put rocks in her chest. She was sinking, sinking. She thrashed her arms and legs. Air! She needed air!

A hand grabbed her by the back of her shirt and yanked her up. Her face breached the water's surface. She coughed and breathed, and coughed some more. The sun burned her eyes.

"Calm down," Hoku said. "Take it slow."

"Necklace—" she managed, sputtering.

"I know," he said. His hand was still on her, helping her to hold her head above the water.

She took in one mouthful of air and then another. Her eyes focused on Hoku. On the freckles on his cheeks. On the paleness of his skin. On the firm, worried line of his mouth. Her mind began to recover from its panic.

She gulped air and nodded. "I'm okay."

"I'll get Dash," Hoku said. "Stay here."

"Hoku, I'm afraid of the water," Calli yelled, her face stricken with panic. "My wings will get waterlogged!"

"Fly to the trees and hide!" Hoku said. "Your bones are too thin for the deep. You have to fly!"

He submerged and headed for Dash. Aluna paddled after him, coughing and keeping her chin raised as far above the surface of the water as she could manage. The ocean used to be her home. She never realized how dangerous it was . . . and how unwelcoming.

She kept an eye on the Upgraders as she navigated the waves. The first monster insects had reached the water's edge, but they would not go farther. A distant buzzing noise grew louder and louder as she inched through the water.

Dragonfliers!

Those despicable machines skimmed over the surf, their translucent wings flapping so fast that she couldn't even see them. What she could see were the twin flamethrowers mounted on each flier.

She scanned the sky for Calli and saw the winged girl heading to the trees. *Good.* Calli had spent her whole life trying to be invisible. That had to count for something now.

The rhinebra bolted from the water, and three of the Upgraders broke off from the group to chase it down. She saw Dash struggling to stay afloat near the shore, each wave buffeting his body. Hoku surfaced between them and then disappeared back under the water. *Swift as a seal,* she urged him.

They were never going to survive. The four of them were separated, wounded, flailing. The Upgraders were fresh, powerful, fast. She was supposed to figure out some brilliant plan that enabled them to defeat the Upgraders, make it to the HydroTek dome, and save the world. Instead, they were going to die alone and afraid, half killed by the ocean that used to be an ally.

It was her job to lead them, and she had led them to their death.

Salt water splashed into her face, as if the ocean were slapping her. The cold sting woke her up. This was no time for self-pity—and certainly no time for giving up.

The first dragonflier headed for Dash.

"Watch out!" she yelled.

Dash heard her and ducked under a wave as double gouts of flame shot from the dragonflier. The second dragonflier sped toward her as the first one hovered over Dash's location. Where was he? He hadn't resurfaced yet. How long could he hold his breath?

She scanned the waves for Hoku but couldn't find him. Had he gotten to Dash already? Was he keeping Dash under the water? She wanted to go help, but soon she'd have her own Upgrader to deal with.

A slimy hand wrapped around her left ankle and pulled.

Aluna yelped in surprise and kicked. The thing let go for a second, then grabbed her again. She kicked harder, but whatever was attacking her tightened its grip. Could the Upgraders swim? She smashed the heel of her right foot into the thing holding her.

Another slick, rubbery hand grabbed her free ankle. Aluna gulped air. Her attacker yanked, and she was dragged under the water.

Down, down, down. She slid through the water. Pressure built around her lungs, slowly squeezing them tighter and tighter. She kicked and squirmed harder as her panic grew.

Whatever was pulling her slowed but did not release her ankles. A dark shape appeared in front of her. She recognized its huge black eyes and slick gray skin immediately.

"Deepfell!" she blurted out.

She realized her mistake too late. Down this deep, she'd drown before she could find her way to the surface again for another gulp of air. If the Deepfell didn't kill her first.

The Deepfell darted its head forward, as if it were going to head butt her. Instead, the flat gray lips of its mouth pressed against hers. When it pulled away, a bubble formed between their mouths. A bubble filled with air.

Aluna breathed.

The Deepfell holding her legs released its grip. She stayed where she was, grateful to have the air, and grateful to be far away from the Upgraders.

Even if that meant temporarily surrendering to the Deepfell.

CHAPTER 38

THE DEEPFELL in front of her—a woman—
motioned for her to follow. Aluna worried that the air
bubble wobbling around her mouth might burst when
she moved, but decided to trust her rescuers. If they'd
wanted her dead, they could have stayed safely underwater and watched the Upgraders kill her. Or worse,
they could have let her drown in the ocean that used to
be her home.

She swam after the Deepfell. The bubble around
her face wavered, but remained intact. She could even
open and close her mouth without breaking the seal.
There wasn't much air inside, so she swam swiftly.

They caught up to another group of Deepfell, and
she recognized a small, pale figure among them.

"Hoku!"

"You're safe!" he answered in her ear.

She saw Dash behind him. He had an air bubble over his mouth and was being carried by one of the Deepfell. He waved with his good hand and managed a weak smile. His eyes were bloodshot. After looking at her, he squeezed them shut again. Ocean salt wasn't kind to visitors, especially those without special ocean-ready eyes.

Hoku spoke in an endless quiet stream to Calli. "I hope you have the radio on. We're okay. We're going underwater with the Deepfell. But not the evil Deepfell. At least, I don't think they're evil. Stay safe. Stay in the trees. Hide. We'll be fine. You have to take care of yourself. Don't let the Upgraders find you. I hope this works. I hope you have the radio on."

The Deepfell escorted them farther up the coast but stayed close to the ocean's surface, probably to keep Dash's lungs from collapsing from the pressure. She grew more comfortable with the air bubble, despite its tendency to tickle her nose as it wiggled.

As they swam, they passed cadres of Deepfell camped along the ocean floor or sparring midwater. She'd never seen so many together in one place. She saw one warrior without a right arm and another without a dorsal fin. In fact, she couldn't spot a single Deepfell without a scar marring its sleek gray skin.

The Deepfell were at war.

Their escorts took them into a cave. They swam through a tunnel that angled up. After a few dozen meters, her head broke the surface of the water. The interior of the cave was as large as the ritual dome back home. They surfaced in a small pool of water, but the rest of the cave contained sand and air, and hundreds of wounded Deepfell.

Aluna's rescuer turned and touched her lips to Aluna's air bubble. The Deepfell inhaled and sucked the whole membrane back into her mouth. She swallowed and smiled, then swam away.

The rest of the Deepfell dragged themselves onto land and headed for the back of the cave, walking like seals instead of people. One of them, a male, beckoned to Aluna and she followed, more relieved than she wanted to be about leaving the water. Hoku and Dash joined her.

Much of the sand beneath their feet was stained red, and it took her a moment to realize that it was blood. But it made sense. Blood in the water meant death. Too many predators would be thrilled to find a secret stash of wounded Deepfell. Great White itself could smell blood for miles. According to legend, it had once swum all the way around the earth to eat a dying penguin. The Deepfell took their wounded out of the water for the good of the colony.

At the back of the cave, they found the command

center of the Deepfell's war operation. Battle plans and accounting tallies had been scratched on thin sheets of shale and were stacked in piles around a lone Deepfell. Unlike the others, he reclined on a raised hammock as he reviewed some sort of report etched into a piece of the rock paper. A thin circlet of shells and coral surrounded his hairless gray head. Despite the fact that he was a mortal enemy of her people, he looked noble.

The Deepfell they were following pointed at the man and squeaked, "Preeence Eekikee," before disappearing into another part of the cave.

The prince looked up when they approached, and Aluna saw a deep scar across his neck, still red around the edges, but mostly healed.

The Deepfell from the beach — the one that she had saved!

Prince Eekikee swung his tail off the hammock and stood on it, tall as a Kampii. She had no idea they could do that. Thick muscles bulged under his shark skin. He could have been the same age as one of her brothers. Now that she thought about it, she'd never seen a Deepfell much older than that. Certainly none as old as her father or the other Elders.

"Come. Here," the prince said, looking directly at her. The words looked painful for him to speak. He held out his webbed hand. She offered her hand in return, and he dropped a small shell necklace into her palm.

She stared at the familiar jewelry in wonder.

"Your shell," Hoku said. "Aluna, your breathing shell!"

She nodded dumbly.

The prince placed his hand on his chest and squeaked. Aluna winced. The prince frowned, clearly frustrated. He thumped his chest again, then said, "Eekikee."

"Eekikee," she repeated. Then she pointed to herself and said, "Aluna." The boys followed her lead. Dash started to say something after "Dashiyn," but stopped himself. Another mystery to unravel, she thought, but for another time.

Prince Eekikee nodded, then hopped over to a pile of circular objects and grabbed one. He held it out for them to see. It looked like a thick collar made out of some kind of black metal. One side hinged open, but it looked like it could snap closed easily enough. It certainly wasn't pretty enough to wear, not even for her.

Hoku took the collar and turned it over in his hand. He brought it up to his neck, as if he were going to try it on. Eekikee knocked it out of Hoku's hand.

"Hey!" Hoku said. He looked at her for support, but she shook her head. The look in Prince Eekikee's eyes was dark. She reached for her talons.

"It is a slave collar," Dash said simply. "No one chooses to put one on."

The prince pointed to the collar, now lying on the sand, and then pointed up. His eyes stayed dark.

"F-F-Fathom," he said. Then he pointed to the wounded all around them. "Fiiight."

"Fathom. Fathom is enslaving his people," Aluna said. "That's why they're at war."

A loud screech echoed through the cave.

The prince listened to the alarm, then squeaked a series of commands to their Deepfell escorts. When they nodded, he dropped to the ground and pulled himself toward the water faster than she'd ever seen a Deepfell move.

"Waaaait," one of the remaining Deepfell said to her, and pointed to a patch of sand by the cave wall.

A young Deepfell male lugged Hoku's satchel and an extremely irritated Zorro into the clearing. The raccoon had clamped on to the handle of the bag and refused to be removed. When he saw Hoku, the little thing went crazy. He scampered over to Hoku and covered his face in a frenzy of tiny licks.

"Glad to see you, too, boy," Hoku said.

The Deepfell brought a small pile of fish that Aluna could have devoured in two flashes, had she not seen the half-starved look on Hoku's face. Dash nibbled one fish but didn't go back for a second. If he got hungry enough, he'd eat, she reasoned, and took a fifth for herself. She ate the last one slowly, savoring the delicate crunch of bones in her mouth.

"My books!" Hoku said.

She looked over. He had spread the contents of his bag in a circle around his spot on the sand.

"The water destroyed them," he said. And then, more quietly, "I can't even read the inscriptions anymore."

Aluna knew this wasn't about the books. "Why did you make Calli fly away?" she asked. "She would have been safer down here with us."

Hoku opened up each of his books and placed them gently on the sand to dry. "Aviars have thin, light bones in order to fly," he said. "If we brought her underwater, she'd be safe from the Upgraders, but the pressure from the ocean would snap all of her bones."

"Oh," Aluna said. "Good choice, then."

"The books did not survive, but we did," Dash said. "You made the correct decision, and you made it quickly in a dangerous situation. It was a victory."

"They weren't *your* books," Hoku said bitterly. He pulled out the water safe and set Zorro to trying combinations. "At least whatever's inside here is still dry."

Aluna opened her fist and stared at the breathing necklace she thought she'd lost forever.

She sat cross-legged in the sand and pressed her

breathing necklace to her throat. Hoku and Dash watched as she twisted the shell, trying to activate the hidden mechanism that would bring it to life. A moment later, she heard a whir and felt its twin tails burrowing into her neck.

She choked and sputtered. For several horrible seconds, she couldn't breathe at all. Her eyes and mouth opened wide as she gasped. She needed air. Her hands clawed at the shell. She needed to get it off of her!

Hoku grabbed her wrists and pulled them away from her throat. "It's okay," Hoku said. "Let it work!"

He stared into her eyes and she tried to focus on his freckles, tried to make herself count them one by one. The pain! Spots swam across her eyes like a horde of ink-black eels.

And then the bubble of tension growing inside her chest burst, and she could breathe. She sucked in great gulps of air through her mouth and felt the glow of the breathing necklace pulsing at her throat.

"Good," Hoku said. "It still has work to do in your lungs, but the worst is over."

She hugged him tight, afraid to speak. The ocean was hers once again.

Click.

Aluna, Dash, and Hoku looked over at Zorro just as the lid of the water safe sprang open.

CHAPTER 39

AS SOON AS the water safe popped open, Zorro tried to shut it again.

"No!" Hoku said, prying himself free from Aluna and rushing to the animal. "Stop!"

The raccoon tilted his head and perked his ears.

"Zorro, stop," he repeated more clearly. "You're all done, boy. Good job." He gave the raccoon a big scruffle between the ears. Figures the little guy would focus on the combination part, not the actual goal of opening the box. In a way, that was Hoku's favorite part, too.

But now that the mermaid box was open, all he could hear was the pounding of his heart inside his chest. *Please, oh, please let it be something worthwhile!*

"What's in it?" Aluna asked.

Hoku memorized the numbers first, before anything happened to reset them: *704404*. Then he took a deep breath and lifted the silver mermaid lid all the way open.

Three items sat inside: a handwritten letter, an old photograph, and a small carved wooden dolphin.

Where was the powerful artifact that was going to save them all? Where was the perfect weapon for defeating the Upgraders?

"Well?" Aluna said.

He looked in the box, searching for a good answer and trying to quell the disappointment that threatened to overwhelm him. "There's a letter," he said. The paper was faded and wrinkled. Someone had written all the words by hand, except for the top part. He read, "FROM THE DESK OF DR. KARL STRAND, DIRECTOR, BIOMEDICS."

"Can you read the rest of it?" Aluna asked.

"Of course," he said. Just because it took him a long time to figure out *biomedics* didn't mean he couldn't figure out the rest. Then he remembered that she couldn't read at all and felt sorry for his reaction.

"Please," Dash said. "I also am interested."

Hoku cleared his throat and started at the handwritten part. Luckily "Karl" had used a steady, even hand when he wrote it, or Hoku's job might have been much harder. "'Dearest Sarah—'"

"Sarah Jennings! Your grandma was right!" Aluna interrupted. She turned to Dash and explained, "Sarah Jennings—known as Ali'ikai—founded the City of Shifting Tides. She was the first Kampii."

"Shhh," said Dash. "Do not interrupt a word-weaver."

"He's not making up the words," she said. "He's reading them. It's not the same."

"Perhaps not to you, but—"

"'Dearest Sarah,'" Hoku repeated, louder this time. When Dash and Aluna settled down, he continued:

"You say you've made up your mind, but I can't let you go without trying one last time to persuade you to stay. I will start with this: We do have a future. We have a future both as a race of people on a struggling planet, and as a family.

Even now, in my own lab, Ratliff and Nazarian are close to the cure. Not only can they stop the spread of Super-Z but they can make sure nothing like this ever happens to humanity again. They want to keep testing, but I know, in my heart, that it works, and that it will save us all. In fact, we'll be stronger than ever before.

If only you were willing to give me more time. . . . Ah, but I know you. When your mind is made up, you are a bulldog. (There won't be bulldogs in your new underwater colony, will there? No bulldogs, no fireplaces, no long, slow hikes at dusk. . . . Can you really give up all those things? Will your new race of Kampii ever love you as much as I do?)

I've enclosed two items with this letter. Do you remember the photo? We'd taken Tomias to his first soccer game. He ate two hot dogs and cheered for both teams. He was so healthy then, and we had so many plans.

The second item you will also recognize. It will pain you to keep it, knowing that I carved it with my own two hands. But you will not be able to throw it away, knowing how much Tomias loved it. Knowing how he put it under his pillow at night and insisted on bringing it everywhere he went. Do you remember that night in San Diego when we spent nearly four hours scouring the beach for it?

Tomias is gone, but we can have that happiness again. We can have another child, or two more, or even six! I can guarantee they'll be safe. I can guarantee that they'll live forever. I'm not giving you empty promises. Not anymore. Not ever again. I can make miracles now.

I can, I will, do anything for you, Sarah. Just don't leave me.
With more than an ocean of love,
Karl"

Hoku pulled the photograph out of the box. Three faces smiled up at him, presumably Sarah Jennings, Karl Strand, and their son, Tomias. Sarah was tall and brown skinned, a much younger version of the sculpture on her monument in the Kampii city. Her crinkled hair was pulled back but not quite contained in a bushy ponytail behind her head. The grinning boy was about six years old and held a spotted black-and-white ball in his hands.

Karl had a shock of brown hair, nicely mussed, and wore the biggest glasses Hoku had ever seen. The man stood slightly shorter than Sarah and had sand-colored skin. One of his arms was around Sarah's waist, and the other rested on his son's shoulder. They stood on a field of green grass, with a blue cloud-spotted sky behind them. It was hard to imagine a more perfect vision of Above World family bliss.

Hoku picked up the wooden dolphin. It fit nicely in his hands. Although it had been crudely carved, certain places along its nose and dorsal fin had been worn smooth. He ran his thumb along the wood, imagining the child Tomias doing the same thing centuries ago.

Hoku closed his eyes for a moment and felt his mother's arms around him. The sounds of dying Deepfell faded into the warm memory. He could smell her hair, could hear the sound of her voice when she was trying to scold him about something she didn't really think was too bad. He could picture her as she talked, trying to keep her face stern, trying to keep the smile from her lips. He didn't always make her proud, but she always loved him. Always, always. And he had left her without even saying good-bye.

"Hoku!" Aluna said.

He snapped his eyes open and the real world came crashing in around him like a tidal wave.

"What else is in there?" she asked. "Weapons? Secrets? Anything we can use?"

He shook his head. "No," he said, dropping the dolphin back into the box. "Nothing except the dreams of dead people."

CHAPTER 40

ALUNA TOOK A STEP toward him. "Hoku—"

He shoved the water safe into her hands. "I'm going for a walk," he said, afraid that if he didn't get away he might do something humiliating and unforgivable, like burst into tears.

He turned his back and headed off before she could stop him. Zorro started to follow him, but Hoku shook his head and said, "Zorro, no." The raccoon sat back on his haunches immediately, eyes pulsing green. Hoku kept walking.

He wound his way along the edge of the cave wall, his brain a jumble. He wanted nothing more than to be back in his family's nest with a big net of fresh clams, planning his next experiment and listening to his parents talk about their day.

A strange squeak invaded his thoughts. He looked around for its source and saw a wounded Deepfell lying on the sand. She squeaked again, louder, and looked straight at him. He headed for her pallet, careful not to kick sand in her face as he walked.

She couldn't have been more than a few years older than he was. Most of her torso was wrapped in cloth spotted with blood. Even for a gray-skinned monster, she looked pale and frightened.

"Akkikoki," she squeaked. "Okok kikka kikka."

He shook his head. "I don't understand."

She reached out a webbed hand, and he took it in his own. Her flesh was smooth and rubbery. It should have been firm and slick with water, but here in the cave, it was dry and soft. Almost frail. He never thought he'd say that about a Deepfell.

He dropped to his knees and stared at the wounded girl. Her eyes were wide and black, set farther apart on her face than his—probably so she could see in more directions while she swam. She didn't try talking again. She sat there and held his hand. He watched her breathe. Her body jerked with each inhalation, as if even the act of drawing in air was painful to her.

He pictured his mother in the Deepfell's place, pain contorting the lines around her eyes and mouth. He pictured Calli, her huge smile replaced by a grimace as she tried to be brave for him. He pictured

Aluna, always so strong, barely able to keep her grip on his hand.

He dropped his head and cried.

The Deepfell girl did nothing. She just lay there, breathing slowly, her hand in his hand. Then, ever so softly, she started to whistle. The sound was high-pitched and faint, the melody haunting.

The Deepfell was singing to him.

He cried while she sang. All the danger and running and fear—it had all been building up inside him. The letter from Karl had made him sad. Sad for Karl and for Sarah Jennings and for their son, Tomias. He was worried about Calli, out there in the Above World all alone, because of him. He was scared, not just for himself, but for everyone he loved.

None of these things were terrible by themselves, but together, all at once? Crushing, as if he'd swum too far into deep ocean.

Eventually his tears stopped and only the Deepfell's song remained. It was beautiful and melancholy, but there was a note at the end of each verse that lifted his spirits. A single note that offered hope. How could the whole song be redeemed by such a small moment?

He thought about Aluna and Dash, Calli and Zorro. They were just like that: small notes in a great big song of despair. The Above World felt vast and cruel and hopeless, but maybe their actions could change the tenor of the world's song. Maybe they were those little notes of hope.

When the Deepfell finished her song, Hoku squeezed her hand gently.

"Thank you," he said, looking into one of her deep, dark eyes. He'd never meant the words more.

Grandma Nani had always said that the Deepfell gave up their humanity to live in the deep ocean. Nani was wrong.

The Deepfell let go of his hand and smiled.

Thinking about his grandma sparked a memory. When she'd given him the water safe, she'd said, *Maybe it holds her memories of the Above World. Maybe it holds far more.*

The space inside the box should have held much more than just a letter and a picture and a wooden dolphin. What if those items were decoys? The whole water safe seemed designed to look sentimental: the silvery mermaid on the lid, the letter, the photo. Grandma Nani said Sarah Jennings was smart. Well, he was smart, too.

He waved good-bye to the wounded Deepfell girl and sprinted back to the others.

CHAPTER 41

WHEN HOKU GOT BACK to the command center, he ignored Aluna and Dash and even Zorro and headed straight for the water safe.

"Are you okay?" Aluna asked. "Did something happen?"

He punched in the combination, popped open the box, and removed the letter, photo, and dolphin. Now that it was empty, he could easily see that the container part extended only halfway through the box's depth. He ran his fingertip slowly along the smooth plastic bottom, feeling for anything unusual.

Then he found it. A small depression at the back, no bigger than a few grains of sand. A button? He pulled out an Extra Ear, straightened one of the wires, and poked the end into the hole.

A small square flap in the bottom of the box swung open, revealing a hidden compartment. He pulled out a thin black rectangle, no bigger than the palm of his hand and thick as a finger. He looked up at Aluna and Dash and grinned.

"I examined that box thoroughly," Dash said. "How did you do that?"

"Because he's Hoku," Aluna replied, as if that explained everything. "What is it?"

"A piece of really old tech," Hoku said. "Wait, I bet there's a way to turn it on."

He found a series of buttons along one edge and pressed them in succession. As soon as he hit the second, the tiny video screen filled with the glowing, spinning symbol of the Kampii seahorse. A moment later, it was replaced by the face of a familiar dark-skinned woman in a small domed room full of air. He recognized her high cheekbones and strong, tired eyes immediately.

Sarah Jennings. Moving as if she were still alive.

"Amazing," Aluna whispered, and crowded closer. Hoku felt Dash on his other side and angled the device so they could both see.

On the device, Sarah looked over her shoulder, at something they couldn't see, then forward again. If he didn't know better, he'd have thought she was looking right at them.

"Hello, Kampii descendant, whoever you may be," Sarah said. Her accent twisted the words strangely, but she spoke with a slow, stately grace that helped him keep up. "I don't have much time, so I will make this brief: I fear that my compatriots, the other men and women who will become the ruling council of our new society, have a different view of the world from mine."

She looked down at something in her hand. He could just make out the dorsal fin of a small wooden dolphin.

"There were bound to be differing opinions," she said. "I recruited strong men and women for this great experiment. It is the rare individual willing to give up everything he or she has — all material, emotional, and cultural ties to the world — and begin a new life, with a new identity, somewhere as dangerous and unforgiving as under the sea."

Aluna snorted.

Sarah Jennings continued, "We need to hide, to stay safe, while the world is so broken. On that point, we are all agreed. But for how long? My fellow leaders would have us hide forever. They would have the City of Shifting Tides become our home, now and for all time. The coral reef would be forever the limits of our world."

She leaned forward, her brown eyes intense. "The world is broken, but it will not always remain so. Eventually, it will be ready for us again. We have a duty—a responsibility—to help it heal. The world needs us, and we need each other. We must not hide forever."

Sarah looked over her shoulder again. When she looked back at them through the screen, she tucked a rebellious twist of graying black hair behind her ear. Her voice came in whispers. "This outpost, Seahorse Alpha, houses information about the world—facts and figures and scientific data, but also the stories of its people. Art, literature, languages, cultures, TV archives, movies . . . every last bit of digital information I have been able to find and download and encrypt in the last few months. Let it be your window to the past . . . not so you repeat the mistakes we have made, but so that you learn from them."

She pulled the mermaid box into view. "Because the people in power are the least likely to encourage change, I will give this recording and this box to my assistant, Christopher, for safekeeping. He's smart and resourceful and has been a good, loyal friend. I have filled the remaining space on this device with information that HydroTek does not want me to have: passwords, formulas, schematics, and the like. They will be useless to you without the computers to interpret them, but I feel better knowing that someone else will have them."

"And so farewell, descendant of mine," Sarah

Jennings said with a sad smile. "I wish you swift currents and Godspeed. And remember: we are not alone. We were not meant to be alone." She reached forward, and the screen fell to blackness.

He didn't understand everything Sarah Jennings had said, but he understood enough. Aluna had been right about the outpost holding secrets. The Elders had been wrong—so, so wrong—about what Sarah Jennings wanted for her people. But best of all, formulas! Schematics! Passwords! All hidden in an artifact so small he could shove it in a pocket.

"I need to see it again," Aluna said. Quiet tears dripped down her cheeks. "Please."

Dash stood quietly beside them, and said only, "A wondrous woman. She must come from a strong bloodline."

A loud screech echoed through the cave, interrupting the spell Sarah Jennings had cast over them. Every Deepfell turned his or her head toward the sound, listening.

Eekikee pulled himself to the clearing while the alarm still blared. He had to gulp air before he could coax his throat to speak. "Cap-turrre," he said finally. He leveraged himself onto his tail and held out his hand fin. A small pearled hair stick sat in his palm. Hoku had seen dozens like it worn by the Kampii women back home. In fact, Aluna's sister—

"Daphine!" Aluna cried.

"No," Hoku said quickly. "It could be anyone's."

"It's hers. It's my sister's," Aluna said. She snatched the hair stick from the prince and pointed to one of the shells. Her finger shook. "I borrowed it last year and broke it."

Hoku squinted and saw a faint line where the shell had been snapped in half and glued back together with sticky jellyfish goo. "No," he said. "It can't be."

Dash muttered a curse.

"What happened to her?" Aluna said, her voice cracking. "She was probably looking for me. This is all my fault. Did they kill her? Tell me!"

The prince looked surprised at her outburst. "No keeeel," he said. He motioned to his neck and said, "Slaaave."

The words hung in the air. Hoku had never seen Aluna both crying and ready to rip something's heart out at the same time. Her fist closed around the jewelry. He could see her gritting her teeth, trying to calm herself down enough to speak.

"I'm going after her," she said finally, her voice low and scary.

Hoku shuddered. She looked just like her father.

"But we have no army and no plan," Dash said. "Your death will accomplish nothing."

"I don't need a plan," Aluna said. "I've always

trusted my instincts, and I'm trusting them now. There's no time to squabble like Elders, discussing plans and never actually doing anything. I need to go. Now. I have to save Daphine, or I have to die trying."

"Then let us go with you," Hoku said. "Me and Dash and Zorro, we can help you! And maybe Calli—"

"No," she said. "Daphine wouldn't have been captured if it weren't for me. I couldn't bear it if you got captured, too. You have to stay safe, Hoku. Don't you see?" She grabbed his arm and pointed to the video device in his hand. "You're the one who has to save us. Sarah Jennings herself just told you so. And I can't protect you when I'm trying to protect my sister."

"But what if—?" Dash said.

"I said no," Aluna shouted. "Do whatever you want, but you're not coming with me. I catch either of you following me, and . . . and you know what I can do."

She glared at Dash, then turned and glared at Hoku, daring either of them to disobey. Hoku wanted to, but she scared him. Aluna-his-best-friend would never hurt him, no matter what. But the Aluna in front of him now? He didn't know her at all.

Aluna turned to the prince. "Thank you for saving us from the Upgraders," she said. "I think our people make better allies than enemies. I hope we can meet as friends again after all of this is over."

The prince bowed.

Aluna smiled grimly. "Can one of your people show me how to get inside the dome?"

Eekikee squeaked and a Deepfell dragged itself over. The prince called some orders, and the Deepfell took off toward the water.

"Stay here and be safe," Aluna said to Hoku and Dash, half ordering them, and half begging. Then the steel returned to her eyes, and she raced after her guide.

As Hoku watched her go, his hands curled into fists. Again? She was leaving him again, after everything they'd been through? Dash still had a broken arm, Calli was out there somewhere on her own, probably afraid and in danger, the Kampii still needed to be saved, and he . . . he was supposed to be her best friend.

No. He was done taking orders.

Hoku turned back to Dash, Zorro, and the prince. "If we're going after her, we'll need a plan."

CHAPTER 42

$\mathcal{A}$LUNA FORCED HERSELF to breathe slowly, despite the pounding in her chest. What was happening to Daphine? Were Fathom and his Upgraders hurting her? Was she really a slave? It was hard to think about anything else, and she needed to focus. *A good hunter stays relaxed and ready,* Anadar always said. Panic was making her stupid.

In the distance, the domed city of HydroTek floated on the water, looking like a giant gleaming jelly-fish. Inside the huge translucent cap, buildings in shimmering silver twisted and flowed to amazing heights. She couldn't make out any details, even when she and the Deepfell crested the water for a better look. Below water level, pipes and machinery and long, thin buildings swayed and churned like a mass of tendrils. She had no doubt that, just like a real jellyfish, those tendrils could sting.

A pod of three Deepfell approached. She thought they were a scouting party, but when her guide gripped his spear and pulled out a knife, Aluna looked closer. All three of the Deepfell wore collars around their necks. *Slaves!* They swam in a tight pattern, their spears raised. She didn't understand Deepfell facial expressions very well, but something was definitely wrong with them. They looked dead.

"Can we rescue them?" she said. The Deepfell raised his spear and bared his sharp, sharklike teeth. He probably wanted to rescue them more than she did. But his grimace only widened into something dangerous, something feral.

"No can free. Only keeeel," her guide said.

She grabbed his arm before he made his first throw. She couldn't watch him murder his own kind, even if they were mindless slaves. The Deepfell twisted to break her grip, but she held on.

"HydroTek," she said, pointing to the dome with her other hand. "I have to get there. I have to save my sister."

They stared at each other. Aluna thought about all the horrible things she would do to whoever hurt Daphine. It wasn't difficult to let the anger swell into something almost overwhelming. And then she let those emotions swim into her eyes. The Deepfell stared at her for a moment, then nodded.

Instead of fighting, they hid in an outcropping of kelp. As the patrol passed, she got a better look at the enslaved Deepfell's faces. They looked as unthinking as fish. Even their mouths hung open. Whoever had enslaved their bodies had enslaved their minds as well.

As soon as they were gone, Aluna and her guide resumed their swim toward HydroTek. She tried not to imagine Daphine as a brainless slave, but the images assaulted her. Daphine with that same slack-jawed idiocy, Daphine with no spark in her eye and no smile on her perfect lips. She'd never forgive herself if that happened. Daphine was the Voice of the Kampii, irritatingly beautiful and graceful and eloquent and kind. No one was allowed to hurt her. No one.

HydroTek got bigger and bigger, until it loomed as large as Skyfeather's Landing in front of her. The tendrils that floated below it didn't undulate in the current as she had thought. No, they created the current. Pipes hissed, artifacts pumped up and down, and Deepfell slaves became more plentiful. She noticed dolphin and shark slaves, too. Even a few great whites were leashed and guarding some of the entrance holes.

But her guide avoided those areas and took her up, toward the surface of the ocean inside the lip of the dome. This close, the dome seemed impossibly large and intimidating. They squeezed into a narrow intake pipe and swam through the darkness. Aluna focused on the gentle swoosh of water around her body, on her heartbeat, and on the distant hum and clank of machinery.

Eventually, they emerged in a shallow pool inside the dome. *Inside HydroTek.*

"Thank you," she said to her guide. And then she added, "May the currents always carry you to safety."

He squeaked once, twice, and then dove beneath the water. He wouldn't wait for her. That had never been part of the plan. When she needed to escape, she was on her own.

Aluna squinted in the sunlight. She had surfaced in a pool surrounded by a ring of dirt dotted with dead grass and matted with garbage. Maybe it had been a pretty garden once, but abuse and neglect had turned it ugly. The sloped curve of the dome loomed on one side, and tall, silvery buildings on the other.

She waded to the edge of the pool and hauled herself out. Something rustled. She peered into the shadow of a building and saw a short four-legged creature digging its nose through a pile of garbage. A dog! She'd seen animals like it at the Aviar stronghold, mostly begging near the eating tables or sleeping by the fires.

"What are you doing in this place, little one?" she asked him.

The dog paused in his hunt and looked up at her. A yellow stain covered the tip of his black-gray muzzle. His ears pointed straight up.

"Same as you," the dog said. "Looking for munchies, dodging Gizmos." He pointed to the pile of garbage with his snout. "This batch mine mine mine. Find your own."

"Dogs talk?" Aluna said. None of the Aviar dogs had.

"Sure, yeah, dogs talk," he said. "You been living under a rock, maybe?" He growled as he spoke, but it seemed more like a necessity of speech than a threat.

She shrugged. "Does under the ocean count?"

The dog's tongue lolled out in a laugh. "Sure, yeah. Ocean even worse than a rock. Very wet. Very cold. Very bad." Then he stopped and tilted his head to the side. "Wait. What Humans live in water?"

"I'm not Human. I'm a Kampii," she said. "From the City of Shifting Tides." And then, because he was still tilting his head, she added with disgust, "We're mermaids."

"Mermaids!" the dog said, his ears quivering. "Wait, no. What mermaid has legs?"

"We get our tails when we're older," Aluna said

hastily. "You saw me come out of the water with your own eyes."

The dog squinted at her, then bobbed its head once. "True, yeah. But no mermaids here. Not yet. You turn around and swim swim swim." He motioned toward the pool with his snout. "Go now. Before he sees you and snatches you up."

"No," she said. "Fathom has my sister. I'm not leaving without her."

The dog lowered his head and shook it sadly. "Many sorries," he said. "My littermates all gone, too. Very sad. But Fathom is strong. Likes parts. All kinds of parts. Parts that make no sense. He takes and takes, even what he don't need."

"You know where he is? Can you take me to him?" Aluna asked.

The dog tilted his head again, thinking. It reminded her of Zorro.

"Sure, yeah," said the dog, wagging his tail. His ears were perky again. "We goes now. Follow follow follow!"

CHAPTER 43

HOKU DIDN'T WANT to enter HydroTek by the same route Aluna had chosen. He had no desire to confront Fathom head-on. That was Aluna's way, not his. He and Dash and Zorro needed to find HydroTek's nerve center, its technological core. Maybe restoring power to the Kampii's breathing necklaces and defeating Fathom and his army would be as simple as pressing a button.

A boy could dream.

Prince Eekikee himself escorted them to the dome. A Deepfell warrior carried Dash so they could all swim faster. Hoku carried his satchel with the water safe. Zorro clung to his shoulder. The little guy didn't need an air bubble and could swim well enough on his own, but not quickly. Besides, Hoku liked the feeling of Zorro's small furry body clinging to his back. It made him feel less alone, and a tiny bit less scared.

Prince Eekikee hid them well in advance of patrols and killed a shark scout with only two thrusts from his spear. The Kampii hunters would do well to fear him; Hoku had never seen anyone so good with a weapon in his whole life. He was suddenly glad that Aluna wasn't here to witness it as well, or she'd be talking about Eekikee's prowess for the rest of their lives.

Eventually, they reached HydroTek, and Hoku's heart soared like an Aviar. The very tip-top of the structure protruded from the water's surface, but that glittery part didn't interest him much. Not compared to what was happening underwater. There, HydroTek's massive coils and artifacts pumped and hissed as if the great city itself were breathing. Intakes and outtakes moved water, creating a warm current that toyed with them as they got closer and closer to its maw.

But even as his chest swelled at the wonder, he had to ask: How could his ancestors build something so amazing when the Kampii could not? The city's Elders knew how to maintain their artifacts, but they never made new ones. They could never build something like HydroTek, not even with all the Elders working together at once.

Unless . . . unless he found a way into the outpost and gained access to all the information Sarah Jennings had hidden. Then, maybe—if the Above World became a safer place—they could build something glorious.

"Alooooona," Prince Eekikee said, and pointed toward the part of HydroTek above the surface. "You," he said, pointing to the dome's underwater innards.

Hoku grinned.

As they wove through HydroTek's metal tendrils, Hoku touched everything within reach, marveling at how some metal was cold and some hot, how some artifacts vibrated and others seemed to hum. When they neared an intake tunnel barred with metal, Eekikee motioned everyone to stop.

The prince and the other Deepfell had little trouble bending the bars wide enough for Dash and Hoku to enter. They couldn't get it wide enough for themselves, but that was fine. Hoku had never expected the Deepfell to enter HydroTek. Prince Eekikee had his own war to fight.

Hoku squeezed into the circular tunnel. Prince Eekikee helped Dash through the bars, careful not to break the breathing membrane over his face. Hoku nodded to Prince Eekikee and mouthed, "Thank you." The prince smiled grimly in return. A moment later, he and the other Deepfell disappeared into the churning murk.

Without their guide, and confined in a dark metal tunnel, Dash seemed close to a panic attack.

Hoku pantomimed breathing slowly. If Dash's breathing bubble popped, there'd be no one to make him a new one.

Dash swallowed and nodded, clearly trying to stay calm.

Hoku pointed to Dash's eyes, then to his own feet. The horse-boy couldn't hear him underwater, but he spoke anyway. "Focus on my feet, but don't get too close. I don't want to kick you in the head."

Dash nodded and smiled weakly. A good sign.

Hoku started up the tunnel, using his hands to feel his way along the metal. It got darker as he swam, and soon even his Kampii eyes couldn't find enough light to see the way.

"Zorro, make light," Hoku said.

Crouched on his back, Zorro obeyed. His eyes glowed green to acknowledge the command and then yellow to illuminate the tunnel.

"Good boy," he whispered. He had no idea how much of Zorro was animal and how much was machine, but he knew the little guy enjoyed a compliment and a good scruffle once in a while, so that's what he got.

They made their way in silence. Hoku stayed

focused on the tunnel in front of him. How many hours had they been swimming? Were the darkness and the cramped tunnel playing tricks on him? Were they heading straight for some kind of ancient industrial grinder?

Calm as Big Blue, he told himself. That's what Aluna would say. She never panicked at times like these. She wasn't here now, so it was his job to stay calm all by himself. Besides, Dash needed him. And somewhere out there, Aluna and Calli and all the Kampii needed him, too.

Eventually the narrow tunnel joined with three others into a larger waterway. The prince had drawn him a diagram of this intersection, and he started breathing easier. They were going the right way. Maybe he wasn't going to get them both killed after all.

Not long after that, they emerged in a place the Deepfell had called the Moon Pool. The air in the small room felt pressurized—just like the ocean— which seemed to keep the ocean from filling up the tiny chamber.

Dash popped up beside him, looking pale and wild-eyed. The horse-boy popped his breathing bubble with obvious joy.

"I hope I never have to do that again," Dash said, and paddled with one hand toward the edge of the pool.

The room was brightly lit and contained piles of equipment—lots of unmarked crates and weird clothes that looked way too big for a person to actually wear.

"Swimming clothes," Dash said. "For people who can't breathe water."

Hoku swam over to the lip of the water and pulled himself out. Zorro, eyes still glowing, hopped down onto the metal walkway.

"Zorro, stop making light," Hoku said, and the raccoon's eyes flashed green before he obeyed.

Dash, who had been drying himself off with a piece of cloth he had found, suddenly stopped and lifted his head. The motion caught Hoku's attention. It looked as if Dash were sniffing the air.

"I hear something coming," Dash said. "Something with eight feet."

"Eight legs?" Hoku asked. Dash nodded.

He hadn't heard anything, but he had long since learned to trust Dash and his odd skills. The horse-boy disappeared behind a large suit of swimming clothes. Hoku was about to do the same when a round hatch dilated open behind him.

CHAPTER 44

T HE CREATURE that scuttled into the room was
Human from the waist up. A Human girl with skin the
color of dead coral and round black eyes with no irises.
Her pale white head was bald, except for a patch of
metal wires in the back that were gathered in a bunch.

Below the waist, the girl's body became a crab. A
giant red, evil-looking crab. A crab with eight chitinous
legs for running and jumping and walking, and two
huge claws for fighting and gripping. One of the claws
held a large metal wrench.

"Ooh!" the crab girl said when she saw Hoku, and
she dropped her wrench. It clattered against the metal
floor so loudly that it made him cringe.

Hoku glanced over to where Dash had been, but the horse-boy stayed hidden. Hoku took a deep breath and tried to stop himself from screaming. *A Dome Mek,* he told himself. *She's just a Dome Mek.*

"Don't hurt me!" he said. "I'm a friend!"

She raised her left eyebrow. "Friend?" she said. "I don't have any friends."

He felt a sudden pang of sympathy for this bizarre crab creature, but not enough of one to let his guard down.

"Well, I'm not a friend yet," he said quickly. "I meant that I'm not an enemy. I don't mean you any harm, and I hope you don't mean me any, either."

She lowered her eyebrow and clicked her eight legs a little closer to him. She had arms like a regular girl, but it was one of the big crab claws that swooped down and recovered her wrench.

"I'm not here to fight," she said very matter-of-factly. "I'm here to fix a clog in drainage pipe alpha-six-foxtrot-four-one-zebra."

"A clog?"

"Yes," she said. "Water hasn't been moving at the appropriate rate for the last hour. I was activated to clear the pipe and restore proper flow."

He had a feeling he knew what had been causing that "clog," namely him and Dash. But he wasn't about to tell the Mek that, at least not while she was carrying a big wrench.

"You said you were 'activated.' What does that mean?" he asked.

The girl frowned, and her shoulders hunched slightly. "When we are not needed, Fathom turns us off in order to conserve power," she said. "If my internal clock is correct, I was last activated more than eight-point-three-six months ago, to install a new lens in one of the camera sharks."

"Camera sharks?" That must be what he and Aluna had seen in the waters around the Kampii outpost, the night before they left the city. Great White had been recording them! Then he remembered what else the crab girl had said. "You've been asleep for eight months? How long were you awake before that?"

"It took exactly thirty-three-point-seven-zero minutes to complete the installation," she said with a sigh. "During the last two days I have been alive, three-point-three-six years have transpired."

"That's terrible," Hoku said, and he meant it. Machine or not, no one deserved to be turned off.

The girl skittered closer, her eight legs moving in quick succession. "We used to be alive all the time," she said. "We love the dome, and we love caring for it.

Our ancestors built it. We are happy to dedicate our lives to its maintenance."

Hoku kept his position as she got closer, despite a strong desire to jump back in the pool and hide. "What happened?"

"Sea Master Fathom," she said. "He activates us only when there is a problem, and then only for as long as it takes us to fix it." She definitely looked sad now.

"But why?"

"Fathom is funneling our power to another location. I was one of the Meks who reconfigured the transmitter to his specifications." The crab-girl looked behind her, then lowered her voice. "He's not killing us, just making us sleep a lot. It could be worse. Fathom had us shut down the generators sending power to the Kampii colonies. We turned them off completely."

"You turned them off?" This time, he did stumble. He fell back against a wall and slid to the floor, suddenly dizzy. His hand went to his neck, to the breathing shell pressed into his flesh. He'd thought the generators powering their necklaces had been accidentally damaged. It never occurred to him that Fathom would have turned them off on purpose, knowing that thousands of innocent Kampii would eventually die.

Unless Fathom could be stopped and the generators restored, all Kampii were doomed to drown.

"He's trying to bring the Kampii to the surface," the

Mek said. "He wants to control all the splinters of the ocean—both the Deepfell and the Kampii. He claims that victory over the shark-people is fast approaching, but he hasn't been able to locate the Kampii. He has only caught one so far, and he plans on using her for parts."

Daphine.

"So it's a trap," Hoku said dully. "He wants to find us, and we jumped like fish, right into the dolphin's mouth."

"You're . . . one of them?" the girl asked.

Hoku looked up. She was standing next to him, smelling of sea salt and artifact oil. An image of Calli and her bright eyes filled his mind. He wished, more than anything, that he could hold Calli's hand right now. Or at least know that she was safe.

"Yes, I'm a Kampii," he said. "And you've just told me that my best friend has walked into a trap, that her sister will be killed for parts, and that all my people are going to die."

The girl's eight crab legs folded until her torso was almost as low as his. He expected her to say something comforting. That's what Aluna or Calli would have done.

Instead, she said, "I wish I could help, but I have to fix the clog in drainage pipe alpha-six-foxtrot-four-one-zebra."

He stared at her while her words penetrated the dark thoughts in his head.

"Wait a minute."

He stood up so abruptly that the girl scrambled backward to get out of his way.

"You're going to let my people die? You were created to protect me and this dome and all the Kampii. And now you're going to let us all die?"

The girl looked at him with lidless black eyes. "It's not my fault!"

"You'd rather fix a stupid clog in a drain than try to save us."

"If I help, I will be shut down," she said. "My dreams are so empty. I'm scared of the darkness. I don't want to be trapped there forever!"

He hadn't thought of that. Now he felt bad for trying to guilt her into helping. For better or for worse, Aluna had rubbed off on him. All he cared about was his own mission. He kept forgetting that other people had lives, too.

"What's your name?" he said.

"Technician one-zero-zero-seven-seven-one," she said. "But at one time, I was also Liu."

"Liu," he said. It was a pretty name, much nicer than a string of numbers. "I'm Hoku. How can we— how can *I* help you?"

Liu stared up at the ceiling while she thought.

Eventually, she said, "I wouldn't mind going back to sleep if I had something pleasant to dream about. . . ." She hooked her hands together behind her back. Her cheeks blushed pale pink.

Hoku narrowed his eyes. Where was she going with this?

"I'll take you to the control center, if you give me something in return." She took four skittering steps closer. "My price is a kiss."

Now it was Hoku's turn to blush.

"But I have a . . ." Was Calli really a girlfriend? "And Aluna would . . ." Would probably laugh. "And I don't know how . . ." But he did know how to kiss, sort of. "And you . . ." Are a crab-girl, he wanted to say, but wasn't Calli a bird-girl? That certainly hadn't stopped them from kissing.

"Enough!"

Dash shoved aside the swimming clothes he'd been hiding behind and strode over to where they were standing. He turned to the crab-girl.

"Beautiful lady, I am Dashiyn," he said, touching two fingers to his heart and bowing his head. "I am honored to meet you. If you deem me a suitable substitute for our Kampii friend, I would be happy to render the requested price."

The crab-girl clapped her hands with glee. "Why, yes!" she said. "You will do nicely—"

Before she could finish speaking, Dash slid his good arm behind her back, looked into her eyes for several long moments, and then kissed her.

Even though he wasn't playing a part in it, Hoku could tell it was a good kiss. Both Dash and Liu had their eyes closed. Their faces pressed together firmly, but not awkwardly. He and Calli hadn't had a chance to work on that part yet. But the biggest reason he could tell it was good was because both of them seemed to forget he was even in the room.

When it was over, Dash stared into the girl's eyes for another long moment, then pulled one of her hands to his mouth.

"Thank you," he whispered, then kissed her knuckles. His eyes never left hers.

Liu bobbed a curtsy, her face more flushed than ever.

"No, thank *you*," she said in the same hushed tone he had used. "Now I won't be afraid to go back to sleep."

They smiled at each other, and Dash gently released her hand.

The girl turned to Hoku, her eyes suddenly full of life. "We'd better hurry," she said. "The control center isn't far, but I probably don't have much time." She turned and scuttled out the hatch.

He looked at Dash. For the first time, Hoku didn't

see the horse-boy's broken arm or his claustrophobia or his fear of being underwater. He saw a boy who already knew who he was and what he was capable of. He saw a leader.

Then Dash turned to him and, with panic in his voice, said, "Please don't tell Aluna."

Hoku laughed.

CHAPTER 45

THE DOG TOOK OFF down the street, weaving between two buildings at a fast trot. Luckily his legs were short. Aluna jogged after him and managed to keep up.

"Who lives here?" she asked. The tall silvery buildings were etched with waves and glinted in the sunlight.

"Dogs and Gizmos and Meks," the dog said. "Cats and rats and Mess-ups."

"That's not very helpful," she said. Gizmos were probably Upgraders. Whatever a Mess-up was, she didn't want to meet one.

The dog ignored her. "Middle Green is where Fathom keeps his toys," the dog continued. "Those that don't become Gizmos or Meks or Mess-ups. Faster now," he said. "Run run run."

The mangy four-legged thing burst into a full-out gallop. She had no idea something so little could run so fast. She pumped her legs to keep up.

They wove through the HydroTek dome. She barely had time to absorb all the wonders. Even covered in garbage, the city gleamed and sparkled. It reminded her of the story of Atlantis, a floating city out of legend. Supposedly, the Atlantis Kampii tribe grew too curious about the Above World. They sailed their city closer and closer until one day Atlantis beached itself on the shore and was overrun by Humans. HydroTek was too beautiful to be the creation of savages. She saw the stamp of Kampii craftspeople everywhere.

The dog zigged and zagged through tiny streets, under arches, and around glorious statues and defunct fountains. She wanted to slow down and examine everything, but sightseeing would have to wait.

They were heading toward the heart of HydroTek. Or, if it didn't have a heart, they were heading toward the center. "Middle Green," the dog had called it. The animal seemed to know the way well, and she was happy to let him lead.

She wondered what Dash and Hoku were doing. Maybe she should have brought them along. She could picture Hoku leaning against one of the buildings, panting and begging her to take a break. And Dash. He would have run and said nothing. She wanted to know his story, but she respected him too much to ask. If he wanted to tell her, he would.

Calli was out there somewhere, too. If anything happened to her, so soon after the girl had embarked on her first adventure, Aluna would never forgive herself.

"Birds!" the dog said, and darted for an alcove in one of the buildings. "Find shadows! Take cover!"

She followed him into a shadowy indent and pressed her back against the cool stone.

"I don't hear—"

"Shhh," the dog warned.

She clamped her mouth shut and listened. A moment later, she heard the flapping of hundreds of tiny wings.

The birds flew like a school of fish, darting out of the street they'd been heading for in tight formation. When one bobbed in the air, they all did. When one cut a sharp left, the others followed so fast it seemed as if they were operating with a single brain.

"Beautiful," she whispered.

"Deadly," the dog said quietly. His whispery voice was a soft, low grumble. "Rip you to shreds while you scream scream scream. Saw them take down a Gizmo once. We go now," the dog said, and slipped around the corner, away from the flock. She followed quietly, stealing one last look over her shoulder to watch the birds careen up toward the sun.

The buildings grew taller as they approached the center, where the dome was highest. Aluna craned her neck up but couldn't see all the way to the top. There was nothing so big back at the colony. She didn't even see how buildings could stand so tall without collapsing. Hoku would probably know.

The dog slowed to a trot. "Gizmo guard soon," he said. "Let me talk."

"You got it, friend," she said. "I'd rather kill an Upgrader than talk to it."

The dog nodded. "Talk easier than kill. At least now."

Suddenly the street ended and the buildings gave way to great green trees and grass and bushes. This is what the dog meant by Middle Green.

They headed to an opening in the foliage — and to the Upgrader who seemed to be guarding it.

The man was tall, but his body was short. He would have been exactly Aluna's height if his head hadn't been detached and mounted on a metal shaft that raised it up a meter higher. When his disembodied head swiveled around and saw them, he said, "Yo, stop, yo!"

"Sure, yeah, Giraffe," the dog said. "Let us in.

Going to see him." The dog pointed his snout toward Aluna.

Giraffe looked down his nose at her. She didn't particularly enjoy her view up his very wide nostrils. Only when she lowered her gaze did she see the evil-looking gun that had replaced his left arm.

"Master Fathom don't need no more Humans, Barko," the Gizmo said. "You should know that."

She started to say, "Oh, I'm not—" but the dog interrupted her.

"My problem, not yours," he said with a growl. "Let me in in in."

"Easy, easy," Giraffe said. His gun arm lowered and pointed toward the ground. "But I warned you, Barko. You come out with a second butt instead of a head, you remember that I warned you."

"Sure, yeah," said the dog.

Giraffe shuffled to the side. His head bobbled a bit but stayed in place. Aluna couldn't understand how he was even alive.

The dog nosed her in the back of the knee. She took the hint and walked quickly into the tree-lined path that Giraffe had been guarding. Barko stayed on her heels.

Middle Green seemed like a beautiful forest. The trees were lush and green and swayed as if there were a breeze. Hidden birds chirped from the branches. She even caught a glimpse of a tiny puffed tail. She wondered how bad Fathom could be if he lived in a place so wondrous.

And then she saw the cages.

CHAPTER 46

DOZENS OF LARGE plastic cubes, each bigger than her nest back home, lined the widening dirt path. Aluna stumbled to the first cage and saw a Deepfell floating inside. She recognized the slave collar around his neck and the dead look in his eyes.

The second held a young man that looked like a Kampii, except he had a long, sinuous snake body where his fish tail should have been. His tail coiled around and around. Gold hoops hung from his ears, and half of his long, dark hair had been shaved to stubble. His eyes were bloodshot, but there was still intelligence in them, still some spark of life.

She walked over and put her hands against his cell.

Suddenly, he pounded his fist against the plastic and shouted. She jumped back. His words were muffled by the cage.

"I don't understand," she called back.

"Shhh!" Barko said. "No yelling. No yelling!" He danced around nervously and looked up the path. "Faster now, mermaid. No time for the Mess-ups!" He bolted forward, and she had to follow.

She wanted to stop and talk to all the creatures trapped in the cages. They passed a dolphin and a baby shark, a huge white bird and a striped cat so big that Aluna's whole body could have fit inside her mouth.

Another cage held a creature that was Human from her head to her waist and horse below that. An Equian! Her back left leg had been replaced with a metal blade that sparked as she stomped. Deep red gashes and scars ringed the metal where it connected to the horse-woman's flesh.

The dog pulled Aluna along. Her stomach knotted tighter and tighter as they wove quickly through the captives. So many had been altered. She saw metal tusks added to a deer and a huge tortoise with jagged razors attached to the rim of his shell and some sort of saddle mounted on his back.

So much suffering, so much loneliness, so much pain and loss. Sadness rolled from the cages in waves, suffocating her heart. What kind of person could do this? What kind of monster? She couldn't save only Daphine, not anymore. Now she had to save them all.

Barko bounded down the path, ignoring all the cries and dead eyes of the captured creatures. Aluna felt tears well in her eyes and trail down her cheeks, but she didn't stop. She couldn't. There was only forward.

The path emptied them into a bright clearing surrounded by cages, some occupied, some empty. She didn't have time to study their occupants. They had arrived at the very center of Middle Green, at the very center of HydroTek. And the man—the *thing*—crouched by the last cage with his back toward them could only be Fathom, so-called Master of the Sea.

He likes parts, the dog had said, and Aluna finally understood what he'd meant. Maybe Fathom had looked Human once, but now he was a patchwork monster. Two dorsal fins jutted from his shoulders, fins that must have belonged to Deepfell before they were ripped off and reattached. His left arm had been split into two. One limb ended in a mechanical hand, and the other had some sort of artifact control pad screwed onto the end. The bottoms of Fathom's legs had been extended to twice their normal height, with dull-black metal bars wrapped in wires and tubes.

She couldn't even identify the other bits of flesh and metal stitched and embedded all over his body. Some oozed blood as she watched. Worst of all, the back of his skull had been replaced by some glasslike material. She could see right into his brain.

When he turned and rose, Aluna gasped. Not only was Fathom's face still fully Human, but she recognized his tousled brown hair and glasses from the photo Hoku had pulled from Sarah Jennings's water safe.

Fathom was Karl Strand.

But how? That letter was written hundreds of years ago! Karl and Sarah were together before the Kampii even existed. How could he still be alive?

Fathom smiled, looking even more like the man from the photo. But when he spoke, it wasn't to her.

"Well, dog," he said. "What have you brought me today?"

The dog sketched a nervous doggy bow and said, "A mermaid, master! A mermaid for your collection!"

Aluna looked at Barko, surprised at his betrayal, but the dog ignored her gaze.

"Pity, dog, but there will be no reward for you today," he said. "You see, I already have a mermaid."

Fathom motioned to the water-filled tank he had been inspecting when they arrived. Aluna had assumed it was empty, but it wasn't. The occupant had been cowering in the far corner, curled into a ball. When Fathom activated the control device in his double arm, the creature yelped and swam obediently to the front of her enclosure.

Fathom's mermaid was Daphine.

CHAPTER 47

$\mathcal{D}$APHINE!" Aluna yelled, and bolted for her sister's cage. Daphine had a slave collar around her neck and an ugly metal scope sticking out from her face where her left eye had once been.

Her face, her beautiful face. Aluna would smash the cage to pieces with her bare hands if she had to.

"Stop her," Fathom said simply, and pressed a sequence of buttons on his arm device. A dozen Upgraders swarmed into the clearing. Aluna recognized Giraffe, his head wobbling as he ran.

They were too close, too fast.

A man with thick muscles and bright-red skin leaped at her, but Aluna ducked and the man sailed over her head. She rolled forward and unclipped Spirit and Spite, her talons. They were already spinning by the time she vaulted to her feet. The three closest Upgraders took a step back, apparently uncertain how to handle the whirring weapons.

A woman wearing bulky goggles raised a harpoon gun. Before she could fire, Aluna sliced Spirit across her face. The Upgrader yelped and fell back, clutching at her eyes. Aluna dodged and headed for Fathom. She could fight his minions forever, but he was the one she needed to destroy.

Spirit and Spite sang in her hands, cutting the air and creating a whirlwind of slashes and cuts. She yanked Giraffe's legs out from under him and jumped over another Upgrader's knee spike. Still, her enemies were coming too fast, too strong. She couldn't even recognize some of their weapons, let alone determine how best to disable them.

"Let her be," Fathom said. "Let me see what this child can do."

Instantly, the Upgraders lowered their weapons and backed away. Some were bleeding or holding wounds, but not enough of them.

Aluna wasted no time. She screamed and ran straight for Fathom, talons spinning. She whipped Spite at his head, aiming for his bespectacled eyes. He blocked the talon with one flick of his hand. The sharp metal weapon bounced off his arm with a spark and sailed back toward Aluna's head. She changed the direction of her swing and diverted it toward one of Fathom's legs, intending to yank it out from under him. Again, her talon sparked off the unnatural metal and bounced back toward her.

Fathom laughed.

She circled him, striking with her weapons again and again. She spun to get more speed and power with her attacks, but they glanced off him each time. Finally, the talons moved too fast, even for her. She failed to redirect Spirit and the talon's point clipped her across the forehead. She felt a slow trickle of warmth slide down the side of her face.

Fathom punched at her with one of his metal hands. His fist slammed into her chest. In the next flash she was flying backward through the air, gasping for air. She crashed into Daphine's cage and dropped to the ground. Luckily, she'd tucked her chin to her chest and managed to take the brunt of the hit with her shoulder, not her skull.

"Not a bad showing for such a small unadorned creature," Fathom said. He rubbed his chin with four slender metallic fingers. "I wonder what you could do with longer legs? Or perhaps some horned implants on that thick head of yours? Such a nice blank canvas!"

"Aluna, is that you?" Daphine said in her ear.

Aluna groaned. She could see her sister floating in

the cage behind her, but couldn't find the air to speak. Black spots zigzagged in front of her eyes.

"You see, my father taught me that there is always room for improvement," Fathom continued. "For a long time, he has looked for ways to preserve the flesh, to make it impervious to disease, famine, and even the humiliation of aging. But my goal is somewhat grander. I want to improve life, to combine the best of every life-form into one perfect example of superhumanity."

He turned to Daphine and pointed to the scope that had replaced her eye. "Is she not far more beautiful now that she has been improved?"

Daphine shrank away from him. "Swim, Aluna," she said. "Go! Warn the others!"

"Oh, does my mermaid pet know this little intruder?" Fathom said.

Aluna struggled to her feet. Fathom walked closer, moving gracefully on his bizarre extended legs. He punched more buttons on the artifact attached to his arm.

"Aaaah," he said, staring at the device. "I thought I recognized you, girl. One of my recon sharks got a scan of you a few months ago."

Aluna thought back to her days at the colony, to the day before the ceremony. The day she'd found Makina dead in the kelp, Great White had cast a glowing green net out of its eyes. The shark had been taking her picture.

"Is that how you found my"—she stopped herself before she said *sister*. Fathom didn't need any more weapons—"that mermaid?"

"Why, yes!" he said jovially. "I thought at first you were merely a silly Human child, but the way you swam and the way your breathing device glowed, I knew I had finally found the elusive Kampii! I knew sabotaging your breathing necklaces would drive you out of hiding when they eventually started to fail. I did not predict that my first catch would be such an incredible beauty. How fortunate that she was traveling with only one guard!"

Fathom put his hand on Daphine's cage. "Sadly the male escaped, but I cannot regret letting him go. Not when we came home with this prize," he said. Then, quietly he added, "I will enjoy fixing her many flaws and weaknesses. Then, when she is truly perfect, she will take me to the fabled City of Shifting Tides, so that I may improve all of her people. Yes, yes. My own army of mermaid-Meks!"

Daphine retreated to the corner farthest away from him, a wild look in her eye.

"Now, now, my pretty," he said to her. "No need to fear." But all Aluna could see was terror on her sister's face. All she could hear were Daphine's whimpers in her ears.

"Please, let her go," Aluna said. She pushed herself up against the cage, aware that Fathom and his Upgraders could kill her within seconds. "Take me instead."

Fathom stared at her. Aluna's heart thundered in her chest, wave after wave crashing against her ribs.

"Take you?" he said with a harsh laugh. "Why would I want to take you, little girl? You don't even have a tail! You have no beauty upon which to build."

Tides' teeth! Of course Fathom wouldn't want her. She wasn't even good enough to be a slave.

Unless . . .

She fumbled with the pouch hanging from her neck. Her fingers felt stupidly thick. The Upgraders raised their weapons, but Fathom waved them off. Finally, she managed to untie the drawstring. Two items dropped to the ground: her mother's ring and the Ocean Seed. Aluna shoved the ring back into her pouch as fast as she could, then lifted the seed and held it out for him to see.

"The seed of transformation," Aluna said quickly, holding up the dull-brown Ocean Seed. It was cool and soft between her fingertips. "If I eat it, I'll grow a tail."

She thought about swallowing the seed, about losing her legs forever. She would lose the Above

World, too—from Skyfeather's Landing to the distant desert where Dash's people lived. She'd lose the trees and the campfires and the feel of wind running past her face.

And she'd be Fathom's slave—his *possession*—so she'd lose the ocean, too.

She gritted her teeth and said, "I'll get a tail, and you can watch it grow."

CHAPTER 48

Lᴜ ʟᴇᴅ Hoku and Dash and Zorro on a wild run through a dozen white corridors. Hoku would have sworn they were all identical if not for the different patterns etched into the surfaces: starfish, dolphin, Big Blue, sunfish, kelp, wave. When they reached the section marked with the City of Shifting Tides' seahorse design, he knew they were getting close.

The control room door stood out from the others. Instead of a little pad of numbers next to the handle, there was a huge artifact mounted on the wall. The door itself was ink black and imposing and looked thoroughly impenetrable.

Liu scuttled up to the device and stuck her face against it.

"Retinal scanner," she said simply, as if Hoku would understand. But he almost did understand. The machine was scanning her eyes! There must have been some form of identification hidden in them.

The red light over the door turned green with a loud buzz, and a mechanism inside the door shifted.

"Come on," Liu said. She grabbed the door and swung it out. "Gentlemen first!" she said, motioning to Dash.

Hoku couldn't tell if Dash was blushing under his sand-colored skin. Liu had been going on and on about the kiss since it had happened. How could she skitter so fast and talk at the same time?

Inside, the control room was large, vaulted, and packed with gleaming artifacts. Machines hummed from every wall. Lights flashed. Portions of the wall displayed graphs and charts that moved and beeped and *monitored*. He turned in place, trying to make sense of the chaos.

"Quickly, I will show you what to do," Liu said. She headed for the station with the biggest set of moving pictures above it. "This is the main computer." Her two front claws started pressing buttons while her human hands pressed letters at an alarming speed. Words started appearing on one of the screens. "We need to restore power to the Kampii generators before—" she started to say, then froze, her hands and claws hovering over the computer, her mouth half open.

"Before what?" Hoku asked.

"Before she is put back to sleep," Dash said, frowning. He walked over and waved his good arm in front of Liu's face. She didn't even twitch. He turned to Hoku. "It is your room now."

"But, I don't—"

"Hoku, it is your room now," Dash said. And all of a sudden, the horse-boy was a leader again. How did he turn that on and off? "Use it to save Aluna and your people," Dash said.

Hoku took a deep breath. Save Aluna. Save Daphine. Save the Kampii. Maybe even save himself. He took another breath for good luck.

"Okay, let's do this." He headed over to Liu and gently pushed her aside. Her crab legs scraped across the floor. "Zorro, connect to this . . . computer."

The raccoon hopped onto the desk and poked his tail at a socket Hoku hadn't even seen. The animal's eyes flashed green.

"There's a flashing red light here," Hoku said. "Should I push it?"

"I do not know," Dash answered. "What will that do?"

Hoku shrugged. "There's one easy way to find out."

"Wait. What if—?"

Hoku pushed the button.

The air exploded with alarms. Red lights flashed. The noise—*the noise!* Hoku covered his ears with his hands and saw Dash do the same.

"Zorro! Turn off the alarm!" Hoku yelled. The creature's eyes flashed green again and the noise stopped as suddenly as it had started. Hoku lowered his hands, but his head was still filled with shrieking echoes.

"That didn't work," Hoku said. He looked over to see if Dash was okay and found the boy flat on his stomach, his ear to the floor.

"They come," Dash said. "At least six, maybe more. I do not know how many legs they have."

Barnacles! They didn't have much time.

"Zorro, uh . . . restore all power to the Kampii," he said. Zorro's eyes glowed yellow and he tilted his head. "Zorro, deactivate . . . uh . . . whatever Fathom did?" More yellow glow.

Dash pulled the huge black door closed.

"It will not latch," Dash said.

Hoku saw another eye-scanning device on this side of the door. "Push Liu to the scanner," he said. "Her eye is the key!"

Dash did as he was told but couldn't maneuver Liu's eye close enough to the device. She'd been hunched over the keyboard when she stopped moving, and her eyes were in the wrong place.

"Zorro, lock the door," Hoku said.

The raccoon's eyes flashed red, meaning he understood but couldn't obey the command.

"It is no matter," Dash said. He pulled his sword from his satchel and expanded the blade. After moving Liu to the far end of the room, he positioned himself by the door. "I will give you the time you need. Just . . ."

"What?" Hoku could hear footsteps thundering through the corridors.

"Work quickly," Dash said.

Hoku nodded grimly and stared back at the array of blinking lights and knobs and strange glowing letters and pictures. Grandma Nani's words echoed in his ear: *Hoku, my boy, it's time you had an adventure.*

CHAPTER 49

ALUNA HELD the Ocean Seed in front of her and steadied her wobbling legs against Daphine's cage. This wasn't supposed to be how it happened. The rescue, the transformation—any of it. She'd followed her gut coming here by herself, and this time, her gut had failed her. Just as she'd failed everyone else.

"I've never seen a Kampii grow its tail," Fathom said, his voice crackling with glee. "As pretty as this one is, I would trade her, yes. Take the pill and I will free my pet, release her back into the ocean. She can go braid her hair and play with the dolphins all day."

Aluna brought the seed closer to her mouth. "The transformation takes many days. Remove her collar now and free her."

"Oh, don't be silly," Fathom said. "You might be holding a piece of candy, not a genetic resequencer. But I will make you a bargain: I will remove her obedience collar, then you will swallow the pill. When I am satisfied that it is working, I will release the mermaid."

It was more of an offer than she thought she'd get.

"If you don't free her, I'll escape. Or kill myself. And then you'll never get to see my tail. Do you understand?" Aluna said. He could grab her and force the seed down her throat right now, but he didn't. He seemed delighted by their negotiation.

Sea Master Fathom nodded, pressed a few buttons on his device, then pointed it at Daphine. The thick metal collar around her neck clicked open and sank to the bottom of her tank. Both of Daphine's hands went to her neck, and Aluna saw her sister take in a huge breath.

"My father will be so pleased when I tell him about this," Fathom said, clapping two of his three hands together happily. "He has always hated the Kampii."

"Who is your father?" Aluna asked.

"Before the modern age, he was known as Karl Strand," Fathom said.

Aluna sputtered, "Karl Strand is still alive? It's been hundreds of years—how is that possible? And if he is truly your father, why do you look just like him?"

Fathom laughed. "Oh, no," he said. "I am merely a clone of the great and mighty Karl Strand. I was created from his genetic code, from his very flesh—when he still had some. He tasked me with bringing the ocean realms under our control. How could he trust such an important task to anyone other than his own genetic child?"

Clones! Fathom was a copy of Karl Strand!

"Was Sky Master Tempest a clone, too?" Aluna asked. She wanted answers, and unlike the Kampii Elders, Fathom seemed inclined to actually give her some. And why not? She would be his slave soon enough.

"Ah, my brother Tempest, may his memory fade to dust," Fathom said, resting two of his hands over his heart. "Yes, he was a clone, but an inferior one. You see, the process is imperfect. We all share an illustrious genetic heritage . . . but not all of us are our father's equal.

"Tempest was greedy," Fathom said. "He was given the title of Sky Master and ordered to destroy the Aviars if he could not tame them, but that wasn't good enough for him. He wanted to rule them. To turn them into his own personal army. But the Aviars are savages. Unlike more civilized people, they chose to fight to the death rather than to submit to his will. They battled like devils against him. Technically the Aviar leader struck the killing blow, but it was my brother's hubris, his unbelievable arrogance, that destroyed him."

Aluna stood up straighter and raised her chin. She was proud to call the Aviars and President Iolanthe her allies.

"Tempest was foolish to disobey our father. You see, Karl Strand has a plan," Fathom said. "He will unite all the people of this land—be they birds or fish, horses or snakes. He will collect us, bring us together, make us strong. Under his rule, we will conquer life, death, and the very earth herself."

Aluna shuddered. She wanted the Kampii to be less afraid of their own tails, to come out of the water, to be a part of the world. But not if that world was ruled by Karl Strand and his crazy clones.

"Don't look so disgusted, mermaid. It will be a world of incredible beauty," Fathom said, motioning to the Upgraders surrounding them. "A new civilization of advanced Humans. Faster, stronger, and more durable. The best parts from all the races and splinters!"

Fathom bent over in a flash, his head was just half a meter from Aluna's. Up close, she could see his Human brown eyes more clearly, could see the lines around his mouth, the wrinkles near his eyes.

"You see, not all of us are weaker than our father,"

he said quietly. "Some of us, like me, are his betters. Do you not marvel at the improvements I have made?" He stood up and spread his arms wide, displaying all his fleshy add-ons and oddly integrated parts. "When the time comes, we shall see who sits upon the throne of the new age. Yes? We shall see."

He stood there for a moment, grinning. Was he waiting for her to cheer? To clap? To proclaim her allegiance? All she could think about was running, and all she could focus on was keeping her legs from doing just that.

"Enough chitchat," Fathom said. "I have removed the mermaid's collar. Now take the pill. Take it now, or I will destroy you both and collect more samples from your precious coral city."

The Upgraders raised their guns and swords and knives and needles, and Aluna had no choice. She pressed her hand against the plastic of Daphine's enclosure, trying to draw strength from her sister's presence.

"Don't do this, Aluna," Daphine said quietly, the scope on her left eye whirring as it focused. "He already has me. There's still time for you to escape."

"The Kampii need you," Aluna said. Her brothers, her father, the entire colony — they were all better off with Daphine than with her. No one could argue with that logic. Before she could change her mind, before she let the fear overtake her, she dropped the Ocean Seed into her mouth and swallowed.

At first, the seed felt like a rock lodged in her throat. She wanted to choke, to cough it back up and spit it on the ground. It tasted like poison. It *was* poison. There was no cure for a tail. There was no reverse seed. And then it was down, an ugly lump in her stomach ready to wreak its chaos on her insides.

"Someone get me a fresh collar," Fathom said to his Upgraders. He turned to Aluna. "I have a new slave."

Two of the Upgraders left the clearing.

Collar. Slave.

"No, no, no," Daphine said, shaking her head. She sank to the bottom of her tank. "No, no, no."

"Don't worry, Daphine," Aluna said. "I'll be okay."

She'd never lied to Daphine, not about anything important, not until now. But her sister was still too fragile from her ordeal. Too *broken*. She wasn't the same Kampii who'd raised Aluna from a youngling and kept four headstrong men in line every day. If Fathom kept his promise, Daphine would return to the City of Shifting Tides. Under the water, surrounded by her friends and family, she'd find her strength again.

Fathom pointed another pair of Upgraders. "You two. Get one of my medteks and bring the recording equipment. Fast. If she so much as sprouts a scale before you get back, you'll be dragging yourself around with your elbows!"

The Upgraders grunted and fled the area. Four gone, Aluna thought, but eight was still too many, even if she could find a way to defeat Fathom himself.

It would be so much easier to give up. To stop looking for solutions to an unsolvable problem. Fathom was too strong, his army too big. The seed could render her helpless at any moment, and Daphine was useless in her current state. Aluna had no allies, since she'd stupidly turned away Hoku and Dash, even after they'd begged to help.

She was finally out of options.

CHAPTER 50

METAL CLANGED against metal. Behind Hoku, Dash fought the Upgraders at the door, keeping them outside, giving him time. Hoku didn't look. He couldn't. Dash's survival depended on it.

"Zorro, start all the power," Hoku said. "Zorro, restore power to the Kampii city. Zorro, shut down the Upgraders!"

None of it worked. Zorro's head was frozen at a tilt, and his eyes alternated between red and yellow flashes.

"Fathom is redirecting the dome's power," he said to himself. A gout of flame shot through the room. He could feel it singe his back. A second later, a huge piece of metal clanged to the floor and the flames stopped.

Dash had a shield covering his broken arm while his sword flashed in his other hand.

"Zorro, save the Kampii. Zorro, stop sending power to Karl Strand. Zorro, shoot electricity at Fathom."

Yellow. Yellow. Yellow.

Hoku smashed both his fists onto the desk, mashing buttons and triggering changes in the screens. He spared a quick glance over his shoulder, expecting imminent death, but saw Dash still up and fighting. Somehow, he'd kept them bottlenecked at the door.

His eye fell on Liu, still frozen. If only she'd stayed awake another few minutes. She could have told him what to do. *Think,* he told himself. *Think!*

He had to restore the Kampii generators and save his people.

He had to stop Fathom so he could never harm the Kampii again.

He had to wake up the Dome Meks, rescue Daphine, and save Aluna.

Behind him, Dash yelped and dropped his shield. His left arm, the one Aluna had broken, dripped red.

But first, he had to find a way for him and Dash to survive for the next five minutes.

Hoku looked back at the crab girl.

"Zorro, wake Liu."

Yellow.

His gaze fell to the girl's shirt, to a number stitched along her collar. His heart was beating fast. Too fast. He only had seconds or it was all over.

"Zorro, wake technician one-zero-zero-seven-seven-one!"

Zorro's eyes glowed green.

Liu stirred. When the first Upgrader made it past Dash and charged toward him, the Mek girl scuttled across the room, raised one mighty claw, and bashed the Upgrader in the head.

Hoku didn't watch. He couldn't. He had work to do.

CHAPTER 51

"Do you feel anything yet?" Fathom asked. "Pain? Discomfort? The subtle shifting of your genetic code?"

Aluna felt the Ocean Seed inside her, but as far as she could tell, it was just sitting there in her gut doing nothing. Why wasn't the seed working? The transformation was supposed to begin immediately. Back in the City of Shifting Tides, the Elders carried the young Kampii from the ritual dome to the medic dome as soon as they swallowed their seeds. It was an essential part of the ceremony, both symbolically and out of necessity.

Fathom wanted a show, and since Aluna wanted him to release Daphine, she had to give him one.

She faked a wince and dropped to one knee, trying to remember the time Anadar had walloped her in the stomach with the flat of his spearhead. "Barnacles," she hissed. That sentiment, at least, did not require much acting.

"Excellent," Fathom said, and tapped some buttons on the device attached to his arm. "Now, how would you rate the pain on a scale of one to ten, ten being the worst?"

"Five," Aluna said through gritted teeth.

"Hm," he said, twisting his mouth into a frown. "There should be more pain. I have read all the research. Perhaps this will help."

He pulled back one of his extended metal legs and kicked her in the gut.

Aluna tumbled across the grass, over and over, and landed on her stomach.

"Now?" Fathom asked.

"Eight," she coughed into the ground.

"Don't lie to me," he said. "I may decide that I prefer my other mermaid after all. She already has a tail. It won't be difficult to remove."

"I'm not lying," Aluna said quickly, and she wasn't. She stayed on the ground and crushed her cheek against the cool earth, wondering if he had cracked any of her ribs. She tried to breathe through the pain, but breathing only made it worse.

"Aluna? Are you there?" Hoku's voice sounded in her ear like whale song in the empty ocean. A beacon.

"I'm using the computer to project my signal as far as I can. I won't be able to hear you."

"I'm here," she whispered into the grass. "I'm here!"

"Tides' teeth, I hope you're alive," said Hoku's voice. "If you're out there, please listen. I've almost got it figured out. Zorro and I will—watch out!"

Was he talking to Dash? He had to be. They were both alive, and they were both in the dome!

"Sorry, they're coming too fast," Hoku said. "But we're sending help. Hang on, Aluna. Stay alive. Wherever you are, whatever's happening to you, you're not alone. Do you hear me? You're not—no! Stop!"

His voice cut off abruptly.

"Hoku!" Aluna's heart beat wildly.

In three strides, Fathom was hovering above her. "Who are you talking to?" he asked.

Up close, she could see spikes and scales on his belly, could smell oil and burned flesh. His so-called upgrades had ceased being functional ages ago. What he had done to himself had no reasonable explanation.

"No one," she said, trying to scramble out of his kicking range. "I'm not talking to anyone."

Stay alive, Hoku had said. She had no idea where he was or what he was doing, but she trusted him. Deep down, she trusted him more than she trusted anyone in the world.

"Ah, it's your aural communicators!" Fathom said,

clearly pleased with himself. "I saw them in the schematics. I should have known you wouldn't be so stupid as to come here alone." He looked around the clearing. "Where are they? The range is only a few dozen meters, if I remember correctly." He motioned to some of his waiting Upgraders. "You four. Fan out and search the woods. Kill every intruder you find."

The Upgraders grunted and started to jog for the trees. Aluna used the distraction to maneuver into a crouch.

"Wait!" Fathom said. He turned to look at Aluna but spoke to his minions. "When you find the other mermaids, make sure they scream before you kill them. I want this one to hear every second of their suffering."

"No!" Aluna yelled.

Her friends were somewhere in the dome, trying to save her because she was ridiculous and swam off without them. Her father had been right. In so many ways, she was still a child. Well, it was time to grow up and take responsibility for her bad decisions.

Aluna unclipped her talons and charged.

CHAPTER 52

H OKU HAD TOLD ALUNA they were sending help. He'd told her she wasn't alone. Now he had to prove it.

Liu swung her wrench, her claws, and even her legs. Somehow Dash was still up, fighting by her side with just one good hand. Even so, the number of Upgraders crowded around the control center door never lessened.

They needed more help than just Liu. They needed an army.

"Zorro, wake more Meks."

Yellow.

"Zorro, retrieve the names of all HydroTek Dome Meks and wake them up. Wake them all up!"

Yellow.

Glowing words pulsed on the display screen in front of him. At the same time, an inhuman voice spoke them aloud: "Current password grants insufficient security clearance to complete that action. Level Seahorse access required."

"Hoku," Dash yelled. "We are losing ground. I cannot—"

Out of the corner of his eye, Hoku saw Dash crumple. Liu stepped in to cover his spot, protecting his body with her six remaining legs.

"Passwords," Hoku muttered, and pulled out the device he'd found in the water safe. He pressed the power button, and a spinning seahorse floated into view. Sarah Jennings said she'd stored forbidden information inside the tiny box—all of HydroTek's secrets. Well, right now, he only wanted one.

"Zorro, disconnect from the computer."

The raccoon pulled its tail off the magnetic port and scampered out of the way. Hoku held the device over the spot and felt the familiar tug of the magnet pulling the artifact into place.

The screen glowed and the computer's voice spoke. "Device detected. Accessing password. . . ."

Hoku held his breath. Metal clattered on metal behind him. The screen went blank.

"Password accepted. Clearance Level Seahorse. Proceeding with command."

Lines of tiny words streamed up the screen—so many he couldn't read them nearly fast enough:

ACTIVATING DOME TECHNICIAN 001072
ACTIVATING DOME TECHNICIAN 001086
ACTIVATING DOME DEFENDER 001102
ACTIVATING DOME LEADER 001114
ACTIVATING DOME DEFENDER 001116

. . . .

The list went on and on and on.

CHAPTER 53

ALUNA CHARGED, her talons spinning in tight whirls around her body.

Fathom hopped back impossibly fast on his metal legs, and Aluna heard a *snick* from behind her. Upgraders! She dodged too late. A blazing harpoon grazed her thigh and she screamed. The wound wasn't deep, but it stung.

"Catch her!" Fathom yelled. "Damage her arms if you have to, but leave her legs intact!"

The Upgraders charged. Some headed for her, and some ran to protect their master. If Fathom hadn't sent so many to the woods, she would have been dead in one flash of a tail. Now she had a chance.

She spun her talons faster as the Upgraders circled her. Good. They wouldn't be able to use their missiles and their flamethrowers now, not without the risk of hitting one another. A man with a silver head stepped in swinging a glowing red sword. She sent her talon Spite to disarm him, but with a twitch, the Upgrader sliced through Spite's chain. The tip of the talon flew off and landed out of sight. Aluna's heart thudded faster. The man grinned. She feigned fear to lure him into a lunge, then sidestepped, letting the Upgrader behind her figure out how to deal with the tip of his blade.

A woman with spikes growing out of her arm attacked next. Aluna dodged the swing, then jumped up on the woman's arm and vaulted over her head. The Upgraders were used to dealing with front and back, left and right. But Aluna learned to fight in the sea. She also knew how to use up and down.

She landed hard behind the woman and yelped. Her wounded thigh burned.

Sound erupted in her ear: Hoku screaming.

"No!" she yelled. The Upgraders must have found him!

"I did it! I did it!" his voice echoed in her ear.

And that's when she saw them. A stream of people with bodies shaped like crabs and lobsters, with wrenches and pipes and bits of metal gripped in their human hands. They swarmed into Middle Green and threw themselves at the Upgraders, weapons and claws swinging.

Aluna yelled again, this time in triumph.

Cones of flame shot across the sky. Metal clanked against metal. Men and women screamed. A snake-man—the one she had seen earlier in the cage—slithered past her and struck at the Upgrader named Giraffe with fists so fast that they blurred together in the air.

The Upgraders she had been fighting were now struggling against dozens of the newcomers. Aluna limped through the chaos, dodging blades and poison needles. She found a long metal spike and hefted it like a spear. The air smelled of smoke and oil, of sweat and ocean salt.

An Upgrader with spinning blades instead of hands charged her. She stepped quickly to the side and batted him from the air with her spear, shark-style. Fast and quick. He landed on the ground with a thud and a howl as one of his circular blades cut into the flesh of his other arm.

Where was Fathom? She hadn't been so far from him when the fight started, but now she couldn't find him. If only she were taller! In the ocean, height never mattered. In the Above World, she felt like she was always standing on her toes in order to see. Maybe she understood Giraffe a little bit after all.

"Aluna! Help!"

Daphine's words screeched inside her ears.

"I'm coming!" she yelled, her heart stuttering in her chest. She ran for Daphine's cage, ignoring the pain in her leg, ignoring the splashes of blood and screams surrounding her from every side.

When she found Daphine, Fathom was standing over her with a long jagged blade in his hand. Her sister's cage had been shattered. Daphine struggled in a pool of water two meters from Fathom's feet, trying to pull herself away from him on shaking arms.

"Leave her alone!" Aluna said, spinning her makeshift spear.

Fathom looked over his shoulder at her, a small twisted smile on his lips. "You will not play fair while this one lives," he said. "Without hope, you will truly be my slave."

He raised his sword.

Aluna was too far away. She'd never make it in time. *Daphine, sweet Daphine!*

And that's when a brown-haired girl with wings dropped out of the sky, landed right between Daphine and Fathom, and pointed her spear at the Sea Master's heart.

CHAPTER 54

CALLI!

Aluna was relieved to see the girl was holding her spear properly for a change. But it wouldn't matter, not if Fathom attacked her. Calli was no match for him.

Aluna kept running. She was still too far away, but Calli was giving her time. *Brave, foolish, wonderful girl!*

"Stand back," Calli said grimly.

"Aviar!" Fathom hissed, but surprisingly, he did as she said and took a step away from her. Away from Daphine. "I've long wanted to catch one of you alive. There's so much I could do with a pair of wings. As homage to my brother, of course."

"My mother killed him, you know," Calli said. She sounded strong, but Aluna could hear the waver in her voice, could see the tip of her spear beginning to quiver. "She ran her spear right through Tempest's throat."

One of Fathom's hands went to his neck.

"All the more reason for me to kill you, Aviar," he said, and lifted his sword arm to strike.

But Calli had done her job. She'd distracted Fathom long enough. Aluna yelled and swung her metal spike like a spear. It smashed into Fathom's sword and bent it nearly in two. She stopped running and dug her toes into the mud that the water from Daphine's cage had created.

"Fight me," she said, panting.

Fathom dropped his mangled sword and turned on her. Behind him, Calli pulled Daphine out of danger. More winged women fell from the skies and entered the fray. Aluna thought she recognized High Senator Electra's distinctive hawk wings only a dozen meters away.

While she was distracted, Fathom struck. Two of his arms punched out. One sparked against her metal spike, and the other slammed into her shoulder. She'd seen them coming and fell back to absorb the blows. But he was faster, so fast. Her left arm went numb from the force of the impact.

Aluna shifted her spear to her good hand and adjusted to a single-arm grip. When Fathom punched with his third arm, she knocked his fist to the side and swept her spear into a spin. Spinning protected her body and disguised her attacks.

"This world doesn't need you, or your father," she said. "We don't need to be 'protected.' We don't need to be 'improved.'" Her left arm started to tingle as feeling returned.

"It doesn't matter what you need," Fathom sneered. "You are parts, nothing more. We will control the whole."

He twisted and kicked at her face. She blocked with her heavy spear and sidestepped. Fathom hopped and swung the other leg out in an arc toward her face. She dropped her spear, ducked, and grabbed his foot as it passed over her head. She shoved straight up, trying to push Fathom off balance. The technique would never work underwater, where your enemy could just somersault away.

But Aluna was an Above World fighter now. There were new rules. Fathom flailed his arms and crashed onto his back. He twisted onto his stomach and tried to regain his feet, but his extra-long legs kept slipping in the mud.

Aluna vaulted onto his back and tried to pin him, but he was too strong. He bucked and she grabbed the dorsal fins jutting out of his shoulders to keep her seat. If only she were heavier or stronger! If only she weren't alone.

But wait: she *wasn't* alone. Calli and the Aviars were here. Daphine was here. The crab people were fighting all around her, along with the freed prisoners. And somewhere out there, Hoku and Dash were here, too.

"Help!" she yelled. Her voice sounded impossibly quiet in the din of battle, but got louder and louder with every word. "Help me! Help me keep him down!"

Fathom wriggled beneath her, his multiple limbs sinking into the ground as he tried to push himself up. Aluna clung to him with her weak hand and tried to slam the bottom of her spike into the back of his skull, where only glass protected his brain. One of his elbows jerked back and struck her in the temple. Her head pulsed with pain. Her vision clouded. She lost her grip on the spike.

She cringed, expecting another blow, but it didn't come. When her vision cleared, she saw Daphine clinging to one of Fathom's arms and Calli to another. The snake-man prisoner had wound his long tail around a leg. Even Barko the dog was there, bloodied but determined, his jaws around one of Fathom's ankles.

"Get off me!" Fathom screamed. "I'll harvest you all for parts! Karl Strand will hear of this!"

"Well, if he does, you won't be the one to tell him," a familiar voice said. Aluna looked up and saw High Senator Electra, her face cut and bleeding, her wing scorched, her eyes fierce. The Aviar lifted her spear in both hands, clearly intending to drive it into the back of Fathom's skull.

"No!" Aluna said. "The device on his arm—it controls everything!"

Electra began her swing but changed the direction at the last moment. Her spear point smashed into the muddy earth, piercing the artifact on Fathom's arm.

Sea Master Fathom screamed.

"Alive," Aluna said, to herself as much as to the people around her. "We can take him alive."

High Senator Electra spat. "This is your fight," she said. "We'll do it your way." She flipped her spear over and smacked the butt into the side of Fathom's head. Aluna felt his body relax.

"You did it," Daphine said in her ear. "Aluna, my sweet, sweet sister. You did it."

"He's out!" Calli yelled with a whoop.

Aluna's head felt as if it were barely attached. Her stomach lurched and she wondered, idly, if she might pass out. All around, the sounds of battle clanged in her ears. Several nearby Upgraders surrendered as soon as their leader fell.

"Sharks," Aluna mumbled as she fell into darkness. "They never expect you to fight back."

CHAPTER 55

ALUNA SAT on the edge of a pool at HydroTek's rim and toyed with the bandage on her leg. Just beyond the clear slope of the dome wall, the ocean spread blue and glittering to the horizon. Somewhere out there, the City of Shifting Tides was waiting.

"You're keeping the scope?" Aluna asked. She already knew the answer, but she wanted to hear it from Daphine's lips.

Her sister surfaced, water cascading off the glinting metal scope that had replaced her eye. Daphine's long hair lay sleek and perfect against her head and neck, except where Fathom had shaved it off for his operation.

"Hoku has restored the power to our breathing shells, so the Elders will be tempted to continue their hiding," Daphine said.

"But Fathom and Karl Strand know where the Seahorse Alpha outpost is. And the Trade Rock. It won't be long before they find the City of Shifting Tides itself," Aluna said.

"Exactly," her sister said. "As the Voice of the Kampii, I will be a daily reminder of the cost of turning too far inward and ignoring the Above World. Karl Strand *will* find us. And if we're not ready when he does, then my fate—or worse—awaits all Kampii. Hiding is no longer an option."

"We need allies, not isolation. We're at war," Aluna said. "Not even Father will be able to deny that when he sees what happened to his favorite child."

Daphine stuck her tongue out and swam closer. Aluna fought an urge to recoil. She still wasn't used to her sister's mutilated face. Daphine relaxed against the pool wall and splashed her tail in the water.

"He'll be happy to see you, you know," Daphine said. "He was angry, of course, but only until he realized you were gone."

Aluna studied her hands, pretending to examine the calluses. Her sister stopped splashing.

"You *are* coming home," Daphine said, suddenly serious.

"How can I? We captured Fathom, but who knows how many of Karl Strand's clones are out there? He wants to take over the Above World. Our victory won't stop him—it'll just anger him. You said it yourself: it's just a matter of time before they find the City of Shifting Tides. The Kampii will never be truly safe until Karl Strand is dead."

"But you took the seed, Aluna. I saw you."

"Then why don't I have a tail?" Aluna asked. "It's been almost a week. Back home, the transformation starts right away."

"Ocean Seeds are most potent when they're hot," Daphine said. "The one you took had grown cold. It's still working inside you—just slowly." She rested her hand on Aluna's arm and squeezed. "Come home, Aluna. Talk to him. If you don't want to stay after that, then I'll help you pack myself."

Talk to her father.

She was a hero now, a warrior. But would he see her any differently? Would he look at her and see anything besides a defiant child?

"I'm sorry, but I can't," she said. "Not yet. Maybe not ever."

Daphine smiled sadly. "You'll have to say good-bye to the Above World eventually. It might take weeks or it might take months. But you'll have to say good-bye."

"I know," Aluna said quietly. She could feel the

seed in her body, shifting things around. Most of the time she could ignore it, but twice now the pain had made her scream. Whether or not it gave her a tail, the Ocean Seed would not let her forget the choices she'd made. "But there's a war to fight, and even if I don't make it to the end, I want to play my part in as many battles as I can."

"Have you told Hoku about the seed?" Daphine asked.

Aluna shook her head. She hadn't told any of them. She looked at her sister. "Can it be our secret? Please?"

"Oh, little one." Daphine rose up in the water and wrapped her arms around Aluna. "For you, I would do anything. You have already done everything for me."

Hoku strolled through Middle Green with Aluna and Calli and watched the technicians clean up after their old master. Liu scurried around with the other Meks, stopping to wink at Dash every chance she got. Hoku glanced nervously at Aluna, but she didn't seem to notice.

Most of the Upgraders were gone now that their slave collars had been removed. He doubted they'd seen the last of them. Some Upgraders hadn't been slaves at all, but Fathom's willing henchmen. And he was sure that some of them had scurried off to report to Karl Strand. Not that Strand didn't already know. When Hoku had woken up all the Meks, he'd used all the power Fathom had been sending to his father. Karl Strand would notice, all right. He'd notice and want revenge.

The Dome Meks were already working on their defense systems, but to Hoku, it wasn't enough. As long as the Kampii generators were here, his people would be in danger. Someday, he'd have to do what the Aviars had done—take back the power and the control and make the Kampii wholly self-sufficient.

Fathom was imprisoned in a stasis pod, just like the ones the Dome Meks used for extended sleep periods. Hoku had voted for a more painful and humiliating incarceration, but in the end, logic won out. If Fathom was a genetic copy of Karl Strand, then there was a lot they could learn by studying him, both mentally and physically. Not to mention his access to Strand's tactical information. Aluna was right. They'd be foolish to destroy him.

"Hey, look, there's Dash!" Aluna said.

Hoku watched Aluna jog ahead, content to stroll more slowly with Calli. The three of them joined Dash under the shade of a huge tree. The horse-boy was squeezing an apple with his new mechanical hand. The goal was to squeeze it as hard as he could without completely pulping it. The medteks had tried to save his mangled hand, but it had taken too much damage during his fight with the Upgraders.

Next to Dash, Zorro sat behind a pile of smushed apples, happily gorging himself.

"Zorro is going to get fat eating all of those!" Aluna said.

"Zorro saved my life," Dash said. "He gets as many apples as he wants."

"Well, then Calli gets an apple, too," Aluna said. "I've lost track of how many people she's saved."

Calli blushed and stuttered, "Then you and Hoku and Dash should get a whole orchard!"

Hoku grinned and motioned to a spot under the tree. He and Calli sat side by side, a little closer than they used to, but still not as close as he'd like. Aluna sat next to Dash and reached a finger toward his new arm.

"Does it hurt?" she asked.

Hoku could tell that she still felt guilty about breaking it back in the SkyTek dome. If it hadn't been so useless during the fight, Dash might have been able to defend himself longer.

"I cannot feel much with it," Dash said, shrugging. "But it is strong, not so easily broken. I will grow accustomed to it." He smiled at Aluna. It was a very different sort of smile from the one Dash used with Hoku.

Aluna blushed and didn't take her hand off his arm.

"So, when are we leaving for the desert?" she asked.

The Equian woman they'd saved, Shria, had relayed some terrible news. Another of Karl Strand's clones—Sand Master Scorch—had been seen in the desert. If they stood any chance of rallying the Equians against him, they needed to move fast.

"We leave tomorrow, early, if that is acceptable," Dash said.

"And I'm going with you," Hoku blurted out. He'd wanted to tell Aluna sooner, when they were making plans, but he'd never found the right time. "I know I should go back to the Kampii, but I can't. Not yet."

She looked up at him, her eyes wide with surprise. He rushed on.

"I've always needed you, Aluna. You've looked out for me and taken me on amazing adventures," he said. "But it's all different now. I'm not the same. Nothing is the same. I'm figuring things out, more every day. Maybe now . . . I can help in ways that you can't. And besides, this is my fight, too."

"It's *our* fight," Calli corrected him.

Hoku looked into Aluna's eyes, and suddenly her arms were around him. She hugged him tight, hugged Calli, and laughed her big belly laugh.

"I promise not to send you away again, or to leave either of you behind," she said. "I used to think I could do everything myself, but I can't. Not in the Above World. You've all saved my life, and I won't forget it. You make me stronger than I am by myself." She smiled grimly. "What did Sarah Jennings say? The world needs us, and we need each other."

Hoku had said that nothing was the same, but he knew he was wrong. Aluna was still his best friend, and he was still hers. Underwater or above it, they were in this fight together.

ACKNOWLEDGMENTS

First of all, thanks to Stephanie Burgis and Christopher East. They read each chapter of *Above World* as I wrote it and made me keep going. They are both incredible writers, cheerleaders, and unconditional friends. Thanks also to Sarah Prineas and Greg van Eekhout for almost daily support and inspiration on a whole heap of levels. Great friends do more than help you with your book—they help you with your life.

Thanks to my agent, Joe Monti, for believing in me and this story, and for encouraging me to include even more martial arts. Thanks also to Barry Goldblatt for creating a family, not just an agency.

Thanks to Sarah Ketchersid, my wonderful editor, for loving the book even more than I did most days. Her insights made *Above World* the book I wanted it to be. The whole Candlewick team has my gratitude, including Liz Zembruski, Kathryn Cunningham, Rachel Smith, Hannah Mahoney, Maggie Deslaurier, Martha Dwyer, and everyone in sales and marketing.

I have some of the best friends in the world, and they give me some of the best critiques. Thanks to Sally Felt, Michael Jasper, Samantha Ling, Eugene Myers, Tim Pratt, Erik Ratliff, and Shelley Stuart. *Above World* also went to the Blue Heaven novel workshop with Paolo Bacigalupi, Tobias Buckell, Sarah Castle, Deb Coates, Charles Coleman Finlay, Daryl Gregory, Sandra McDonald, Paul Melko, Sarah Prineas, Catherynne M. Valente, and Greg van Eekhout. These guys kept me from looking like an idiot (at least with regards to this book).

Thanks to my World of Warcraft guild. (Don't laugh!) They've been with me on this journey from the beginning, particularly: Andrea, Andrew, Andy, Bill, Brenda, Danielle, Erin, Jamie, Leslie, Lisa, Mike, Mikiel, Paul, Rachel, Rob, Roe, Shelley, Steven, Tom, and Tommy.

Thanks to my martial arts family at White Lotus Kung Fu: Master Douglas Wong, Master Carrie Ogawa-Wong, Master Phil Jennings, and the rest of my brothers and sisters.

For all-around awesome advice, support, and friendship, I want to thank Christine Ashworth, Claudia Hoffman, Heather Shaw, and my buddies at SAGE and Cosmic Toast Studios.

And last, thanks to my family: Mom, Jeff, Jason, Maya, Griffin, and Cassell. I love you.